...that you think of me?"

"We're strangers," he said. "What should I think?"

To Daniel's astonishment, she worked at the fastenings of her robes, and they fell like water to her feet. Beneath them she was naked. And breathtaking. Her body was sweetly curved, full-breasted and full-hipped, her legs shapely and strong, her waist supple.

"You cannot abide losing control, Daniel," she said. "Now I give you a choice. You may prove to yourself that I cannot influence you. . .because I want you, and I will do nothing to make you want *me*."

'"I made no attempt to influence you," Isis insisted.

"I made no attempt to influence you," Isis insisted.

DARK JOURNEY

SUSAN KRINARD

MILLS & BOON

First Published in Great Britain 2016
By Mills & Boon, an imprint of HarperCollins*Publishers*
1 London Bridge Street, London, SE1 9GF

© 2016 by Susan Krinard

ISBN 978-0-263-92171-7

89-0516

Our policy is to use papers that are natural, renewable and recyclable products and made from wood grown in sustainable forests. The logging and manufacturing processes conform to the legal environmental regulations of the country of origin.

Printed and bound in Spain
by CPI, Barcelona

Susan Krinard has been writing paranormal romance for nearly twenty years. With *Daysider*, she began a series of vampire romances, the Nightsiders series, for Mills & Boon Nocturne. Sue lives in Albuquerque, New Mexico, with her husband, Serge; her dogs, Freya, Nàhla and Cagney; and her cats, Agatha and Rocky. She loves her garden, nature, painting and chocolate. . .not necessarily in that order.

Foreword

For thirty-five years after the end of the war between Opiri[1] and humans, the greatest hope for lasting peace lay in the self-contained mixed colonies established along the western seaboard of the former United States of America. These colonies—unlike the slave-holding Opir Citadels, which kept captive humans as blood donors, and the human Enclaves, which rejected all Opiri as monsters—demanded full equality between Opiri and human members, and encouraged the willing donation of blood from human colonists.

For many years, such relatively small colonies provided the only working examples of truly peaceful coexistence between humans and Opiri. But rumors of a new kind of mixed colony began to spread: tales of a former Opir Citadel turned free city, populated by hundreds of citizens both human and Opiri.

Never before had the experiment of equality been attempted on such a grand scale. In the original colonies, every member knew every other member; humans were well acquainted with the Opiri who would live on their donated blood. In a city, such personal acquaintance would be far less likely, and the government would have to be cor-

1 Colloquially known as "vampires" or Nightsiders.

respondingly complex to ensure a steady supply of blood from cooperative humans, to distribute it fairly, to properly apportion work among the citizens, and to prevent less well-adapted Opiri from reverting to the old ways of asserting dominance and obtaining blood by force.

Doubting that such a system could be maintained for any length of time, the Western colonies sent ambassadors to the new city of Tanis. If such a city-state could survive, the hope for a permanent end to war might be realized. If it failed, many on both sides of the divide would regard Tanis as proof that coexistence on anything but the smallest scale might never be achieved.

—From *The Armistice Years:*
Conflict and Convergence

Chapter 1

It was time.

Daniel moved through the woods to the edge of the field, making one last check to be certain that his clothes were appropriately dusty. Cattle grazed in the waning light, and in the distance Daniel could make out the small white forms of sheep. Farther on stood more fields, green with crops, and beyond that…

Tanis. The former Citadel of Tartaros, rising beside the river, its odd but impressive silhouette revealing its nature as a place where—if the stories were true—humans and Nightsiders, or Opiri as they called themselves, lived side by side in peace and equality.

They lived the same way in Avalon, the colony to which Daniel had escaped when he'd fled the Nightsider citadel Erebus, and in Delos, the compound he had governed in the far north of Oregon, where Opiri, humans and half-bloods worked together to fend off common enemies.

He'd given up his command of Delos and returned to the place where he had first been free. But his reunion with old friends and comrades had been incomplete.

His father had disappeared. Ares, former Bloodmaster of Erebus, had gone east in search of the mysterious half-domed Citadel at the foot of the mountains. He'd wanted to find out if it was truly possible for an entire city to maintain the equality that only smaller settlements and colonies had managed since the end of the War.

Daniel had serious doubts that such a thing was possible. Nevertheless, since Ares had not returned, he had volunteered to complete his mission. And if Ares's disappearance had something to do with his going to Tanis, Daniel would find that out, too. No matter what role he had to play.

For now, that role meant blending in among the human field workers as they ended their workday. The path between the fields widened to a dusty dirt road, bounded on both sides by pastures. By the time Daniel reached the crops, the last light of day was reflecting off the several towers of the former Citadel and glinting on the surface of the river behind it. Workers—humans—gathered along the road to return to the city, while other figures, white-haired Nightsiders, arrived to take their places.

It was just dark enough for Daniel to slip in among the retiring workers, just another man in a plain shirt and pants and work boots. He didn't let on that he could see everything as if it were full daylight; as far as the people of Tanis would know, he was fully human.

He lingered at the back of the group as the workers started toward the city gates, talking in low voices. One of the women shot a curious glance Daniel's way, but said nothing.

The human workers stopped as a flood of artificial light fell over them from the parapet walk above the gate made of immense logs bound together with steel, which would require the efforts of more than a few inhumanly strong Nightsiders to open. Opiri looked down on them from the walk, and they appeared to be armed.

Clearly the people of this city feared attack. But from whom?

Daniel braced himself for some kind of screening or

check on the workers, but no one seemed to pay any particular notice as they passed through a smaller door just to the right of the gate. They entered a large, canopied courtyard, where other humans and a few Nightsiders spoke to the workers, tallied the day's harvest or engaged in activities Daniel couldn't identify. Daniel noted that there seemed to be little mixing between the Opiri and the humans.

Not a good sign, Daniel thought, in a place supposedly devoted to peaceful coexistence between humans and the beings they used to call vampires. But he didn't have much time to think about it; the humans were passing through one of the doorways at the other end of the courtyard, moving more quickly as if they were eager for food and rest. Again, nobody stopped them, and they entered an open area like an immense, railed balcony that was part of a raised causeway circling the inter wall of the city. Two wide ramps on either side of the landing descended to the lower part of the city. The humans hurried down the ramps, paying no attention when Daniel fell behind.

Waiting until all the humans had left the landing, Daniel moved to the railing. His gaze followed the causeway, exactly like the one in Erebus where Bloodlords, of lesser rank but far more common than Bloodmasters, displayed their Households in grand promenades, showing off their wealth and power, accompanied by a train of their favorite serfs.

Daniel forced himself to look away to the city below. A single main avenue ran through the center of the city, terminating at the base of the largest tower. Unlike Erebus, the former Tartaros's towers were clustered at the far end of the Citadel, piercing the half dome that protected the area from the sun. Once, such towers would have been occupied by the wealthiest and most powerful Bloodlords and Bloodladies, Bloodmasters and Bloodmistresses, shrouding blocks of lesser buildings in their shadows.

Closer in lay the low town, where Opiri of lesser rank would have made their homes, a maze of structures interspersed with plazas and small parks. The town glittered with lights like distant stars.

Tanis.

Daniel ground his teeth together, resisting the overwhelming emotions that took hold of him in that moment. He hadn't set foot in any Citadel since Ares and his allies had helped Daniel and dozens of human serfs get out of Erebus, but he had not forgotten one moment of pain or humiliation, not one day of being chained like a dog or forced to give blood to a ruthless master and other Opiri of his master's acquaintance.

This Citadel had changed, yes. Half of it was now open to the sky. Human workers left and entered the city without being subjected to checks or examinations.

But that didn't mean Tanis was like Delos or Avalon or the other mixed colonies. It would be a miracle if it were.

"A lovely sight, is it not?"

Daniel stiffened and then forced himself to relax. The woman who had come to stand beside him at the railing spoke softly, without concern or threat. But the hairs at the back of his neck prickled with recognition even before he turned to look at her.

The first thing he noticed was her hair. Glossy and black as a raven's feathers, it fell past her shoulders and almost seemed to move of its own accord as she spoke, tempting any man within reach to run his fingers through it.

But the hair framed something even more remarkable: a face of astonishing beauty by the judgment of human *or* Nightsider. Her chin was firm, her brows finely shaped, her eyes nearly black with the slightest tinge of deepest purple, her lips full. The skin of her face and bare arms was golden bronze. Hints of her figure appeared beneath the layers of her flowing, semitransparent robes—a hip here, a breast or shoulder there. Daniel had no doubt that this woman's body was as sleek and perfect as her face, hair and voice.

And there was something more about her that Daniel felt all the way down to his bones: a profound charisma, a pull that Daniel had experienced before, and not only in Erebus.

Surely she couldn't be what his senses told him. Not with hair like that or eyes so dark or teeth as blunt as any human's.

But Ares's hair was just as black, an anomaly among pale-haired, pale-skinned Opiri. And he knew of other anomalies. Daniel, for instance, lacked the sharp Nightsider cuspids of *his* kind, the half-breed offspring of a Nightsider father and a human mother. *He* looked nothing like a normal dhampir, and had no need for blood.

She was not what she was pretending to be.

"It *is* beautiful," he said, as if he believed she was only another human sharing the view.

"It isn't often that our fellow humans come here," she said, every word as rich and smooth as sun-warmed honey. "I often wonder why that is so."

Daniel gripped the railing, breathed deeply and unclenched his fingers. "Memories of a darker past?" he said.

She ran her fine-fingered hand along the railing and gazed at him until he had no choice but to look at her fully. Her eyes were not only striking; they were wise and perceptive and sharp with intelligence.

"Were you one of the original inhabitants?" she asked. "I do not recognize you as a former serf of Tartaros."

"No," he said. "I came here for refuge, after I escaped from another Citadel."

"How long have you been here?"

Daniel leaned against the railing. "In Tanis? A few months," he said.

"Not long enough to forget what your life was like before," she said, sympathy in her voice. "This still must be very strange for you—a Citadel without masters and serfs."

He smiled with one side of his mouth. "Can you read minds?"

"No. But I have had many years of experience in understanding people."

Many years. Daniel looked at her out of the corner of his eye. How many? he wondered. A hundred? A thousand? Certainly far more than the twenty-odd years her body and face suggested.

"May I know your name?" she asked, moving closer to him.

It didn't matter what he called himself, he thought. It was highly unlikely that anyone here would know him from Erebus, Delos or Avalon.

"Daniel," he said.

"I am Isis," she said.

He held his breath for a moment and then let it out slowly. How appropriate that her name should be that of a goddess, as Ares's was that of a god.

If Ares *had* been here, she would certainly know.

"You have just come in from a shift in the fields," Isis said, breaking the silence. "You must be tired, and hungry."

He went on his guard. Her concern seemed a little too intimate. And she was standing too damned close, close enough that he could smell her fresh, citrusy scent and hear the beat of her heart.

"Where do you work, Isis?" he asked.

"In the administrative offices," she said. "It is an easy job compared to the fields."

"We all do what we're best suited for," he said.

"That is how it is supposed to be, is it not?" she asked, her lovely lips sliding into a faint frown. "The more difficult the work, the higher the reward."

"You don't agree?" he asked.

"'Difficult' is a subjective concept. Should one person be given more credit for being able to do what another person cannot?"

"There is no perfect system," he said.

She cocked her head. "And I think you were no ordinary serf, Daniel," she said, sliding her hand closer to his.

The comment was too personal, and definitely unwelcome. "I had a decent education in my Enclave before I was sent to the Citadel," he said coolly.

"Or perhaps you were never a serf at all?"

He stared at her, suppressing his anger. This was the interrogation he'd expected if he'd been caught entering the city, but it wasn't proceeding at all in the way he'd imagined.

But I was *caught,* he thought. This was no chance meeting.

"Oh, yes," he said, very softly. "I was a serf, for many years."

"In what Citadel?"

He was prepared for the question. "Vikos," he said, naming a Nightsider Citadel in the area once known as northern Arizona.

"And you escaped?" she asked.

"Bloodlords don't release their serfs."

"Except here," she said.

He pretended not to hear her. "Where did *you* come from, Isis?" he asked.

"I was never in bondage," she said, looking down at her slender hands on the railing.

"Then why are you in an isolated Citadel instead of in a human Enclave?"

"Perhaps because I believe in what this city represents. There are many like me, or this place could not exist." She met Daniel's eyes. "Of all the refuges you might have sought when you escaped, you chose Tanis rather than a human compound or even another Enclave. Yet surely you have good reason to hate Opiri?"

"I don't hate them," he said. "My own fa—"

He broke off, appalled at what he had been about to say. It was she, this woman, who threw him so off balance with her allure and questions and keen observations. It was as if she'd known him before.

She came from outside, he thought. From some other Citadel, where she must have been a Bloodlady of distinction, an owner of many human serfs.

"The majority of humans here are former serfs, aren't they?" he asked. "Do *they* hate all Opiri?"

"No. I must seem rather foolish." She smiled again. "In which ward do you live?"

This wasn't a question he'd expected. He knew too little about Tanis to answer.

"I need to get home," he said suddenly. "It's been pleasant talking to you, Isis. Maybe we'll meet again."

"I am certain of it," she said. Behind her, men in olive-drab uniforms—both of them Darketans, children of Opir mothers and human fathers, human in appearance save for their sapphire eyes and sharp teeth—advanced on Daniel with shock sticks in hand.

"What's going on?" he asked, backing away in seeming confusion.

"Please go with these men," she said, her voice still as musical, her face every bit as flawlessly beautiful as before. He felt the push of her "influence," that particular gift limited to the most ancient and powerful Bloodmasters and Bloodmistresses.

But he was fortunate enough to be virtually immune to the lady's subtle power. "Why?" he asked, his gaze fixed on the guards.

"I know you are not a citizen of Tanis, Daniel," she said.

"We do not allow strangers to enter our city without first being questioned and screened."

"You turn away refugees?" Daniel asked.

"Only those incompatible with our way of life," she said.

"Do you enjoy spying on your own kind?" he asked, still playing along with her masquerade.

She blinked several times. "You were recognized as an outsider when you entered the gates," she said. "My purpose was only to determine if you were a threat to us."

"A threat?" he said, holding his arms out to his sides. "How?"

"Please, Daniel, go peacefully. You will not be harmed."

"And if I refuse?" Daniel asked.

Moving almost more quickly than Daniel could detect, the two guards lunged at him. One of them caught his left arm. He swung around, defending himself without thought, and punched the guard in the face with his fist. The second guard grabbed his right arm and twisted it behind him.

Everything within him, all the instinctive desire to be free, urged him to keep fighting. Panic nearly overwhelmed him, but he pushed it down. He bore the pain silently and allowed the other guard to jerk his other arm behind him. Manacles locked around his wrists.

He gave Isis a long, cold look. "They were wrong about this place," he said as the guards pulled him away. "And you're wrong about me."

"Come quietly," the Darketan guard said. "You don't have anything to be afraid of."

"Wait," Isis called after them as they turned for the archway. "I will accompany you."

The two guards inclined their heads…deferring to Isis, Daniel thought, as if they were still in a traditional Citadel. Daniel knew that they, like him, were feeling that indefinable magnetism, whether she intended to use it on them or not.

Head down, Daniel slipped into his role as a down-trodden serf.

Letting all the resistance go out of his body, Daniel allowed the guards to escort him back down the left ramp. He was aware of Isis behind them, though her footsteps were almost inaudible to his sharp hearing. He still didn't understand how an Opir of her obvious stature would be employed in meeting and questioning outsiders, unless her work could be considered evidence of real equality in Tanis.

But he was still a prisoner, and he couldn't afford to remain one. Nor could he risk being ejected from the city without getting the answers he needed.

The ramp ended abruptly at ground level in the low town and led out onto a wide plaza open to the sky. Clearly designed to be as welcoming as possible, adorned with decorative murals, many benches and large planters filled with flowers, the plaza was deserted save for a few humans strolling along tiled water channels cut into the concrete. They smiled and bowed to Isis as she passed by, and some of the men stopped and stared as if they had never seen anything so beautiful. On every side stood recently built, multistory buildings; above, the stars were so numerous and bright that it felt more like twilight than full night. The partial dome at the other end of the city cast a deeper, almost sinister shadow.

They crossed the plaza toward a cluster of tall buildings. The guards headed for one of the larger structures and pushed Daniel through the door.

A large reception area was dominated by a desk attended by a human receptionist sorting through a stack of papers. She immediately rose to her feet and stood alert while another pair of uniformed Darketans materialized from a corridor behind the desk. Three pairs of eyes made note of Daniel and then focused on the woman behind him.

"Isis," the receptionist said, her voice a little breathless, her smile very bright. "How may we serve you?"

"I will require a private room," she said, sweeping past Daniel and the guards.

The receptionist's gaze fell on Daniel. "Will you require more guards?" she asked with a worried frown.

"I need none," Isis said, glancing at Daniel with a slim, raised brow. "I do not think our friend will cause any trouble."

"Yes, Isis." The receptionist nodded to one of the guards behind her, who strode back into the corridor. A few moments later he returned and nodded to Isis.

"If you will come with me," he said.

With Isis striding ahead of them, Daniel's guards led him past the desk and into the corridor. It was dim and plain, punctuated by a dozen identical doors. The escorting guard stopped at one of them, unlocked it and inclined his head to Isis.

"If you need assistance—" he began.

"I know what to do."

The guard held the door open for her. The room was as featureless as the corridor, with gray walls, a single table and two chairs.

"Unbind him," Isis said. Daniel's guards exchanged glances and unlocked the manacles. Putting on a mask of confusion and fear, Daniel shivered and rubbed his wrists.

"There is nothing to be afraid of," Isis said, catching his gaze. She believed his panic was real. She took his arm, and he felt the power of her nature, magnified a hundred times—warm, soothing, almost magical. As the door closed behind them, she led him to one of the chairs at the single table.

"Please, sit," she said.

Daniel took one of the chairs and watched Isis as she sat at the opposite side of the table.

"Now," she said, "it will be easier for everyone if you cooperate. Nobody will hurt you, but we must know why you are here."

And that, Daniel thought, was precisely what he couldn't tell her.

Chapter 2

Daniel pitched his voice a little high to suggest nervousness and clasped his hands under the table. "I told you," he said. "I came here for refuge."

She smiled almost sadly, her teeth perfect and white. Once again Daniel felt the impact of her fascination, the seductive call of predator to prey, the effortless ability to bring "lesser" creatures under her control. Once again he shook it off.

"You came secretly, without declaring yourself," she said. "Why would you take such an approach?"

Avoiding her gaze, he stared at the tabletop. "I had to be sure," he said.

"Sure of what?"

"That the stories about Tanis being a refuge were true."

Isis spread her own delicate hands on the table. "I can assure you that they are." She spoke with sympathy, and Daniel was aware that his body was responding to her naturally seductive body and the warm scent of her skin. His mind was clear enough, but his heart was beating too fast, and another part of his anatomy was very much at attention.

"What are *you* afraid of?" he asked, bringing his body back under restraint.

It was the wrong thing to say—certainly nothing a wary and frightened former serf would have asked. Maintaining the balance was tricky at best.

He wasn't sure he could keep up the pretense.

She studied him, her dark eyes intent on his face. "I told you—we make certain that newcomers can live with our rules and will be comfortable beginning a new life here," she said. "The same concerns apply for both humans and Opiri. But there are those who have come to observe our city in secret so that they can take reports back to their people."

"You mean spies?" he asked in a much quieter voice, edged with alarm. "Why would anyone do that?"

"Some of them fear us, Daniel. We believe that the Enclaves and the Citadels throughout the west have learned what we have accomplished and may regard us as a threat to the separate worlds *they* have built, though those worlds are built upon hostility and a truce that might fail at any moment."

Isis was right, Daniel thought. He remembered the mad Bloodlord in the northwest who had nearly started another war because he had stolen half-blood children and recruited rogue Freebloods—lordless Opiri—with the intent of attacking the Citadels and, eventually, the human Enclaves, as well. The Armistice had always balanced on the head of a pin, and a stiff wind could blow it off and plunge the world back into chaos.

"Do you think some Citadel or Enclave would attack you?" he asked.

"We do not know. But it is possible they may send agents to observe us, so you see that we must screen everyone who seeks sanctuary in Tanis. There can be no exceptions."

So they must have screened Ares, Daniel thought. "What do you want from me?" he asked with feigned anxiety.

Her expression turned grave. "At the causeway," she said, "you said you escaped from Vikos."

"Yes," he said, after a calculated hesitation.

"That is at least a five-hundred-mile journey," Isis said, "much of it through mountainous territory. You came so far alone?"

"Yes," Daniel said, looking past her at the drab wall.

"And your supplies?"

"I left them behind when I came into the city."

"Your clothes are not too worn. Did you steal them?"

Daniel didn't answer.

"You must have had help along the way."

"There are…humans hiding everywhere," he said. "Trying to survive and keep away from Opir hunters."

"And none would come with you?"

Daniel shook his head. "They were afraid this was a trap."

"But you were not?"

"In Vikos," Daniel said, "there were rumors that humans here were more than—"

He broke off, but Isis completed the sentence for him. "Chattel?" she said, her lush mouth setting in a thin line.

"Yes."

"And you chose to risk coming here, based only upon a rumor?"

Daniel swallowed, as if debating whether or not to continue. "It was a risk I was willing to take." His jaw tightened. "But I will never let anyone take me prisoner again."

"I understand," Isis murmured.

Daniel imagined that he heard pity in her voice. He had never needed or accepted pity from any human or Nightsider, and he wanted none of hers.

"*Do* you think I am a spy?" he asked. "Who would I spy for? The Enclave that cast me out as a criminal and sent me into slavery? Vikos, where I was treated no better than an animal?"

"It seems unlikely," she said soothingly.

"Very unlikely." He laughed with half-feigned bitterness. "What do I have to do to prove myself?"

"We will keep you in a quiet room for a time, and others will speak to you. Once we are certain you are no threat, you will have the opportunity to—"

Daniel jumped out of his chair, nearly knocking it over. "You'll lock me up?"

"You will be comfortable. Nobody will—"

"No manacles," he said, working his fists. It was barely an act.

She rose slowly. "We have no intention of binding you. That is not done here, except when it is absolutely necessary." She moved toward him, her white-and-gold robes swirling around her feet. Before he could back away, she touched his hand, her fingers—warm and soft and gentle—stroking his arm. Her influence washed over and through him.

"You must understand that not all Opiri are like the ones you knew in Vikos," she said. "I will prove it to you." She released his hand. "Can you trust me?"

Daniel knew how easily she could make most humans accept anything she said, do anything she bid without the need for compulsion.

He let her believe she was succeeding.

"I trust you," he said slowly.

"*I* am Opir," she said.

He put the length of the room between them, keeping his gaze unfocused and his voice on the edge of panic. "You have…dark hair," he stammered. "Your eyes…"

"Nevertheless," she said, "I am what you humans call a Nightsider, and I would never do you harm."

Don't overplay it, Daniel told himself. "You tricked me," he said, pressing himself against the wall.

"It is easier for new humans if one of their own kind introduces him or her to our world, but it is the work I have chosen, and my appearance makes it possible." She removed the caps from her teeth. "You did not guess, Daniel?"

He dropped his eyes. "No, my lady."

"I am only Isis here." She searched his face. "You never suspected? You were not playing a game to deceive *me*?"

"How could I?" he whispered.

"Because I think you know that most Opiri never consider the possibility of being deceived by a human." She paused, as if carefully choosing her words. "Even if you had attacked me when I found you, there would be no punishment. We understand a former serf's justifiable fear and anger."

"We? Did you feel the same when *you* owned serfs?"

"I never kept any human in bondage, nor did I take part in the War."

"But you hunted humans for blood."

"I never killed," she said. "But I saw much suffering. Six years ago I was among those who discovered this Citadel after it had fallen into chaos and savagery. I began to realize what life on our world could be."

"And you changed it?"

"I can take little responsibility for what Tanis has become. All our citizens have shared in the work. We established new laws, expelled the worst of the Bloodlords and freed the serfs, giving them the choice of whether to remain under a new regime based on equality, or go their own way in freedom."

"How many stayed?"

"Most chose to take a chance with us."

"And the Opiri? Did they agree to abide by your new laws and give up their Households?"

"Those who did not were quickly removed from the city."

"But you've still got former serfs living with their former masters."

"We have many immigrants from other Citadels and Enclaves, people who have no experience of Tanis as it was." Her eyes were bright and earnest. "There is safety here. Safety we must maintain." She stroked his arm. "I see more than one man in you, Daniel. You are an enigma. I think you pretend to be a fearful and defiant serf now, but that is not what you were when we first met. Whatever the purpose of this act, it is unnecessary…unless, of course, you mean us ill. And I do not believe you do."

If she had been any other woman, human or Opiri, Daniel would have interpreted her lingering touches as an invitation. But he already knew better, even if his body continued to react as if she might invite him to her bed as a willing partner.

Manipulation. Deception. She was as controlling as any Bloodmistress with dozens of serfs at her command.

Once again he shut down his body's response. "You will still hold me here," he said, "whether you believe it or not."

"I would understand your true nature, Daniel, and your reason for coming to Tanis."

"I've given my reason."

"Yet now you doubt that what you sought is real, simply because you were brought in for questioning." She lifted his chin with her soft hand. "I do not expect you to understand this all at once. But if your hope brought you here, it will help you to see with new eyes, and leave behind your old habits of servitude. If you choose to stay."

"When you haven't even decided whether or not to make me leave?"

Isis sighed and shook her head. "You are in need of fresh clothing, a good meal and rest. We shall discuss these matters in greater detail at another time." She let her hand drift down his arm. "Let me show you to your quarters here at the Center. When you have been cleared, you will be given a tour of the city and time enough to see what we have to offer. Then you shall be granted a chance to apply for citizenship...if that is what you desire."

He dropped the mask completely and straightened, glad to shed the false weight of fear and submission. "And what is the price?" he asked.

"As you must know," she said, "every citizen is expected to do his or her part, human or Opiri."

"Humans have to give blood," he said.

"Willingly," she said. "But you must have known that." She tapped on the door, and the guards opened it.

"I will take Daniel myself," she said.

The guards' faces tightened with worry, but they made no protest. Isis, Daniel thought, had them in the palm of her hand.

He followed her along the corridor to a door at the rear of the building. A second, smaller building stood on the other side of a narrow garden. Summer flowers nodded gently in the breeze left by Isis's passing as if they, too, offered obeisance.

"These are the visitor's quarters," she said. "They are used only until the prospective citizen has been properly introduced to the city and is assigned a permanent residence. I hope you will find your room comfortable."

The room she indicated was near the back of the building. She opened the locked door with a key hidden somewhere among her robes and invited him inside.

It was more or less what Daniel had expected: a bed, a small table, two chairs, a small chest with a lamp. An inner door led to a bathroom. There were no windows.

A thread of real panic worked its way through Daniel's gut. He hated small, windowless rooms. He hated being a prisoner. But he'd known it might come to this, and so he stepped inside.

"I will see that food and drink are brought immediately," Isis said. "Clothes will come after I report the sizes you require." She looked him up and down with a faint smile. "I think I have already made an accurate estimate."

An intensely physical tension rose between them as Daniel realized that she had been as fully aware of his body as he had been of hers.

Her smile faltered, and he had the sense that she was startled by the change in the air, as if she had suddenly lost the use of a tool she had wielded with ease all her life.

What would she do, Daniel thought, if he let her see just how little under her influence he really was?

She must have seen something in his eyes that alarmed her, for she looked away and backed toward the door. "I will speak to you again soon," she said. "Rest well, Daniel."

In a moment she was gone, and the door lock engaged. Daniel sat down on the bed and stripped off his boots, dirty shirt and pants, trying to distract his thoughts from Isis and the sense of walls closing in around him. He stepped into the shower and imagined that the water was washing away the memories, but they were never far from his thoughts. Part of him still lived in that tiny, dirty cell Lord Palemon had kept him in when Daniel wasn't being used or punished for defiance. Even his good years with Ares and his time in Avalon and Delos hadn't erased that cell from his mind.

When he walked out of the bathroom, Isis was standing by the door. A tray of food and a pitcher of water lay on the table, but Daniel barely noticed them. Isis wet her lips and stared at him, and his body reacted exactly as it had before. This time there was no concealing it.

"I am flattered," Isis said huskily.

"It's no less than you expect from any man who comes near you," he said.

Her brows drew down. "You are discourteous, Daniel."

"And you aren't used to discourtesy, are you? You don't have to order anyone to get what you want."

Her dark eyes sparked with anger, bringing out the deep purple lurking within them, and Daniel laughed inwardly. She wasn't so different from the Opiri he'd known in Erebus, or even some of those he'd met outside in the colonies. She summoned respect, even if she didn't acknowledge it.

"You're a Bloodmistress," Daniel said bluntly. "You were born to influence others."

He was surprised to see distress in her expression. "What do *you* know of it?"

"Do you deny it?" he demanded.

She wrapped her arms around her chest and shivered. "You are wrong."

"A pity you never had a chance to own another intelligent being," Daniel said. "Then you could have had absolute power."

"I do not want it!" She gripped the edge of the table, her knuckles turning white against her golden skin. "You do not know me. You see only what you wish to see."

"Then you *do* deny it, in spite of all the bows and smiles and deference everyone shows you, as if you were the goddess your name implies."

"I made no attempt to influence you," she insisted, her golden skin turning pale.

"Maybe not consciously," he said, relenting a little, "but instinctively. Because you are what you are."

"That is truly what you think of me?"

"We're strangers," he said. "What *should* I think?"

To his astonishment, she worked at the fastenings of her robes, and they fell like water to her feet. Beneath them she was naked. And breathtaking. Her body was sweetly curved, full-breasted and hipped, her legs shapely and strong, her waist supple.

"You cannot abide losing control, Daniel," she said. "That is your rebellion against your old life. Now I give you a choice. You may prove to yourself that I cannot influence you...because I want you, and I will do nothing to make you want *me*."

Chapter 3

Lust shone in Daniel's pale blue eyes, but he made no move toward Isis.

He was disciplined, she thought. Disciplined and proud, yet willing to set aside his pride to play the serf if he thought it was to his benefit.

But he had also accused her of trying to dominate others with her influence. Surely that could not be true; she had sworn to give up such power long ago.

At the moment, Daniel had all the power. *Dangerous* was the word that kept coming to mind, even though he was still a prisoner. His body fascinated her; every part of him was whipcord muscle and lean grace, like one of the wildcats that roamed the wilderness. His skin had been bronzed by exposure to the sun, and his eyes were bright and keen in his tanned, handsome face.

She had never met a human who had such an effect on her, not in all her long years of life, though she had known thousands upon thousands of men; men who had worshipped her as a goddess, laying gifts at her feet, willing to serve her in any way she desired.

This man would never serve her. There was a hardness in him, scars she could feel but not see, experiences she could only imagine in spite of her time spent with former serfs. She had always been able to sense what lay in human hearts, had regarded them with sympathy and pity. But Daniel...

He would reject her pity, her sympathy, and any offer to guide him as she did the thousands she had sworn to protect. And still she reacted to his proximity as if she were a starving Opir in the presence of fresh, pumping blood.

How could it be that she should desire a man who was not only a stranger to the city, but an utter enigma to her? How could her body betray her so cruelly? What had she meant to prove by stripping herself and standing before him, a living offering to one who could so easily disdain her?

"Enough of these games," Daniel said in a husky voice, his gaze never leaving hers. The back of her neck prickled as he drew closer. His steps were nearly as silent as an Opir's, his stride loose and easy.

But he was no more relaxed than she was. The physical evidence of his desire had not abated, and his nearness stiffened her nipples and brought her to aching readiness.

"What do you want, Isis?" he murmured. "What are you hoping to gain from this? Are you hungry for blood that doesn't come from a storage unit? Or do you think you'll learn something about me you can't get any other way?"

Anger blurred her vision. He mocked her, but she had made herself a target. She could ignore Anu or Ereshkigal when they derided her for her lack of objectivity in her devotion to mankind, but this was different. This was very personal. She had thrown aside all her pride to prove to this one man, this human...

She reached out and took his hand, laying it on her breast. He sucked in a sharp breath, and his gaze fell to his hand on her skin.

"I want nothing," she whispered, "except to prove that I—"

He caught her lips with his, pressing his palm against

her breast. There was no hesitation in him now. His tongue plunged inside her mouth, and she felt for the table behind her, her knees going weak. He cradled her head in the crook of his arm while he stroked her nipple with his other hand, kissing her mouth and her throat and her shoulder.

Then she noticed the thick scar tissue on his neck, the residue of hundreds of bites never properly healed. She flinched, sickened by the implications of those scars. Not only had he been bitten hundreds of times, but the Opiri who had used him hadn't bothered to mend the wounds they left in his flesh. It would have been a simple matter of altering the chemicals in their saliva to close the wounds and set them to healing.

But Daniel didn't seem to notice her concern. He swept her up in his arms, carrying her easily to the narrow bed. He laid her down and immediately knelt over her, his eyes clouded with hunger. A moment later his mouth was on her nipple, licking and then suckling it while he eased his body over hers. She parted her thighs and arched up against him, moaning deep in her throat.

He kissed her again and slid his hand down her belly to the moistness between her legs. He knew exactly what to do, and in seconds she was gasping, at the mercy of her body's reaction as if she had never known such sensations before. Daniel knew she had surrendered; he pinned her arms above her head, almost tenderly, and kissed his way down her body from breast to hip, pausing only for a moment before his mouth found the center of her pain and pleasure.

His tongue was an expert tool, licking and exploring, making her tremble violently in anticipation. When he dipped it inside her, all she could think of was taking the rest of him, drawing him in, feeling him moving and thrusting and carrying her to the heights.

As if he'd read her thoughts, he slid his body up over

hers and braced himself on his arms. He looked into her eyes and brushed a strand of her hair away from her lips.

"How long has it been?" he asked gently.

Isis didn't want to talk. But she felt him waiting for her answer, withholding himself until she gave it up as she gave up her body.

"Not…since I came to Tanis," she whispered. "I must… remain apart…"

"Why?"

"It is my place…to guide them, show them…the way to live in peace and harmony."

"Humans?"

"They…they need—"

Suddenly his warmth vanished, the weight of his body gone as he rolled away. Instinctively she closed her legs and covered her chest as if she herself were a serf on the block, ready for claiming.

"I am honored that you chose to suspend your noble chastity with me," he said from across the room, "but I wouldn't want to interfere with your work."

She sat up, meeting his steady gaze with shattered dignity, stung by emotions that had seemed so distant for so many centuries: wounded pride, regret, confusion.

But she could not let him see. He must not know how deeply she felt his rejection. The rejection of a *human*, who should have been grateful—

No, she thought. That was the old way, the wrong way. This small error in judgment changed nothing: not her commitment to aiding the humans of Tanis, nor her attitude toward Daniel. It would be as if this had never happened.

She would learn who and what Daniel was, why *he* should have such power to make her forget herself so completely. She would learn *his* weakness.

Rising from the bed, she gathered up her robes and pulled them on, letting them hang loose.

"I thank you for reminding me of my purpose," she said. "I will not make such a mistake again."

To her surprise, Daniel looked away. He turned and walked into the bathroom, and for the first time Isis saw the other scars he carried on his body: the raised pink and brown welts from numerous savage beatings crisscrossing his back, and lower, layer upon layer.

Ill and dizzy, Isis reached for the bed table. Memories. He carried them with him every day, and he could never escape their mark.

Someone tapped on the door behind her. She fastened her robes and opened the door.

"Lady," the human attendant said, color rising in his cheeks. "I have the visitor's clothes. Should I come back at another—"

"No." She smiled at him, and his body relaxed. "I am just leaving." She took the clothes from him and laid them across the bed. Daniel had not emerged from the bathroom when she left.

Still bewildered by the intensity of her feelings—the lust, the fascination, the pity—she gave brief instructions to the guards and sought her own quarters. Unlike most of her peers among the Nine, she preferred to live near the humans with whom she spent so much of her time, in a fifth-floor apartment that held little of the extravagance some high-ranking Opiri enjoyed.

Supposedly, such ranks did not exist in Tanis, and most Opir citizens preferred to live in the towers under the half dome. It was only sensible, since they could not tolerate sunlight.

Once in her apartment, Isis bathed and dressed in fresh robes. Daniel's earthy scent had become entangled with the fabric, and she instructed her maid to have them washed as soon as possible.

She sipped the blood from her small personal store and

found it almost unpalatable. Of course there was no comparison to taking fresh blood from its source, but that was considered a transaction between two private individuals and carefully regulated.

Had Daniel known that, when he mocked her about being hungry for his blood? Did he think she would take it without his express consent?

Her mouth went dry as she thought about what he had done and how tempted she would have been if he had completed the act. If she had so much as touched his neck with her lips…

But that had not happened, she reminded herself. Nor was there any chance of it happening in the future. She would simply find someone else to finish questioning him.

Gathering her composure about her like a heavy day coat, she prepared herself for the meeting of the Nine. She was in no mood to deal with Ereshkigal's sullen manner or Anu's arrogance, but it couldn't be helped. The Elders of Tanis had set policy for the city, and though they did not enact or enforce laws, their opinions had weight with the elected Council of ordinary Opiri and humans. She must be there because she was one of the Nine most personally sympathetic to humans and most protective of their dignity.

She laughed quietly. Had she respected Daniel's dignity? Was she so unaware of her own flaws that a human must point them out? Was she so careless with her power, so accustomed to the influence that she didn't even realize she was still using it?

"It's part of what you are," Daniel had said. But giving guidance was not the same as ruling like a true goddess. The one was necessary; the other was lost in her ancient past.

Still struggling with her conflicting emotions, she called for a shuttle that would carry her through the human sector to the rear of the city and the towers of the Opiri. As always, she felt as if she were entering a different world; as always, it troubled her deeply. There should be no dividing line between Tanis's human citizens and its Opiri, and yet the half dome's shadow was that line. There were times when both races, and the half-bloods, were expected to mingle—as in the forthcoming Games and Festival— but there was always a guardedness, especially on the part of the humans.

Isis had never ceased to hope that would change.

The driver left her at the bottom of the spiraled ramp that reached from ground level to the base of the main tower and the elevated causeway that circled the city. The old Citadel had originally been built with three elevators for each of its six towers, with a single elevator serving a powerful Bloodmaster's Household and the other two assigned to several smaller Households of influential Bloodlords and Bloodladies. Since the reclaiming of the Citadel, the former serfs' quarters had been remodeled, and former Households had been split up to accommodate most of the city's Opiri, even the formerly houseless Freebloods.

But *this* entire tower belonged to the Nine, and nobody questioned their right to it.

Isis took the first elevator past several floors assigned to three of the Nine, stopping at the highest floor. There a large chamber, which encompassed the entire top floor of the tower, served as a meeting room more lavishly furnished and decorated than her own simple quarters. The Nine had confiscated works of fine and decorative arts from the towers' previous inhabitants, and now kept them safe for the people of Tanis.

Isis paused just outside the elevator door to take in the scents and sights of the treasure room, basking in its beauty. On a small pedestal stood a very old sculpture, chipped and cracked, of a serene woman kneeling on one knee, her arms draped with plumage, a sun-disk set between a pair of horns gracefully balanced atop her head.

It was strange to look at it now, when Isis could still recall a time when it had been new. When she had *been* that figure, wearing a winged robe and carrying that same horned crown upon her head.

"Reminiscing?" Bes said, coming to join her. He was an oddity in a world of Opiri, no matter how ancient: short, round and cheerful, with a face that seemed frozen in a constant smile; large ears; and an oiled, curled beard.

Isis turned with a smile. "It is better to think of the future, don't you agree?"

"Yes. But, ah, those were the days."

"You find plenty of amusement with your human friends…at least in their taverns."

Bes laughed. "They do know how to enjoy themselves. Not like—" He grimaced. "'Uneasy is the head that wears the crown.'"

"You do Anu a disservice," Isis said. "He is no king."

"Tell *him* that."

"We are ready to begin," someone called from behind them. It was Hera in her deep blue chiton, a glittering peacock pendant hanging from her slender throat.

Bes rolled his eyes. "Let's get this over with," he said.

They walked around the corner into the meeting area. The space was dominated by a large, beautifully designed round table, and the walls were decorated with murals and works of fine art on every side.

As was customary, Anu sat at the head of the table, Ereshkigal on one side and Hephaestus on the other. Hephaestus stood out from the others with his slightly misshapen body and his limp, but so did Athena and Hermes—Athena with her bright gray eyes, and Hermes with his red-gold hair. Anu, Bes, Ereshkigal, Ishtar, Hera, and Isis herself were dark haired and golden skinned.

They *all* stood out among the pale-skinned, white-haired Opiri, but their differences in appearance only reinforced their position in Tanis.

"Be seated," Anu said.

The others gathered around and took their respective chairs, Isis opposite Anu. Fond of ritual as he was, Anu brought the meeting to order with words in a language nearly forgotten even by the Elders of Tanis, and called upon each of them in turn.

Hephaestus and Ereshkigal, who lived among the Opiri, had little to report. Neither did Anu. None of their people had broken any laws or attempted to take blood from unwilling humans.

"Because they are seldom among humans," Isis said. "How can they face and overcome such temptations if they remain among their own kind?"

"There is peace here, and no taking of serfs," Anu said. "Is that not sufficient?"

Not for the first time, she examined Anu's face, sensing that he was hiding something he did not want her to know. Hephaestus and Ereshkigal seemed to avoid her gaze.

But what would they have to conceal? They had all come to Tanis seeking the same way of life, worked toward the same goals.

Knowing it was better not to air her doubts at the table, Isis listened while Hermes spoke of the half-bloods—chiefly Darketans—under his aegis, and Hera and Ishtar reported on the status of their wards in the human sector. They offered only the briefest and most general commentary, as if "their" humans were of little real interest to them in spite of the Nine's noble intentions.

With Bes it was entirely different. He was his usual cheerful self, offering nothing but praise for the humans with whom he so readily associated. If there were problems, he would never admit it.

Athena, who valued wisdom, assured her fellow Elders that her humans were content. That left Isis.

Immediately she remembered Daniel and quickly dismissed the thought. "We have had record numbers of humans apply to join us here," she said with satisfaction. "It is as if they see our city as a beacon, shining throughout the wilderness."

"How many actually escaped from the Citadels?" Anu asked.

"No matter how harsh their discipline, no Citadel can prevent all escapes. Most of the humans here are prepared to work hard and appreciate the strength of our defenses against outside forces." She glanced at Athena. "They have settled throughout the city... I am surprised that none of you have reported the influx in your wards."

"Of course I am always glad to see more humans in Tanis," Athena said.

"My assistants will have this information," Hera said, fondling the peacock pendant.

"I will look into it," Ishtar said. "I would regret not having greeted them personally."

Isis looked at her askance. Ishtar might consider most humans beneath her, but she was ready enough to take them to her bed for her own amusement.

And am I so much better? Isis thought.

"Have you nothing to say about this human who entered our city without identifying himself?" Anu asked.

Of course Anu would know, she thought. He made it his business to look after all of Tanis, and he had agents who watched and reported back to him personally. He was not secretive about it.

"The human is currently confined to the Immigrant Center," she said. "He was a serf in Vikos. I have questioned him. He has given plausible reasons for entering

Tanis without declaring himself, but of course I will investigate further."

"See that you do," Anu said. "We know the Enclaves and Citadels are watching us for any sign of weakness or vulnerability."

"The Enclaves observe out of fear, and the Citadels with an eye toward conquest and stealing our humans. But I believe this human's story."

"You have never been objective enough where humans are concerned," Anu said.

Isis rose from her chair and met Anu's gaze. "I know my duty," she said, "and have no need to be reminded."

Anu's lip curled slightly under his tightly braided beard, but he nodded his head.

"Very well," he said. "I would have all of you remember that the Games and Festival will soon be upon us. It is time to let yourselves be seen in the human wards—especially Hera, Athena and Ishtar—to remind the humans for whose favor they compete."

"Bread and circuses," Bes said with a laugh. "Let the humans work out their aggressions by legally fighting each other."

Isis winced. She had never liked the Games, which pitted one ward against another. Soon after their arrival in Tartaros, the Nine had agreed that competitions would be an excellent way to give both humans and Opiri an outlet for any hostile impulses as well as a method of cementing loyalty to the Elders of Tanis and thereby ending any lingering conflicts between Opiri and humans. To ensure fairness, Opir competed against Opir, human against human.

But things had changed since those early days. Over time, Opiri had dropped out of the Games, leaving them entirely to the humans. Isis felt that the competitions had outlived their original purpose. The Festival that followed them still served as an opportunity for Opiri and humans to mingle, but the Nine held themselves apart from the city's humans far too often. They should walk among the people, not only during the Games, but on average days when citizens went about their ordinary business.

Isis remembered how angry she had been when Daniel had been "disrespectful" to her. Her reaction had sprung from the habits of millennia, but it discredited her own philosophy. How would Anu react to such boldness from a human?

What would he think if he found out how readily she had given herself to Daniel so soon after they had met?

"I will see to my people," Athena said. The others Anu had admonished agreed with brief nods and sighs. Isis stepped back from her chair and walked away from the table.

"It is not wise to provoke Anu," Athena said behind her. "He is overly proud, but he still has power."

"No more than any of us," Isis said, facing her friend. "We are all equals here." She lowered her voice and touched Athena's arm. "Perhaps you will come to my ward and see the new human. I do not think he is a danger to anyone in Tanis, but another interrogator might learn more than I have."

"Let *me* do it," Ishtar said, joining them. "I can be very persuasive."

"And I have neglected my people too long," Athena murmured.

"If you have failed to acquire enough information from this human," Anu said, slipping up behind Athena, "it would be wise to let Ishtar try."

Chapter 4

Isis considered objecting, but she had no desire for a real quarrel. Anu could be right, and he, too, held part of a long-lost past in his memory. The past Isis tried to ignore but was not yet ready to forget.

So she agreed, and she and Ishtar—the latter in robes that rivaled the most transparent and revealing garments worn in the Egypt of the old days—summoned a shuttle to take them back to the human sector.

"It is the middle of the night, when most humans are sleeping," Isis said when the driver helped them out of the vehicle. "Come to my house and share my wine until morning."

"But any human will be more vulnerable at such a time," Ishtar said. "We should not delay."

Isis knew she was right. Reluctantly she accompanied Ishtar to the Immigrant Center. She knew better than to let Ishtar into Daniel's room, and had the guards bring him to the interrogation chamber.

Dressed in his new clothes, Daniel seemed almost like any other fit human in Tanis. But his eyes revealed nothing when he looked at Isis, and they narrowed to slits at the sight of Ishtar.

He knew Ishtar for what she was, Isis thought. She remembered with painful clarity every accusation Daniel had flung at her: *You don't have to order anyone to get what you want.*

If he thought Isis was a seductress who commanded reverence with her influence, Ishtar would quickly prove that Isis had nothing on her sister of the Nine.

"Is this my new interrogator?" Daniel asked Isis in a calm, cool voice.

Unlike ordinary Opiri, Isis could blush. Even Daniel's few, cursory words carried her back to his bed and into his arms…and reminded her of his final mockery: *I am honored that you chose to suspend your noble chastity with me.*

Ishtar had no concerns about chastity. She moved very close to Daniel, her eyes heavy lidded.

"I am Ishtar," she purred. "I doubt you will find my questions unpleasant."

Daniel smiled a cold, almost cruel smile, ignoring the brush of Ishtar's full, barely covered breast against his shoulder. "Are you finished with me, Lady Isis?" he asked.

She lifted her chin. "I thought it was you who was finished with *me*."

With a throaty laugh, Ishtar looked from Isis to Daniel. "How interesting. Did she not please you, Daniel? Was she reluctant to share her many gifts?"

"You seem eager to share yours, Lady Ishtar."

"I have no prejudice against humans," she said, stroking his chest with a plump forefinger.

"But you're like Lady Isis," he said. "A Bloodmistress used to getting your way."

Instead of showing offense, Ishtar merely laughed again. "I see why Isis had trouble with you," she said. "But if you have any secrets, you will give them up. If not to me, then to another."

"My choice of pleasure or punishment?"

Isis flinched, thinking of the scars. "I told him there would be no punishment," she told Ishtar.

"Then by all means, let us try the former." Ishtar smiled at Isis. "Do you care to watch?"

The room filled with the smell of lust, and Isis couldn't bear it. If she'd had any courage, she would have dragged Daniel out of the room. But Ishtar might succeed where she had failed, and all Daniel would lose was his pride. The city must come first.

She quickly left the room, locking the door behind her, and sat in the reception area. Endless moments passed. The Opir guards offered her warmed blood. She declined.

At last she heard the sound of a door opening and quickly closing again, with no little force. She rose as Ishtar entered the waiting room and swept past her to the door.

"Ishtar," Isis called after her.

The former goddess paused, her beautiful face thin lipped and set. "He did not respond," she said, as if she were speaking of something quite impossible. "He must be made of stone."

With a silent sigh of relief, Isis took Ishtar's arm. "You learned nothing?" she asked.

"Only that he has come for sanctuary, but wished to learn if Tanis was all that he had heard before he let himself be known here."

"As he told me," Isis said. "Surely there can be little more to tell."

"Not if he resisted *me*," Ishtar said with a toss of her black hair. "But perhaps that alone makes him dangerous."

"He *is* different," Isis said, "but we learned long ago that not all humans are the same."

Ishtar blew out a puff of air. "I did note the scars upon his neck. His history must be quite interesting. I should advise Anu to keep Daniel in custody until he has the chance to interrogate the human himself, but I see that you have some concern for him." She smiled slyly. "What draws you to this human, Isis? Perhaps you wish to take him as your consort? I would not blame you."

"You know I have no need for a consort," Isis said, "even if he would agree."

"Yes," Ishtar said with a faint scowl. "By all means, let us not forget that mortals are now our equals."

"It was our goal when we arrived to take charge of Tartaros," Isis said. "To guide, but not to rule."

"Like Bes, you spend too much time among humans."

"If you would look upon them as students rather than casual bed partners, you might see the value in their company."

Ishtar snorted inelegantly. "Let me handle my charges in my own way. They are content enough."

Isis knew she would gain nothing by arguing. At least Ishtar took a personal interest in some of her humans, and it was largely benevolent. She seduced, but did not coerce...though perhaps, with her, there was little difference.

For Daniel, there obviously hadn't been.

"I will go back," Isis said. "Tell Anu that Daniel will be my responsibility."

"I will do as you ask," Ishtar said, her voice silky with insinuation. "But do not let him get into trouble, or we shall both be in trouble with Anu." She shook out her robes. "I think I shall seek out more willing company."

Once Ishtar was gone, Isis returned to the Center. Daniel was still in the interrogation room, standing against the far wall with his arms folded firmly across his chest. His expression seemed carved in stone, as Ishtar had described, but his eyes held an almost feverish look.

He had not been totally unaffected, after all. Isis didn't know whether she should be disappointed that he had felt

Ishtar's sexual appeal or pleased at his strength of will in resisting it.

"Why did you send her?" he asked her. "Did you think that since you failed, she would succeed?"

Isis sat in one of the chairs, angry and ashamed at the same time. "I could not rely entirely on my own judgment," she said.

"I admit that I wasn't expecting tactics like these from you, Lady Isis."

"There are others I could have sent to question you," she said sharply. "They might not have been so accommodating."

"And all without punishment," he said. "That would have been interesting."

She closed her eyes, wondering how this human could defeat her so easily. "I have made myself responsible for you," she said.

"Responsible?" he asked. "Why?"

"It is my decision to set you free, under my recognizance. If you commit any disturbance or prove to be an agent from an Enclave or another Citadel, I will be blamed."

"By whom?" he asked, stepping away from the wall. "I have met two Bloodmistresses in the short time I've been here." He took a step closer. "How many of you are there, Lady Isis?"

"How many of whom?"

"You said you were 'among those' who came here when the Citadel had fallen into chaos. Are there others like you and Ishtar?"

"Yes," she said. "Nine of us were traveling together after the War, seeking—"

"Do they all look like you, more human than Opir?"

Isis paused at the question. The most ancient and powerful Opiri had always borne a closer resemblance to humanity than those who came after. That was the great irony most Opiri did not care to examine too closely.

"You're an Elder," Daniel said, speaking into her silence. "You didn't go into the Long Sleep with all the other Opiri hundreds of years ago."

"How would you know this?" she asked. "How many of my kind have you seen?"

"One," he said. "But we all knew there were more still walking the earth."

"You learned this in the Enclave, before you were exiled?"

"In Vikos."

The serfs there had spoken of it, he meant. But *whom* had Daniel seen? There were other Elders who had chosen not to join the Nine in their quest, but they had seemingly vanished.

"Nine of you," he said, before she could speak again. "All Elders. Who better to enforce the peace? Who better to rule than Opiri wiser and more experienced than nearly all others of their kind?"

"No!" she said, rising quickly. "Yes, we founded this city. But an elected Council of humans and Opiri makes the law and enforces it through the Darketan and dhampir Lawkeepers. The Nine only observe and occasionally advise."

"And they don't use their power of influence on the people of Tanis."

Carefully considering how to answer, Isis hesitated. "We...agreed that every citizen of Tanis should be free in every way."

"Ishtar agreed to this, as well?"

"I am sorry," she said, clinging to her dignity. "It was wrong of me to call upon her."

"I accept your apology," Daniel said, though his expression remained forbidding. "I'd like to meet these other Elders. Unless, of course, they're too busy to see a simple human visitor."

"It can be arranged," Isis said. "But there are other matters to attend to first." She lifted her chin. "I will ask for your promise," she said. "Your oath that you will never do anything to harm Tanis."

Harm Tanis. It was a strange request. Daniel knew all too well that Isis feared some kind of enemy from among humans or other Opiri outside the city, but hurting Tanis was entirely beyond his capability, even if he'd wanted to do it.

The only humans or Opiri who would face opposition from him were those who prevented him from carrying out his mission. His goals hadn't changed; he needed to gather general intelligence about Tanis and find out if Ares had passed through this city.

Isis's description of the Nine had intrigued him, especially as it related to Ares. Ares was, like them, an Elder. If he had carried through with his mission here, it shouldn't take long to find out what had become of him. Not when Isis had been so free with her information. Not when he seemed to have as much influence on her as she'd ever had over *him*.

Something had happened between them...something he hadn't expected or wanted. He still didn't understand why she had been so quick to offer herself to a stranger.

He glanced at Isis, who waited patiently for his answer. Oh, he knew what she *claimed* to want: to assure Daniel that she couldn't or wouldn't try to influence him. She had also claimed to desire him. A Bloodmistress, one of the Elders, wanting a former serf she knew almost nothing about.

That was the part he still had the most difficulty understanding. And yet, whatever her original intentions, she'd responded to him like a woman in the throes of passion, hungry to be touched, to be lost in sensual pleasure. That wasn't something that could easily be faked.

But she'd also told him that he couldn't abide losing control, that it was his way of rebelling against his old life. She thought she *knew* him.

That wasn't why he'd rejected her at the end. It wasn't because she'd implied that humans required her "guidance" and that she had to remain somehow untouchable in the eyes of the city, like some kind of sacred virgin.

He'd stopped because he had felt too much. For her, yes…as nonsensical as that might be.

But he'd also *remembered*: the human women who had been brought to him in Erebus…and the threats that had followed—threats to kill the women if he refused, threats of ugly punishments that would befall them if they failed to perform as breeding stock.

There had been Opiri women, as well. Palemon had lent him out to service them. He had been a useful object, like all his fellow serfs in Palemon's Household.

Leaving that Household hadn't erased what had been done. Neither had Daniel's escape from Erebus, or the years of freedom afterward.

Just as he hadn't appeared to have aged in those intervening years, the memories had remained as fresh as the blood in his veins. In spite of what he'd told Isis, he could still hate.

But didn't hate *her*, even though she'd thrown Ishtar at him. He'd been cruel to Isis because of his own experiences, his own suspicions, but he hadn't thought such cruelty was in his nature. Ruthlessness, yes, when it came to protecting those close to him or under his care. But hurting his only ally would not only be foolish, but unnecessary.

For now, he needed her, in spite of the risks. And as long as he had a job to do, he wouldn't let the memories get in his way again.

"I promise you that I have no ill intentions toward Tanis," he said.

Isis relaxed a little, as if she'd genuinely feared he might refuse to give his word. "I am glad," she said.

"I apologize for my discourteous behavior," he said, holding her gaze.

Her lips parted. "I, too, apologize for any distress I may have caused you. Perhaps we can simply begin anew."

They gazed at each other until Isis looked away. "I can either arrange for you to stay here like most new immigrants," she said, "or find a vacant apartment for you near the plaza. The lodgings will still be plain, but luxury is not a priority in Tanis."

"I never expected luxury," he said. "I only objected to the lock on the door."

Isis flushed again. "After you have rested sufficiently and feel ready, you will be eligible for a tour of the city. We have guides whose particular work is to show newcomers around Tanis."

"I thought that was *your* chosen work," he said. "Pretending to be human so that newcomers wouldn't feel uneasy. Or is your real job to look for immigrants who might pose a threat to Tanis?"

"It is not," she said. "This particular area of the city— the administrative ward, the plaza and the living quarters in the area—are my responsibility."

"Your responsibility?"

"I'm responsible for the welfare of my people."

"You're only concerned for the people in this area."

"No, but I represent them for the Nine."

"Humans, from what I saw in the plaza."

"There are some Opiri," she said, her voice a little defensive. "They work in the offices."

"And other areas of Tanis?" Daniel asked. "The former

Opir quarters in the lower Citadel? The towers? Who's responsible for those?"

She hesitated, sweeping her fall of black hair away from her face. "You asked about the other Elders," she said slowly. "When we took Tartaros from the original Bloodlords and Bloodladies and freed the serfs, we divided the city into nine wards, one for each of us. There are three Opir wards covering the towers, one for the half-bloods and the remainder in the human sector."

"Three Opir wards covering the towers," Daniel said. "The human sector. A city divided."

"Some Opiri do live among humans."

"But there are no humans living in the towers."

Isis shifted uncomfortably. "You have just entered Tanis. You have no right to judge us yet."

"I can only judge by what you tell me. And you've been honest, Isis. Even when what you say doesn't reflect well on this city."

Isis glanced away. "If you have such grave doubts," she said, "why not leave Tanis now?"

"I'm permitted to leave?"

"I can see to it that you are free to do so." She sighed, and her face took on an expression of gentle forbearance and oddly impersonal warmth. "I *do* understand, despite what I may have said or implied."

"Then you will be my guide." When she didn't answer, he moved closer to her…close enough to touch. "You're afraid of me, Isis. You don't have to be."

"Why should I fear you?"

"You're afraid you might want me again."

"Because you are so irresistible?"

He laughed, concealing his bitterness. She swept away from him and strode toward the door.

"Someone will take you to your new quarters soon," she said. "You will remain in the Immigrant Center for now, but there will be no locks." She paused in the doorway. "Exploring without a guide is highly discouraged. I will send one later this morning."

Daniel stood alone in the room for some time after she was gone. He didn't like himself for poking and prodding at Isis, but at least now he was certain that there were others like her and Ishtar in Tanis. After centuries of living among ordinary Opiri, Ares would have met nine of his own kind.

Would he have been tempted to make a new life here, with Trinity?

No, Daniel thought, not without sending word back to Avalon. And to *him*.

Daniel spent the wee hours of the morning in his new quarters, sleeping in fits and starts, haunted by ugly dreams he couldn't remember after the sun rose over Tanis.

But he remembered Isis. She was the first thing he thought of when he opened his eyes. He bathed and dressed, considering how he could get her to agree to show him the city in spite of last night's firm rejection.

Of course, it would be easier with some other guide, someone who wouldn't simultaneously attract him and remind him of the shame of his past. Easier, but not nearly as useful.

If he were more careful, more respectful of Isis—if he kept his physical and emotional distance—he might persuade her to show him more than the average guide might be permitted to do.

Because he already felt that there was something not quite right in this city. It was only gut instinct, but he had learned to trust that instinct long ago.

Isis mustn't know about his doubts, of course. All he had to do was pretend to believe what she did, and she would give him all the help he wanted.

Chapter 5

It was not Isis's intention to go back to Daniel. Like all Opiri, she didn't require sleep, so she had tried to distract herself with books and music and a long stroll through the gardens until dawn brought the realization that she couldn't simply walk away from him.

There were still too many things she didn't understand about him, and she so badly wanted to understand. He had an effect on her that she had never experienced before.

And too much remained unresolved: he had accused her of fearing him because she thought she might want him again. It was a ridiculous notion, and yet part of her *was* afraid. She had gone too far with him, and there was no undoing what had occurred between them.

Still, she could not allow herself to fear anything or anyone in Tanis, not if she was to play her part in the future she envisioned. Surely there could be no question of seduction now. Not on her part. And Daniel would have no reason to touch her again.

Daniel had been correct: she had made herself responsible for him, and she could not fulfill her promise if she put him into the hands of another.

So she dressed in a very simple white gown, casually adorned with a gold sash and a beaded pectoral necklace a human craftsman had made for her. She put on plain sandals and pulled her hair back, just as she would wear it on any occasion when there was work to be done. The unembroidered day coat, with its protective cowl, was the finishing touch.

Instead of summoning a private cab, she caught a shuttle with humans and Opiri on their way to jobs in the administrative offices. It was a pity that Daniel couldn't see her then, among the people like any average citizen.

You have nothing to prove, she reminded herself. And nothing to regret.

When she reached the Immigrant Center, Daniel was pacing in the lobby, each movement imbued with a powerful grace, muscles sliding easily against each other in perfect harmony. He looked up as soon as she entered, and she saw as well as felt the change in him: his blue eyes lit as if a fire burned behind them, and there was a subtle shift in his body, as if he were shedding an invisible weight.

Isis felt her own body respond in spite of all her determination to hold herself aloof, warmth gathering between her thighs and her heart beating more quickly. She smiled at Daniel with the most neutral expression she could manage and approached him as cautiously as she might a lion in the wilderness.

"You changed your mind," Daniel said, his voice warmer than she'd ever heard it.

"Yes. I realized that I was being unreasonable in refusing to guide you."

"I'm glad," Daniel said, bowing his head. The simple act confused and angered Isis, as if he were mocking her with his show of respect.

But he wasn't mocking her. The cynicism she had expected seemed to have vanished, along with the hardness in his face and eyes.

Why the change? she thought. But she knew she should

accept his manner as a gift instead of questioning it. Now she could enjoy showing him the city. If he could come to believe in it as she did…

He might stay.

She shook away the thought and smiled again. "Are you ready to begin your tour?" she asked.

"I look forward to it."

"Then let us begin. We will walk much of the time, but there are areas where we will need other transportation."

Daniel nodded, and she turned for the door.

They began in the main plaza. The sun shone in open sky above, and Isis was careful to keep her cowl over her head when they were exposed to the daylight.

She showed Daniel the multistory apartment buildings the citizens had built after Tanis had been established on Tartaros's foundations. Very few Opiri lived in the apartments, but the humans there acknowledged her and Daniel with smiles and words of greeting. She was relieved that none of them actually bowed or showed her any particular deference, and astonished that she should be thinking about it at all.

Daniel's accusations had made her aware of things she had simply taken for granted.

She pointed out the Council chambers and the Hall of Justice, built in the Greek style with wide stairs and columned porch, and showed him the other government buildings, some adapted from the old, pre-Tanis days, others more recently constructed.

"Your Council is made up of Opiri, humans and half-bloods?" he asked.

"Yes," she said. "They also serve as judges on those rare occasions when a citizen breaks the law beyond the scope of the Lawkeepers and must be evaluated."

"No juries?" Daniel asked.

"Witnesses are called during the hearings," she said. "All testimony is accepted."

"But the Council makes the final decision."

"An elected Council," she said quickly. "All citizens have their vote."

As they left the vicinity of the Hall, they passed a number of Lawkeeper patrols as well as a few guards who served in other capacities, and Daniel noted that none of them appeared to be human. Isis was compelled to admit that guards and Lawkeepers were by custom either half-bloods or Opiri. Daniel's terse nod forced her to realize that the lack of humans in law enforcement would seem strange, even problematic to an outsider.

She had never even thought about it.

"That building, there," Daniel said, indicating the featureless walls of a two-story structure at the far edge of the plaza. "What is that?"

Isis felt a strange reluctance to answer. "The blood depository," she said. "It is where humans go to—"

"Contribute blood." Daniel's expression was neutral, but she felt the tension in him nonetheless.

"As I said before, no human is forced to do it," she said.

"But this city would collapse if the human population refused."

"They know that as well as you do," Isis said, her words sharp with annoyance.

"They'd be compelled to donate in short order," Daniel said, still staring at the building.

"That is why Tanis is built upon cooperation and sacrifice. Our citizens do not allow themselves to surrender to their instincts, no matter how powerful they may be."

"That is reassuring."

But his doubt was apparent, in spite of his attempts to hide it.

Isis was relieved when they caught a private shuttle that took them away from the clusters of multistory buildings and deep into the human sector, where older, lower buildings had once housed the Citadel's many Freebloods, former Opiri vassals who had yet to establish a Household or claim a serf.

"And now Freebloods live in the towers with the ranked Opiri?" he asked.

"Most do," she said reluctantly. "Though many chose to leave and seek their fortunes elsewhere when Tanis was established."

"Rogues," Daniel said. "No Citadel would take in Freebloods from another Citadel, and the only way they can live outside is by running in packs and ambushing free humans or raiding colonies."

Isis knew she shouldn't be surprised by his knowledge of Freebloods. He would have seen many in Vikos. But if he knew about the packs…

"Were you assaulted on your journey to Tanis?" she asked, trying to imagine Daniel fighting off a dozen rogues and escaping with his blood and his life.

"I was able to avoid most of them. But I saw them. I saw what they could do."

"You said that you received help from humans hiding in the wilderness," Isis said. "We know that there are a few colonies in this area and in the mountains to the west, small human settlements that move frequently if they feel threatened."

"I stayed in one for a time. It was under nearly constant attack. People died."

"I am sorry," she said, meaning it. "We are also aware of colonies built upon the same principles Tanis follows, where both Opiri and human citizens are welcome."

"Colonies, not cities," Daniel said. "Before I was sent to Vikos, I heard of them. But it was said that they were no safer than the human settlements outside the Enclaves. Even if they managed to maintain their principles of coexistence, it wouldn't mean much if they couldn't defend themselves from the Citadels and rogue raiders."

And was that, Isis wondered, why Daniel had come all the way to Tanis…to find a place that could defend itself and would still permit him to live in freedom?

She wanted…*needed* for him to see that Tanis was that place.

They left the central avenue and entered the maze of narrow streets between the residential buildings of Bes's ward. The little Opir wasn't there, and most of the human residents had gone to their jobs for the day. The older children were in school, while the younger ones stayed with one of their parents or a caretaker.

The buildings were neat and well-kept, with flower boxes on windowsills and decorations on doors and walls. The small neighborhood plaza was green with trees and grass, crisscrossed with well-tended paths. A few older humans congregated near a bench, gossiping among themselves. They grinned and shouted greetings to Isis, their eyes shining. She acknowledged them with a wave of her hand. A group of children walking with their teacher brought her a bunch of hand-picked flowers. Daniel looked on in silence.

As they turned the corner from one street onto another, a middle-aged man stepped up to speak to Isis, dipping his head in a gesture of respect. He told her of plumbing problems in his building, and Isis promised to see that Bes looked into the situation. Several other men and women approached with similar concerns, ranging from quarrels with neighbors to questions about the Council elections coming up in two months' time. Again, Isis assured them that she would speak with Bes as soon as she was free.

One young mother emerged from her ground-floor residence to greet Isis, holding an infant in her arms. Joy flooded Isis's heart, as it always did when she saw mother and child. Once humans had brought their children to her to be blessed, and mothers had prayed to her for the health of their families.

So very long ago.

The mother slipped the infant into Isis's hands, and Isis kissed the boy's soft, round cheek. Daniel gazed at her with a slight frown between his brows, as if he could not imagine her with a child in her keeping.

"Hold him," she said, gently laying the infant in Daniel's arms.

He held the child awkwardly; not as if he had never done so before, but with an almost excessive caution, as if he didn't trust himself to do it properly. After a moment he returned the infant to its mother with a nod and a half smile.

"Thank you, Lady Isis," the woman said, backing up a few steps before returning to her apartment. Daniel stared after her.

"The boy's eyes," he said. "He's a half-blood. His father was Opir."

"The child's a dhampir, yes. Did I not tell you that we have mixed couples in Tanis? Not as many as I would wish, perhaps, but it is a new beginning."

"Have you ever had a child, Isis?"

She was too surprised to be angry over the impertinent question. "You know it is possible?" she asked.

"I learned in the Citadel that Opir women could give birth in a mating with a male human. It was kept secret because no Opiri wanted to admit that a female of their kind could have a child by a serf."

"Then you know the origins of the Darketans."

"Humans call Darketans 'Daysiders.'" He looked keenly into her eyes. "Unless you spent all your time since the War wandering in the wilderness, you know that the Citadels take them from their mothers when they are hardly more than infants and treat them little better than serfs, even though they rely on them to do their daytime spying in the zones around the Citadels."

"We do not do that here," she said. "Our Darketans

come to Tanis to live full lives as equals. And female Opiri in Tanis can choose to have children by human males if they wish. There's no shame attached."

"And how often has it happened?"

A sharp pain struck Isis's heart as she spoke. Yes, she could have borne a child, if she had ever found a male human for whom she could care deeply enough. But she had never sought one out. It had always been her work to nurture others, and bearing a child would bend her attention away from those who most needed her.

"It's ironic that the Citadels never objected to the wartime practice of Opiri males forcibly impregnating human females," Daniel said.

Ironic, Isis thought. Hypocrisy. She was hardly proud of what Opiri had done during the War, even though she had never been part of it.

But Daniel's voice had hardened, and she wondered why the subject seemed so personal to him. He claimed he didn't hate Opiri, but his words suggested otherwise.

"Why did you wish to know if I'd ever given birth?" she asked, quickly changing the subject.

"It seems as if it would be natural for you."

She relaxed. "Is that a compliment?" she asked.

"It's clear that you would love your children, as all these people seem to love you."

Her mind flew directly to his accusation that she used her power to influence others. Isis was tempted to end the tour there, even though Daniel had hardly seen any of the city. But he was already walking on, his gaze quick and probing as he looked up and down the streets.

She caught up with him. "What is it you wish to see?" she asked.

"Another neighborhood," he said. He paused by the small Lawkeeper station situated at the northern border of Bes's ward.

"What is this?" he asked.

"There is a Lawkeeper station set up at every border between wards," she said, feeling once again as if she had to justify Tanis's laws. "We find these to be practical locations, and they can easily be found by any citizen."

"Then they aren't meant to hinder movement between wards?"

"Of course not! Any citizen may visit any part of the city."

"And are stations located in the Opir wards as well as the human ones?"

"Naturally," she said, "though the stations are located at the base of every tower except the one inhabited by the Nine."

He seemed satisfied with the answer, and they continued past the guard station into the next ward.

It was overseen by Hera, who, Isis knew, very seldom visited her people. Isis rarely came here herself, and almost at once she noticed that something was not quite right. There was refuse in the streets, and no planters of flowers and greenery near the doors. Even the buildings themselves were in less than optimal condition, seamed with cracks and even a few broken windows.

Daniel was staring at one of the buildings, his face expressionless. "Is this one of your bad neighborhoods?" he asked.

"There is no such thing in Tanis," Isis said, struggling to conceal her shock. "Every citizen receives the credits he or she requires to live comfortably, though work beyond the basic requirements can be used for nonessential goods."

"It looks like someone forgot to give these people their share of the common wealth."

Isis was appalled. Hera should never have let things come to such a state. She was the advocate here. Even though she kept her distance from humans, there was no excuse for her failing to care for her charges.

"I will speak to her at once," Isis said.

"Speak to whom?" Daniel said, a grim set to his mouth.

"The sponsor who looks after this ward."

"And who is that?"

Isis was very reluctant to name names, but she could not bring herself to withhold the information. "Hera," she said. "Clearly, she has been neglecting—"

"Hera, Isis, Ishtar," Daniel said, his forehead creased in thought. "Who are the others?"

A human boy appeared on the street, a boy of an age where he would soon move from the schoolroom to his chosen work. His clothes were slightly worn and ill-fitting, and when he saw Isis he stopped suddenly and stared as if she were taking Daniel's blood right in front of him. His expression grew pinched, and he quickly disappeared around the corner of the nearest cross street. Other humans, some older, gathered nearby and gave Isis the same sullen, almost unfriendly stare. Many of them wore Hera's peacock sigil somewhere on their shirts, though they clearly had no reason to thank her for their current circumstances.

One of the larger males moved toward Isis, and Daniel stepped between her and the human. He stared the man down, and he retreated, followed by the others.

Isis touched Daniel's arm and led him back toward Bes's ward. Daniel's muscles were taut as if he wanted to resist her, perhaps even return and speak to the angry humans.

Hera, Isis thought, *what have you done?*

This would have to be brought to the Nine's notice, regardless of Hera's likely animosity. The others would see that she did not fail in her duty again.

But that would not erase Isis's memory of the looks those poor people had given her. She could not remember the last time a human being had shown her even the slightest hostility.

"Why did they stare at you like that?" Daniel asked, echoing her thoughts.

Isis latched on to the first safe explanation that came to mind. "It is nearly time for the Games," she said.

"The Games?"

"Twice a year the human wards hold competitions," she said. "Did you notice the badges on some of the humans' shirts and uniforms?"

"I noticed them. Peacocks."

"Hera's symbol. When the Games are near, many humans wear the emblems of the Elders to represent their teams."

"Only humans?"

Isis glanced away. "There was a time when Opiri participated, competing among themselves. Now they only observe."

"What kinds of competitions?" he asked.

"Racing, jumping, older games that humans remember from before the War."

"No fighting? Wrestling, boxing, martial arts?"

"No!" She stared at him. "We do not condone violence."

"Then those people were hostile toward you just because you represent an opposing team?"

"I have no team in the Games."

"So you didn't anticipate their attitude. You don't understand it."

His challenges came too thick and fast, and she answered carelessly. "It makes no sense to me. Unless they are angry with Hera, and project that anger onto—"

"Isis!"

She snapped out of her thoughts to find Bes gazing up at her and Daniel, a grin on his perpetually pleasant face.

"And who is this?" he asked, staring up at Daniel. "The man who entered Tanis so clandestinely? The dangerous invader?" He shivered dramatically. "Are you quite sure it's safe to let such a monster run around loose, my dear Isis?"

Chapter 6

Daniel stared down at the little Opir, containing his anger and surprise. "I wasn't aware that my reputation had spread," he said, sparing Isis the need to answer. "My name is Daniel, and I promise you that I am no danger to this city or anyone in it."

Bes laughed. "Well said." He thrust out his broad hand. "I am Bes."

After a moment's hesitation, Daniel took Bes's hand.

"A strong grip," Bes said. "Excellent. Though it was amusing to see the look on your face when you first saw me." He dropped Daniel's hand and smoothed the front of his tunic. "What astonished you most? My size?"

"I'm not accustomed to shaking hands with Opiri I've never met," Daniel said.

"But I look nothing like most Opiri. Did Isis tell you about me? Or did you guess?"

"He has met only Ishtar," Isis said cautiously. "How did you know Bes was Opir, Daniel?"

"Survival instincts, perhaps," Bes said in his usual blunt fashion. "Humans have a great capacity for self-preservation."

"Your teeth," Daniel said.

Bes covered his mouth. "How silly of me." He glanced slyly at Isis. "Did you know about *her*?"

"He claims he did not know until I told him," Isis said.

"Well, you do wear the caps so as not to alarm—"

"I believe he *did* guess," Isis said, meeting Daniel's gaze. "But it does not matter now. We were just taking a tour of the human wards."

"I trust you approve of mine?" Bes asked.

"You're one of the Elders?" Daniel asked.

"Isis has told you about the Nine."

"Only a little," Daniel said, his voice clearly indicating that "a little" was not nearly enough.

"I have just begun to show him the city," Isis said.

"Ah," Bes said, belatedly aware of the tension in the air. "Well, I think when you return you will find that my humans are particularly well known for serving the finest beer in the city."

"And that, of course, is what makes Bes so fond of this place," Isis said. "But not even humans can live on beer alone. Are you hungry, Daniel?"

Daniel shook his head. "I'd like to see the other wards."

"Another time," Isis said. "Let us return to the Center."

"I'll come along," Bes offered.

The three of them took another shuttle back to the administrative ward, where a small crowd had gathered in front of the blood depository. Several humans, both men and women, were walking back and forth in front of the doors, chanting and holding hand-printed signs. No Forced Donation, one of them read. Isis didn't have to see the others to guess at their sentiments.

"Forced donations?" Daniel said, his eyes like chips of lapis lazuli. "I thought that didn't happen here. What are they protesting?"

"It is not what it seems," Isis said. She started toward the depository, but four uniformed Lawkeepers had already reached the protesters and had closed in around one female, who began to shout and struggle as a male Darketan caught hold of her.

Isis ran to meet them, Daniel and Bes at her heels. The woman protester was weeping as her hands were pulled behind her, her sign broken at her feet.

"Stop," Isis said. The Lawkeepers in the process of arresting the remaining male and female protesters looked up and hesitated.

"What have they done deserving of arrest?" she asked.

"Disturbing the operation of the depository," one of the Darketans said.

"Let me speak to them," Isis said, aware of Daniel right behind her.

"Wait," Bes said, his wide mouth fixed in a straight line. "I know them. They will listen to me." He spoke to the Lawkeepers, who backed away and watched from a respectful distance as he approached the protesters.

"What is he trying to do?" Daniel asked.

"Calm them. Encourage them to see reason."

Daniel watched intently as Bes spoke to the protesters. The fight seemed to go out of them all at once. Bes gripped one of the men's arms companionably and smiled at the woman. She smiled back. He spoke to the Lawkeepers again, and they removed the manacles.

"What did he say to them?" Daniel asked.

Isis sighed inwardly. This would not be a pleasant conversation, and it must be done in private. "Come to my apartment," she said, "and I will explain."

But he remained where he was, staring toward the doors of the depository with a fixed expression of surprise. An Opir was emerging cautiously, his head swinging back and forth as he took in the small crowd and the presence of the Lawkeepers.

Glancing at Daniel's face, Isis knew that something was very wrong. He *knew* this Opir.

Knew him and hated him.

"Come," Isis said, carefully taking Daniel's hand.

He stared at her blankly. His hand trembled, and it almost seemed as if he had gone to some place deep in his mind, rejecting anything that would restore him to the real world. Unease, strange and unwelcome, coiled in Isis's belly.

But he moved when she tugged on his hand. He followed her as the crowd dispersed, and she took him to her building and her apartment on the top floor. He paused inside the doorway, his rigid expression finally easing into a very ordinary suspicion. He scanned the main room as if he expected a trap.

"It is all right, Daniel," she said gently, afraid to touch him again. "We are alone here."

Daniel met her gaze, and the veil dropped from his eyes.

"Please, sit down," she said. "I can offer something to drink and a little fruit, if you wish."

"No," Daniel said. He continued to stand by the small table in front of the couch until Isis took her seat, and then he perched on the edge of the couch, a muscle in his jaw jumping faintly.

"Who was it, Daniel?" she asked. "Who did you see outside the depository?"

Daniel blinked as if he didn't understand her question. "Why were those people protesting?" he said, changing the subject without warning.

"There are always a few citizens who resent the necessary part they play in keeping our city strong."

"I didn't see any violence. Why were the protesters arrested?"

"It was overzealous on the Lawkeepers' part," she said, equally bewildered by their actions. "It was not necessary."

"Not if you have free speech in Tanis," he said. "Do you?"

"Even your Enclaves do not have completely free speech," she said, "but we do what we can to encourage it here."

"Just not today," Daniel said. "What will happen to the protesters?"

"Since Bes defused the situation, they will be sent home with a reminder not to disturb the peace."

"And if the same people do it again?"

"I do not know," she admitted. "As long as they remain peaceful—"

"What do you do with humans who won't give blood?"

"We encourage them to seek a place that better suits their preferences."

"You eject them from the city."

"Only if we have no other choice, and even then we provide them with all the resources they require. As we discussed, there are human colonies to take them in."

"And packs of rogues to deal with along the way."

"Would you have a society without rules?" she asked. "Would you permit citizens to flout the law at will? Unimpeded aggression among the people of Tanis?"

"Opiri thrive on aggression," he said. "How often do *they* flout your laws? Do they steal blood from unwilling humans?"

"I have never heard of such a thing occurring here."

"If they did, would they face similar punishment?"

"There is no favoritism, Daniel."

He stared down at the glass table and moved a small vase a few inches to one side, his hand clutching the fragile vessel as if it were a weapon. "But humans, of course, need more looking after," he said. "You said it yourself. It is your place to guide." He looked up. "Is that what Bes was doing?"

"He knew those people, and—"

"He persuaded them to back down. He used the same influence you do, even when you don't realize it."

"We have had this discussion before. What I—"

"In this future you envision, can there really be any free will for humanity?"

"We Elders have lived for thousands of years," she said. "Is it so wrong to give others the benefit of our experience?"

"But does your experience apply to humans?" He counted off on his fingers. "Isis. Ishtar. Bes. Hera. They all have one thing in common, aside from being Elders. It isn't just coincidence that you're all named after ancient gods, is it?"

Isis knew the time for prevarication was long past. "You have guessed," she said, lifting her chin. "We once acted as gods and goddesses among your kind, very long ago."

"You ruled humanity, even before the Long Sleep, when most of your kind went into hibernation."

"Humans *made* us what we became."

"But you went along with their delusions. And, eventually, you left the people who worshipped you. You became myth. And then, after the War between your kind and mine, you rose again to rule as you did before."

"That was never our intention."

"Maybe it has nothing to do with your intentions." He smiled crookedly. "Isis. If I remember correctly, she was the protector of mothers and children, the Lady of Magic, friend of slaves. Your ability to influence others would have seemed like magic in ancient times. And you've already proven yourself a friend of slaves, haven't you?"

Isis was beautiful in her injured pride, her head high, her eyes flashing. As he watched her, Daniel could almost forget what he had seen at the depository and in Hera's ward. He could almost accept that everything Isis said was true…all her hopes, her dreams, her faith in Tanis's ultimate success.

"I helped to guide Egypt for over two thousand years," she said, a slight note of defensiveness in her voice. "I did *not* rule. That was the work of mortal kings. I was there for humans who sought my help, and I gave them advice and encouragement when I could." She met Daniel's gaze. "Is that such a terrible thing?"

"And were all your fellow gods so benevolent?"

"Some had almost nothing to do with humanity, but merely took on the aspects of deities created by humans. Bes was a god of mothers and childbirth, as I was, and also a protector of the household. He is a good Opir."

"At least his intentions are," Daniel said. "What about Hera? Was she so benevolent?"

"She has changed from the time I knew her long ago," Isis said with obvious regret.

"And Ishtar?" he asked. "She was a goddess of fertility and sex. She still uses her powers for seduction to get her way, no matter what you and the other Nine intended."

"*You* did not respond."

"Maybe that's because I was thinking of another goddess."

The words came out of his mouth without any thought behind them, but he realized at once that they were true. He had been thinking of Isis every moment that Ishtar had been doing her best to seduce him. Isis, with her dark eyes and lovely body and her odd trust in him. Trust he'd done little enough to earn.

"If you…think well of me," she said, "you cannot believe that I have *ever* used my influence to harm any human."

Daniel stepped around the table, coming very close to her. "You've been honest with me, more than you had to be. I saw you with that baby and his mother. You weren't faking your affection." Very cautiously he touched her cheek with his fingertips, doing his best to ignore the rush of desire that came with the contact. "You weren't faking in my room, either, were you?"

She trembled. "Perhaps, as you suggested, I wished to learn something about you that I couldn't get any other way."

"You must have had a thousand lovers when you were a goddess. Ordinary men would have fallen at your feet without your lifting a finger."

Her hand covered his. "I do not think there is anything ordinary about you, Daniel."

He wondered if she had guessed what he really was.

"There's nothing unusual about me," he said gruffly, withdrawing his hand.

"Maybe *you* cannot see it. But I know your past was a difficult one and that you survived it. Not all humans can say the same."

For a moment he thought she was going to ask him about his life as a serf. A chill enveloped his body.

Then his sense returned to him and he smiled. Isis stood very still for a long moment, barely breathing, her skin flushed. He was half-tempted to take her in his arms and finish what they'd begun yesterday.

But physical attraction wasn't enough. Neither was mutual admiration, though he wasn't sure how he'd earned hers. She was still a Bloodmistress—a goddess—and he still had his work to do.

"Who are they, Isis?" he asked. "The rest of the Nine?"

She clasped her hands in her lap. "You will probably recognize their names," she said, her voice a little unsteady. "Athena, Anu, Ereshkigal, Hephaestus, and Hermes."

"Greek and Babylonian," he said. "Anu, I don't know."

"Ancient Sumer," Isis said. "He is the eldest and wisest among us, and he leads the Nine." She seemed about to go on and changed her mind. "Anu, Hephaestus and Eresh-kigal are the guardians of our Opiri."

"Ereshkigal," Daniel said. "Goddess of the Underworld. Appropriate enough."

"Do you think Opiri belong in such a place?"

The words were spoken half in jest, but Daniel took them seriously. "Certainly not the Opir I'm looking at right now," he said.

He took his seat and leaned forward, his elbows on his knees.

"Were there any others?" he asked. "Some of the old gods who came with you to Tanis?"

She frowned, a delicate crease forming between her brows. "There were a few others. When we came to Tar-taros, one left us to make his way alone. There were a few who wished to rule by the old customs. We did not welcome them among us. And there was one other who came to us for a very brief time, not long ago. His name was Ares."

"The Greek god of war," Daniel said softly.

"Yes. I never met him in the past, and saw him only twice while he was here. He said he had come to find out if Tanis was what he had heard it to be, as you did. But he left soon after he arrived." She searched Daniel's eyes. "Why do you ask?"

He left soon after, Daniel thought. But where would he have gone?

"I saw Ares once, in Vikos," he said. "He was one of the few Opiri who treated serfs decently. I didn't realize then that he might actually have been a 'god.'"

"Strange. Ares spoke of coming from the region of Ere-bus, far to the west."

Immediately Daniel was on his guard. "We heard he was traveling, but the rulers of Vikos would not have let him stay to challenge them. Rumors among the serfs suggested that he was seeking a place like this after leaving his Citadel."

"We know that the rulers of Vikos are aggressive and greedy for power. Ares might have been lucky to escape with his life."

But of course Ares had almost certainly never been there at all. It was all part of Daniel's invented backstory.

"He seemed wise and controlled when he came here," Isis said, as if she hadn't noticed Daniel's silence. "If he once served as a god to humans, he had clearly left that life far behind." She paused. "He had a mate with him when he came to us, a dhampir woman whom he treated with great respect. I believe her name was Trinity."

Daniel kept his breathing to a normal pace. "Why did they leave?"

"I did not actually see them depart, but my last words with them were of making a new life."

"They didn't say anything about their destination?"

It was clear from her expression that she wondered about Daniel's interest. "I was under the impression that they intended to return to their home."

Daniel knew that it would be wise to drop the subject for now. "I hope he found what he was looking for," he said.

"A pity he could not have found it here," Isis said. She gazed at Daniel for a long moment. "Perhaps you will answer a question for *me*. Why did you react so strongly when you saw that Opir emerging from the depository?" She searched his face. "You dodged the question before. But surely the answer is not so terrible?"

"It doesn't matter," Daniel said, looking away.

"It does to me." She rose, and her bare feet whispered across the floor. "I saw the hatred on your face. Who is he?"

Daniel took a deep breath. "His name is Hannibal. He was a vicious Bloodlord, a close ally of my first owner."

"Anu's advisor," Isis said. "I have met him. Your description of him does not seem—"

"Everyone in Vikos knew his reputation. He was an evil man, Isis. He could never stay in a place like this without his own Household and serfs. He would never give up that life."

"And yet he has."

"He lives among the other Opiri in the towers?"

"Yes."

"And he has never caused any trouble here?"

"Not that I have heard."

"Opiri like Hannibal don't change," he said. "If you're worried about spies, Isis, I'd watch him more closely."

Her hand touched his shoulder. "An agent from Vikos?" she asked.

Daniel hesitated. He had chosen to say that *he* came from Vikos to keep the Tanisian's attention away from the western colonies near Erebus, in the event that the Opiri of Tanis proved hostile. Hannibal's presence could prove a danger to him, for the former Bloodlord would know who and what he really was. Daniel had no idea where Hannibal had been over the past several years, but Ares had fought Hannibal and exiled him from Erebus after the overthrow of the Citadel's original government. Hannibal would surely be very happy to take revenge on his enemy, by any means possible.

"You can't believe anything he says," Daniel said.

"Even though he has acted only in good faith and followed our laws?" she asked. "A powerful Bloodmaster like Ares wanted something beyond serfs and divinity. Surely this one, too, can learn."

He took her by her shoulders. "Is it that you only see the good in people, Isis? Is that your blindness?"

She pulled free. "And is yours constant suspicion, a refusal to see what is good or even to hope?"

Grabbing her slender waist, Daniel looked into her eyes. "I've been wrong before."

He kissed her. She stiffened for a fraction of a second and then relaxed in his arms, returning his kiss fully and eagerly. She, a goddess once adored by millions, wanted a man like him as much as he wanted her. He had been a serf, helped found a colony, fought Freebloods, governed a compound where Opiri and humans lived in relative harmony.

But in the end there was nothing more than this.

He swept her up in his arms and carried her to the small bedroom off the living area. The bed's wooden footboard and headboard were decorated with ancient Egyptian motifs and carvings of human figures going about their daily tasks, from harvesting grains to fishing in the river. A woman held a child to her breast, and birds dipped and dived among the rushes.

Isis followed his gaze. "There are some things I do not wish to forget," she said.

Daniel laid her on the bed, staring at the carvings. Isis pulled his head down and kissed him. At once he was inundated by dreams of another time and place, the cool of night on bare skin and the smell of a river as the flower-scented boat glided along, the oars pulled by bronze-skinned men in simple white kilts, singing as he held Isis in his arms.

Unembarrassed by their presence, he unfastened her gown and untied the sash. She wore nothing underneath. Her wide necklace glowed against the golden skin above her breasts, and her bracelets chimed softly as she stretched her arms over her head.

There were no words between them, nothing to break the spell.

She wrapped her thighs around his hips and sighed as he eased inside her. Her breasts rose and fell with each short, sharp breath. She was smooth and warm and wet, drawing him in, and he began to breathe harshly as the pace quickened and she arched up to meet his thrusts. He kissed her breasts, one and then the other, and licked the warm skin of her shoulder. She pulled him closer with agile fingers and pressed her lips to his neck.

When her teeth penetrated his skin, he could hardly hold himself back. A different kind of ecstasy gripped him as the blood flowed, though some distant part of him knew that he should struggle, push her away, prevent her from taking what so many of her kind had stolen by force.

But the blood continued to flow, and he finished inside her with a low grunt of satisfaction. She came a moment later, her teeth still embedded in his neck, her arms holding him tightly against her.

He opened his eyes, and the fragrant deck was gone, the black arc of starry sky and the cool river vanished. He and Isis were naked, and Isis's lips were at his throat.

Chapter 7

Pulling free, Daniel rolled off the bed, retreated to the door and stared at her. He had lost himself completely, and he still saw Isis as she had looked in the dream: glorious skin dappled by moonlight, nipples rouged; hair spread across the cushions; kohl painting her beautiful eyes.

"Daniel?" she said with obvious concern, rising on her elbow.

He touched the side of his neck. There was no blood.

"What did you do?" he asked hoarsely.

"I do not understand."

"You used your influence. You made me see—"

"I did nothing!" she said, snatching up her robes and wrapping them around herself.

"I saw another place, with a river. An ancient time."

Her eyes widened. "I had nothing to do with what you saw."

Had it all been his imagination, then? Daniel wondered. An inner vision of another age, meant to distance him from this one, to hold reality and the painful memories at bay?

But at least some parts of it had been real.

"You were about to take my blood," he said.

She sat straight up. "Do you think I would…unless you asked me, I would never…"

Daniel grabbed his clothes and pulled them on with short, sharp jerks. "I'm sorry," he said. "I didn't know what I was doing."

She tied her sash as she rose, her body supple and soft and alluring. "You were always in control of your mind and your body," she said, hurt and anger in her voice. "Are you saying that the only way you would want me is if I influenced you?"

Her words froze him in place. The thought that she would need to force him to make love to her was beyond absurd.

But he had felt her teeth on his neck. She could have licked away the blood and healed him before he emerged from his dream. They had been together long enough that she wouldn't be able to ignore his blood—the smell of it, the sound of his pulse, the ease with which she might claim it.

"I did not take your blood!" she said, eyes flashing. "I know your past. I would never force you to relive it." Her lips thinned. "But it is more than that which troubles you, is it not? Perhaps if I were human, it would be different. How long has it been for *you*, Daniel?"

There was no mockery in her words, but Daniel flinched anyway. He should lie and tell her that this was simply a casual thing with him, as it seemed to be with her; that he took lovers as easily as he breathed.

"I think it has been a long time," she said. She sat on the couch, her robes settling about her. "Even before the Nine came to Tanis, it had been many years for me." She gathered up one of the hand-woven throws and bunched it into a ball. "Until you came, I was not even tempted. I am not like Ishtar, Daniel. It has never been so simple for me, even in my days as a goddess."

"How could it be anything but simple for someone with virtually unlimited power?"

"And again the cynicism," she said, a note of sadness in her voice. "You have hardened your heart."

"I am what I am."

"What your time as a serf made you," she said. "Again and again you test yourself, to prove...what? That nothing can make you surrender even a little of yourself to another?" She rose and drew very close; he could smell the clean fragrance of her air and the undertone of sexual desire. "What did they do to you in Vikos, Daniel? Why do you feel such shame?"

"I am not asha—"

"I saw the scars on your back. I know you suffered great brutality. But that is not all, is it?" She touched his face. "I want to help. I want to understand, and do what I can to show you that—"

Blind with unreasoning anger, Daniel walked out of the apartment. He strode back to the Center and went to his room, where he washed his face and stared at himself in the mirror.

Again and again you test yourself, to prove...what? she had said. *That nothing can make you surrender even a little of yourself to another?*

She saw into him so easily, Daniel thought. There had been a few lovers since his escape from Erebus, brief affairs with human women that had never lasted. His desires had always been under rigid control. Twice, Isis had punched through those barriers, and the second time hadn't been a seduction. *He'd* begun it.

Daniel glanced at the clock. It was late afternoon, and he needed somewhere to go...away from Isis and her soft, sympathetic reassurances, the murmured promises of a woman who was still Opiri. He made certain that he was presentable and walked out into the reception area. Nobody took any notice of him as he left the building and crossed the plaza. He turned immediately for the first human neighborhood Isis had shown him, Bes's ward. He thought of the people protesting at the depository, wondering if he might find them and speak to them.

Keeping his eyes and ears open, Daniel moved casually past the idle Lawkeepers at the border of the neighborhood. Men and women were coming home from their daytime employment, some dusty from the fields or stained with grease from maintenance work, others in trim clothes suitable to office jobs. Daniel leaned against the wall of an apartment block and watched without paying any particular attention, blending in as best he could.

He loitered as the workers entered their buildings, some greeting children who had been anticipating their return. They behaved like anyone glad to be home after a long day's work, without sullenness or resentment. But after night fell, Daniel noted some of the men and a few women leaving their apartments and moving in one direction, singly or in pairs. He followed one man along several well-lit streets to a building set apart from the others, the double doors flung open and the sound of music emanating from inside.

Soon after, Daniel smelled the unmistakable scent of alcohol. He recognized the place as a tavern, and when he cautiously entered he found the men and women engaged in loud conversation, drinking and even dancing to the rhythm of a guitar and drum.

The closest Daniel had been to such a place had been the mess in Delos, but alcohol was served only on special occasions. Here it seemed to flow freely enough and, again, nobody seemed to notice Daniel entering the large room. Communal tables were scattered all over the tavern, and the smell of cooking permeated the air, making Daniel remember that he hadn't eaten in some time.

But he didn't have any of the local scrip to exchange for food or drink, so all he could do was slip quietly into an unoccupied corner and continue to listen. The people were as varied as they would be in any crowd of humans; only a handful, he noticed, wore Bes's emblem of a sheaf of wheat sewn on their sleeves or the shoulder of their shirts or jackets.

For the most part, conversation was of the kind one might hear in any gathering: good-natured complaints about work, gossip about fellow humans, jokes and the occasional burst of song.

But at least one group was different. Daniel focused on their speech, blocking out the rest.

The complaints of these men and women were not so good-natured, and their faces were grave and discontented. They muttered rather than speaking loudly, and bent over their drinks as if they held secret messages to be guarded from prying eyes.

"The bloody Games," said a thin man with a trace of a beard. "They should be done away with."

"Won't happen anytime soon," an older woman said. "As long as so many human citizens take them seriously..."

"And as long as it serves *their* purpose."

"Keep the humans distracted, so they don't realize how much better the Opiri have it in the towers."

"There's no proof," the older woman said. "We can't know—"

"The human servants who work for the bloodsuckers say they live in luxury," a big man said.

"Hugh, you know the human servants like to boast to make themselves feel better about working for the Opiri."

"You've seen them parading around the plazas and walking on the causeway at night, dressed like royalty," the man they had called Hugh said. "Where did they get the clothes and the jewelry? They've been keeping what was left at the fall of Tartaros just for themselves." He swung his bearded head to glare at each of his companions in turn.

"I say that we're lucky to get half the resources the blood-suckers do, even if we're the ones keeping them alive."

"The Nine favor them," the thin man said. "And as *they* go, so goes the Council. We'll never be anything but peons to them."

"Hush," the woman said. "That's enough. It's too—"

She broke off just as one of the other men at the table noticed Daniel's clandestine observation and stared straight into his eyes. Daniel looked away, but his lack of food, drink or company was a dead giveaway. He rose and started for the door.

Hugh blocked his exit.

"Who are you?" the man asked in a deep voice. "You aren't from around here. What do you want?"

"Company," Daniel said. "I'm new in Tanis, and I'm still getting used to the neighborhood."

"Oh?" a young woman asked, her short hair dyed bright red and her sleeveless shirt deliberately torn to look worn and ragged. She looped her arm over the big man's shoulders. "I don't recognize him, Hugh. Don't they usually have welcoming ceremonies for newcomers?"

They, Daniel thought. Other humans? Bes, perhaps?

"I asked them not to bother," Daniel said. "In any case, I was just leaving. I didn't realize this was a private party."

"Or maybe you just didn't want to be noticed," Hugh said, matching Daniel's soft tone.

The woman smiled at him. "Why don't you tell us the truth? It'll make you feel better."

The "truth" might serve him well this time, Daniel thought. "I wanted to see for myself if Tanis was what it's supposed to be," he said.

"You don't know?" the man said.

"I've seen things—"

"What things?" the woman asked, leaning toward him.

"A demonstration," he said, "at the blood depository."

Hugh and the woman exchanged glances. "And that made you curious?" she asked. "Maybe you wondered why people were protesting?"

"Yes."

"I'll tell you," Hugh said, whispering close to Daniel's ear. "I think you came here to learn something, all right, but it isn't for yourself. You aren't welcome here, and if we find out you're spying for the—" He stopped, grinding his teeth.

"You think I'm watching you for the Opiri?" Daniel asked. "Why would they spy on you?"

"Just shut up and leave," Hugh said. "Don't come back, ever."

Daniel weighed the man's words. Hugh was certainly disaffected with life in Tanis, and his belief that the Opiri were spying on humans had clearly been sincere.

But was it a plausible fear, or merely paranoia based on habitual dislike of Opiri? Daniel knew that he was going to need to talk to these people again in the near future. He needed to find out exactly what lay behind their discontent. And he'd have to prove, somehow, that he wasn't what they thought he was.

"I'll go," he said, backing out of the tavern. By now, every face was turned toward the door, and Daniel knew he wouldn't go unrecognized the next time he entered the area.

Hugh and the woman stood at the door and watched him walk away. He considered going on into Hera's ward, but he'd certainly stand out there, as well. Instead, he turned back to Isis's ward, wondering what she had planned for him now...or if she'd simply wash her hands of him once and for all.

He couldn't let her do that. She was still his best source of information, and she had met Ares. He would simply have to make sure that he didn't fall under her—

The sound of conflict behind him brought him to a halt just as he reached the ward's border. Raised voices were backed by the low rumble of an angry mob.

He glanced at the Lawkeepers at their station. They seemed not to hear. Instead of alerting them, he jogged back toward the tavern.

Arrayed in front of the building were perhaps a dozen humans, both men and women, some with fists raised and others with bottles in hand. Standing opposite them were six ordinary Opiri, white haired and pale skinned, their deep purple eyes filled with contempt. They wore finer clothes than the humans, and bore themselves with the common arrogance of their kind.

"The law says we can go where we choose," one of the male Opiri said. "This tavern is open to all citizens of Tanis."

Hugh stepped forward, fists working. "You come here to cause trouble, not to drink with us."

"Your bigotry against us is apparent," the Opir said.

The humans growled and shifted. The Opir gestured to his comrades and moved toward the tavern door.

"We've been curious to taste your human beer," he said, "and find out if it is the pig swill they say it is."

Another man in the crowd stepped forward. "You can't taste anything but blood," he said. "And you won't find any here."

The Opir bared his teeth. "You are ungenerous with your blood, you humans," he said. "You would starve us."

"And you would drain us dry," Hugh said.

The two leaders strode toward each other, the human with a bottle in his hand, the Opir ready to attack. Daniel managed to get between them just in time, anger and contempt kindling in his chest.

"It's obvious that you *did* come here to cause trouble,"

he said to the Opiri. "I suggest you leave before someone reports your behavior."

"Reports?" the lead Opir said. "Where are the Lawkeepers? They care nothing for what goes on here."

"Bes may feel differently," Daniel said, working to keep his instinctive hatred under control.

"Bes," the Opir spat. "He betrays his own kind for the sake of humans."

And he clearly doesn't frighten these Opiri, god or not, Daniel thought. He faced the Opir with his hands loose at his sides. "If you start a fight," he said coldly, "nobody will blame these people for defending themselves."

"And how will they do that?" a female Opir said. "With their blunt teeth and their weak bodies?"

As if to prove her point, the lead Opir slipped around Daniel and struck at Hugh, knocking the bottle out of his hand and scratching his wrist with long fingernails. He grabbed the man's arm and licked up the welling blood with evident relish.

Daniel moved before any of the other Opiri could react. He spun around and struck the lead Opir hard across the shoulder near his neck, hooked his foot around the other man's ankle and sent him tumbling to the ground. He downed the second Opir who attacked him, making no attempt to spare him pain, and was engaged with the third when the rest broke away. They snarled and threatened, but in the end they retreated, dragging the two fallen Opiri away with them.

"My God," someone said behind Daniel.

"What the hell was that?" Hugh said, clasping his injured wrist with his other hand. "How did you move so fast?"

Daniel expelled his breath, letting the anger go with it. "Training," he said.

"I've never seen a human bring a Nightsider down so easily."

"It wasn't as easy as it looked," Daniel said. He noticed a woman emerge from the tavern with a moistened cloth, which she wrapped around the big man's wrist. He never looked away from Daniel.

"Why did you interfere?" he asked.

"They attacked you."

"You could have gotten yourself killed."

"I doubt it."

Voices exclaimed and argued. The big man offered his hand.

"I'm Hugh," he said. "I'm glad *I* didn't make you angry."

"Hugh," Daniel said, taking his hand. "I'm Daniel."

"And you just got yourself into a hell of a lot of trouble, if the bloodsuckers have their way."

Chapter 8

Daniel looked around at the humans he had just saved. "I should fear the Opiri because I fought back?" Daniel asked, wiping his hands on his pants.

Glances were exchanged, but nobody spoke.

"I've met Bes," he said cautiously. "You're supposedly his responsibility. He can't accept what those Opiri did in coming here."

Hugh frowned at the pavement. "Bes is all right," he said. "But his effectiveness…" He looked right and left and lowered his voice. "You're obviously not what we thought you were—"

"Unless this was all part of a setup," the redheaded woman said.

"—but you'd better get out of here," Hugh said, as if he hadn't been interrupted. "They'll claim you started it."

"I have nothing to hide. Has this happened before?"

"Not like this," Hugh said.

"But Opiri have harassed you in the past?"

Hugh shrugged, his beard bristling like a boar's.

"And *have* you reported this to the Lawkeepers?"

"Didn't you hear the bloodsucker? They don't care what goes on here."

"Then how can they enforce the law?"

The young woman rolled her eyes. "They just won't enforce it on our behalf."

"Maybe I should report the incident myself," Daniel said.

"Don't be stupid," Hugh said. "You're a newcomer, and they aren't likely to listen to you." He leaned toward Daniel. "*We* don't want or need the attention."

"You were ready to fight them yourselves."

Hugh scowled. "It was a mistake. If those Opiri complain, the Council may—"

"Careful, Hugh," the woman said.

"I don't think he'll report us," Hugh said grimly.

"I'm still trying to understand," Daniel said. "Why did they come here to harass you?"

"Why shouldn't they? We're insects to them."

"And all the Opiri here feel the same way?"

"Enough of them do."

But Isis didn't seem to know it, Daniel thought. Or she pretended not to.

"You don't like the Games," he said. "You said they were to keep humans distracted from the advantages Opiri citizens have over humans."

Hugh folded his arms across his chest and stared at the ground.

"All right," Daniel said. "I heard nothing here today. I just happened to be near the tavern when the Opiri showed up."

Gruff gratitude crossed the big man's face. "It might be a good idea for you to leave Tanis, but somehow I don't think you're going to do that."

"I see no reason to."

"I hope you're right. We'll do what we can to put them off your scent, but that doesn't mean the Opiri you beat won't talk."

"Admit they were defeated by a human?"

"Just take my advice. Lie low for a while. If they bring you in, tell them only what you have to." He hesitated. "Once this blows over, there are others you might want to meet. I'll see what I can arrange." He gripped Daniel's hand again, slipping something long into Daniel's palm.

It was a knife in a leather sheath. "Weapons are illegal in Tanis, unless they're carried by Lawkeepers," Hugh whispered. "Keep it hidden. Good luck."

Very much aware of the weapon, Daniel tucked it under his shirt and turned toward the border again. He knew he'd done something very dangerous, not only in attacking the Opiri but also by displaying his strength and speed. Along with his training, it made him the equal of almost any full Nightsider.

It was the anger, he thought. It usually manifested itself in wariness and suspicion, as he'd so often shown with Isis, but he'd let it out this time. He could tell himself it was for the people at the tavern, but in his heart he'd been happy to put the Opiri in their places. If they felt so secure in attacking humans in a human neighborhood, they could have done worse than scratch Hugh's wrist.

He'd guessed that the Opiri wouldn't be quick to admit they'd lost a fight to a human. They might not even remember his face from among all the other humans. But rumors would spread, and if Hugh was correct, the authorities would see no reason to give the benefit of the doubt to a newcomer.

But one good thing had come out of this. Now he had solid evidence that the "peace" in Tanis was troubled, and—unless this incident had been a freakish exception—that the supposed cooperation between Opiri and humans might only be a patch over a festering wound.

Had Ares discovered the problem? If he had, it seemed even more peculiar that he hadn't reported back to Avalon.

As for Isis...

Daniel refused to believe she'd been deliberately lying to him about the state of the city. She genuinely believed what she said about Tanis, about the second chance it gave to humans and Opiri alike. If what Daniel had seen in Bes's domain was commonplace, surely she'd know about it.

Unless she didn't *want* to know.

Hugh had suggested that he leave the city. If he did, he'd have a reasonable report to take back to Avalon, and he'd avoid the complications that might come once the incident was discovered. But only half his work would be finished; Ares was still missing. And the idea of abandoning Isis was like a fist to the gut.

Goddess or not, he reminded himself, *she's Opiri. No matter what she believes, she'll always choose—*

"Daniel!"

He looked down in surprise. Bes stood before him, smiling, his broad hands on his hips. He looked like a doll, his clothing of many mismatched colors and his beard and hair entwined with ribbons. It was as if he wanted to appear the clown.

Was he playing a part assigned him, ineffectual and harmless?

"Visiting my people?" Bes said cheerfully.

"Did I break a rule by coming here?" Daniel asked.

"Well, newcomers are not generally permitted to run around Tanis without a guide." Bes rocked on his heels. "Does Isis know you're here?"

"I left her not long ago," Daniel said.

"Ah." Bes's dark eyes shone. "She likes you very much."

"She seems to like everyone."

"She has a big heart." Bes grinned, revealing the pointed tips of his cuspids. "I knew her when we were both caretakers in Egypt. She is as generous now as she was then." His smile faded. "Did you come to find out what happened to the protesters at the depository?"

"They were released, weren't they? You made sure of that. In fact, after you spoke to them, they seemed to have forgotten why they were there."

"They had concerns. I listened, and eased their minds."

"But their grievances haven't been addressed, have they?"

"I like your boldness, Daniel. But there are matters you can only understand when you have truly become one of us."

"So Isis has told me."

"Follow her lead. She will look after you." He glanced past Daniel. "I always join my people for a beer at this time. You should return to your quarters and take your evening meal."

Join them for a beer, Daniel thought. Would he spy on his own people, or did he genuinely enjoy socializing with them?

Either way, some version of the brief fight was bound to come to his attention. His loyalties would become very clear then.

Bes nodded pleasantly and strode away on his short, slightly bowed legs. Daniel watched him until he had rounded a nearby corner and started back for the administrative complex.

Isis was waiting for him in the lobby of the Immigrant Center. Her eyes were angry, but she projected her usual serene, cordial demeanor.

"Daniel," she said, "you should not have gone out without telling me."

"I apologize," he said.

"Where did you go?"

He saw no reason to hide the truth. "To Bes's ward."

"Why did you go alone?"

"I wanted to see how the humans here behave without the presence of an Opir guide."

The anger in her eyes faded. "Did you expect a change in behavior?"

"I didn't know what to expect."

"And what did you learn?"

"That the people there enjoy their beer."

Suddenly, she smiled. "Yes," she said. "Bes's people are very good-natured."

Daniel felt deep regret that she'd eventually learn what had happened in Bes's ward. In less than forty-eight hours he had come to desire her, respect her, admire her for her kindness and dedication, in spite of his suspicion of her natural powers. Now, absurdly, he felt that he had to protect her.

"I would hear of your visit," she said. "Will you dine with me?"

"As long as I'm not on the menu."

He spoke before he thought, but Isis only smiled, closed-mouthed. "Only if you wish to be," she said. The words were laced with innuendo, and Daniel thought she wasn't entirely speaking of blood.

Considering how he'd behaved before, it was a brave thing to say, putting her pride at risk again. She'd forgiven him his previous rejections, but he couldn't give her what he sensed she wanted now: that he surrender himself, accept her help in matters too personal to share with anyone.

"I think I should stay here tonight," he said. "I have a feeling you're neglecting other work because of me."

"Perhaps I am," she said, her voice soft with disappointment. "But I have a proposal for you, and I must speak to you in private."

"Come to my room," Daniel said.

Isis followed him to his room and leaned against the door. Carefully avoiding the bed, Daniel stood close to the opposite wall and waited tensely for her to speak.

"We have not yet completed your tour of the city," she

said. "You cannot judge us without seeing all of it." She took a deep breath. "I wish you to visit the towers."

Daniel's heart beat a little faster. She'd said that visiting the towers wasn't encouraged for newcomers, but how often did the Opiri welcome human visitors of any kind? The Opir gang had claimed that any citizen could, by law, visit any area of the city.

But he suspected that, except for the servants, humans very seldom went to the towers Hugh had mentioned. If they did, they'd leave with information the Opiri might not want spread throughout the human wards.

Of one thing Daniel was certain: Isis still hadn't heard of the incident with the Opir gang, or she'd surely never have made the offer. And she'd only encourage such a visit if she believed that Daniel's opinion of Tanis would only improve as a result.

"What do you want me to see?" he asked.

"You clearly still harbor many doubts about the Opiri here," she said, her eyes sparkling with enthusiasm, "and I know that that doubt extends to those like me and Bes as well as Hera and Ishtar. Several of my peers would be glad to speak to you in a private setting."

If he were to believe Hugh's warnings about facing repercussions from the fight, Isis was essentially suggesting that he walk right into the lion's den. It was certainly a quick way to find out how Tanis's justice system worked... or if it worked at all.

Not with Isis there to protect me, he thought ironically. He knew she'd step in if he got into trouble, and he didn't want that. He didn't want to put her in the position of opposing her own people if the Council decided to punish him.

"There's something I have to tell you first," he said, getting directly to the point. "When I met with the humans in

Bes's ward, a group of Opiri came by the tavern to make trouble. One of them attacked a man there."

Her eyes darkened in shock. "Opiri attacked humans?"

"And I retaliated."

"You *fought* Opiri?"

"They had no reason to be there except to harass the people who live in the neighborhood."

He told her briefly what happened, and she folded her arms across her chest, shaking her head slowly. "I cannot believe such a thing has occurred," she murmured. "You defeated two Opiri?"

"Arrogant, overconfident Opiri who didn't expect any resistance."

"Why did you not report this to Bes or the Lawkeepers?" she asked.

"I was told that some blame might fall on the humans involved. I couldn't risk that."

Isis straightened. "The Opiri were clearly at fault. I would never allow the humans or you to be—"

"I didn't want you interfering," he said.

"Why?" she asked. "You would not have been able to hide this from me indefinitely."

"You told me that if I committed any disturbance, *you* would be held accountable."

"I…overstated the case. I do not fear for myself—"

"But you do think your people might do something to me?"

"The Nine do not lay down punishment."

"They have no say at all?"

Her gaze flicked back to him. "The testimony of the humans involved will hold equal weight with that of the Opiri. There is no separate law. You will have every chance to explain what happened."

"You accept my account?"

"I believe that you defended the weak from those who

would take advantage of them. I am ashamed that such a thing happened in this city. I assure you, it was an aberration."

"Then you don't think I'll be locked up."

"Nobody would dare," she said, the mantle of her instinctive power flaring around her. "I know this will be dealt with fairly and properly. If the Opiri are guilty, they must face judgment." Her brow creased, and she spoke as if she were thinking aloud. "My peers already know about your clandestine entrance into the city. Even before Ishtar came to question you, I told them that I did not believe you intended harm to Tanis. But it might help to let others among the Nine meet you and recognize for themselves that you would never commit a crime against Opir citizens."

Daniel knew she was playing a contradictory game with herself, wishing to believe the city's justice system was fair, and yet recognizing an advantage in making Daniel known to the Opir powers that be. He couldn't bring himself to call her out on her inconsistency.

"Would I be meeting all of the Nine?" he asked.

"I would take you to see those closest to me," she said, "and then to Anu."

"And he might tilt the judgment in my favor, if I convince him that I'm...what? A properly deferential human in the presence of a god?"

Isis stared at him in confusion. "Have I not made clear that we do not rule here as gods?"

"Yes," he said, "you've made that clear. If you think I should go, I will."

Suddenly she seemed uneasy. "Keep in mind that you would be one of only a handful of humans in the tower. Anu will have Opiri guests with him. The others may, as well."

"It won't be the first time I've been outnumbered."

"And your memories of your past as a serf? Will they cloud your thinking?"

"They won't—"

"Can you forget the scars on your back when you walk where Opir Bloodlords once kept their Households?"

"Have you told them about my past?" he asked.

"They know you were a serf from Vikos."

"Then why do you seem to be having second thoughts?"

"I only want to make sure you understand." Her sharp cuspids dented her lower lip. "What of Hannibal? What if you meet him there?"

"Do you expect him to be with Anu?"

"It is possible. Does he hate you as you hate him?"

"I wasn't *his* serf. Why should he stoop so low as to hate a human?"

She cast him a probing look. "I would meet with Hannibal myself, but not if such a meeting would upset you."

"I'm not an animal, Isis. I can restrain myself. But confronting Hannibal now wouldn't be a good idea." He reached toward her, dropping his arm before he could touch her. "It'll be all right, Isis. The only thing I ask is that you not interfere if any of the Opiri confront me about the incident with the gang."

"How can I make such a promise?"

"If you trust the objectivity of your people, you have nothing to worry about."

Her beautiful face was tense with anxiety. "There is one other thing I should have mentioned before. You and I have been seen together twice, and some may think it odd that I give so much time to a newcomer. Rumors travel quickly in Tanis. It is very possible, even likely, that it will be assumed…that the others may believe…"

"That we have a relationship?" Daniel said with a crooked smile. "That we're lovers?"

Isis lifted her chin. "Yes. And also that I am taking your blood."

"You said such private exchanges aren't unknown."

"They are not. But among the Nine, only Ishtar regularly consorts with humans in that way."

"Will it shame you in front of your own people?"

"*I* am not ashamed."

They gazed at each other, and the gentle defiance in Isis's eyes warmed Daniel like a fire in the dead of winter.

But he had an idea that the visit Isis proposed might be more complicated than she'd originally let on.

"Isis," he said, "I know you're doing this for my sake. If it's going to make things difficult for you among your own kind—"

Her jaw set. "Let there be no more arguments. We will go. I will make the arrangements."

Turning abruptly, she left Daniel to consider the decision he had made. If he accomplished nothing else, he would make clear to the Opiri in authority that Isis had nothing to do with his behavior and that he had disregarded her warnings by walking the city alone.

And if he was lucky, he might meet Opiri in the tower who knew more about Ares's visit than Isis did.

Isis returned an hour later with an attendant, who carried another meal on a tray. Isis held a shirt and pants over her arm, made of a finer weave and quality than the ones Daniel had been given before. The shirt had a high collar, as if designed specifically to cover the neck area, and the pants were closer-fitting. The shoes were low, cloth-and-leather boots with simple embroidery on the sides.

"Aren't my regular clothes and boots good enough?" Daniel asked.

"It is only right that you should look…" She trailed off, glancing at the clothes in her arms.

"Less like a serf?" he asked.

"Like what you truly are. A man anyone must respect."

She was truly worried for him, Daniel thought. What did that say about the Nine? "I'll do as you advise," he said.

"Eat first. They will not have much human food in the towers."

"Even though they can eat it themselves?"

"It may not be available to—"

"Human visitors?"

"Do you intend to challenge every word I speak?"

"I apologize," he said, realizing that his sharp tongue was a way of dealing with a situation he believed could be extremely unpleasant for him and Isis. "I trust your judgment."

She nodded without meeting his eyes. After quickly finishing the meal, he began to dress. Isis turned away, but the familiar tension was there again, bringing with it images of Isis's lithe body and her response to his. When he was finished, she turned around and looked him over with critical eyes.

"You look very fine," she said.

He bowed. "I appreciate the compliment."

"Must you always—"

He took her hand, running his thumb over her knuckles. "I'm not joking, Isis. If it made this easier for you, I'd wear a sack over my head."

Laughter burbled from her throat. "Please, do not cover your very attractive head." She sobered and met his gaze. "We should not go."

He kissed the back of her hand. "It'll be all right. I promise."

They gazed at each other, and Daniel found himself on the verge of kissing her parted lips. But now wasn't the time for him to forget himself. This was a serious business, and he would have to watch his step every second... especially for Isis's sake.

Chapter 9

The towers were dark under the looming shadow of the half dome, but Isis noticed that Daniel didn't hesitate as he climbed the ramp to the elevators that would carry them up the tower. His back was stiff but his demeanor was cool and calm, and she wondered how he could be so detached.

I never should have suggested this, Isis thought. Word of the fight would have reached Anu by now, and he might already prefer to believe the Opiri's account of the incident. But even he had to abide by the laws that prevented the Nine from directly interfering in the Council's work. He would certainly not suggest any punishment.

Isis was more afraid of the anger Daniel so carefully tried to conceal. It was his well-being that concerned her.

And when, she wondered, had his welfare become so important to her...almost as important as the welfare and future of Tanis? It was both astonishing and dangerous, and yet it had come to pass without her fully realizing how it had happened. It was not merely physical attraction, though that was part of it, nor Daniel's courage or determination. It was all these things, and she could no longer seem to remember that he was only a single human in a city that must care for every one of its citizens equally. As *she* should.

It will pass, she thought. Daniel might choose to leave Tanis anytime. He could be exiled if he were found to have provoked the fight. Even if he cared a little for her, even if he desired her, he was not bound to her. Nor could he ever be.

She knew that he would never allow anyone to bind him again.

They stopped in front of one of the three elevators, each one clearly marked with the symbols of three of the Nine: a sheaf of wheat for Bes; the eight-pointed star for Ishtar; a peacock for Hera; a lion for Ereshkigal; for Hephaestus, a flame; for Anu, a bundle of twigs from the tamarisk; the owl for Athena; for Hermes, the caduceus, its serpents coiled about a staff; and for Isis, outstretched wings.

"I will take you first to Hermes and Athena," Isis said, gathering her own courage. "You may speak freely to both of them."

Daniel gave her a slight nod of acknowledgment, but his attention was on the House symbols. "Three of the Nine live in each third of the tower?" he asked.

"There is ample room," she said. "It is not as if any of us has true Households in the old sense."

"Your emblem is here, but this isn't where you live."

"A suite has been set aside for me, should I choose to occupy it," she said. "But I prefer to stay where I am." She pressed the button. The elevator arrived almost immediately, and she and Daniel stepped inside.

"If at any time you feel we should leave—" she began.

"I'll tell you, and you do the same," Daniel said, still preoccupied. She wondered how much of that distance was acknowledging and defeating his own fears and memories, the ones he swore would not affect him.

She had come to know him too well to doubt that it was a struggle, silent though it might be.

The elevator reached the third level, occupied by

Athena. Isis was eager for Daniel to meet the former goddess, for she had every quality Isis admired: temperance,
wisdom, compassion and a commitment to civilization and
justice. Though they had seldom interacted in the ancient
past, Athena, Bes and Hermes were those of the Nine to
whom Isis was most closely allied.

As Isis began to knock on one of the doors in the semi-
circular lobby, it opened to reveal Athena, clad in comfortable robes cut in the ancient Grecian style. She smiled,
closed-lipped, at Isis and then Daniel, offering her hand
to him.

"You are Daniel," she said in her low, pleasant voice.

Daniel inclined his head, and Isis wondered if he had
noticed how reluctant Athena was to show her teeth. She
had always been uncomfortable about her Opir nature and
need for blood, considering it something almost shameful
rather than a heritage she had no power to change. It was
the one area where her level-headed wisdom failed her.

Isis was not proud of being Opir, but neither was she
ashamed. It was simply what she was. Daniel had accepted
that.

Except where it comes to my taking his blood, she
thought, remembering his reaction when he'd thought
she'd done so without asking him first. And who could
blame him?

"Come in," Athena said, stepping aside. "When Isis told
me she was bringing her new human to the tower, I was
most eager to meet you."

"Not *my* human," Isis said hastily. "A newcomer who
has agreed to let me be his guide."

"Of course." Athena showed no embarrassment, but her
gaze flickered to Daniel's face and then to the high collar of his shirt. She was more than intelligent enough to
recognize the slip she had made in suggesting that Daniel
belonged to Isis.

"Please, make yourselves comfortable," she said. "I have arranged refreshments for you."

A human female brought a large tray of delicacies and laid it on the small table at the center of a ring of semi-circular couches in the Spartan reception room. Daniel stared at the human for a moment, and the muscles in his back and shoulders seemed to lock.

"There are no serfs here," Isis said in an undertone, carefully taking his arm. It was rigid and hard as granite. Granite that could still be cracked.

With a stiff nod, Daniel settled himself and examined the tray. Isis had tasted the honey-drenched baklava before, but when she caught a glimpse of Daniel's expression, she couldn't guess what he was thinking.

"Thank you," he said, perfectly polite, and took one of the sweets. "I didn't expect such a welcome."

"I seldom have human visitors," Athena said. "I prefer to interfere in the affairs of my wards as little as possible, though I may have gone too far in my eagerness to remain objective."

Daniel studied her face with avid interest. "Objectivity is admirable," he said, "and so is allowing the people to rule themselves."

"Of course," Athena said, arching an eyebrow at Isis. "That has always been the plan for Tanis."

"And do the others of the Nine feel the same way?"

Isis froze, startled by Daniel's blunt question. She had made her opinion clear, but he had every right to seek others, and she should welcome his willingness to ask.

Athena, too, seemed surprised. "Isis must have told you that our goal has always been an independent and productive city of equals." She smiled at Isis. "Isis prefers to stay close to the humans of Tanis, to learn as well as to guide. You have been fortunate to have her take your part."

"Especially under the current circumstances," Daniel said, watching Athena's face.

"Ah," Athena said, looking down at the plate. "You refer to the unfortunate event in Bes's ward. A shocking incident."

"Daniel was only trying to protect Bes's humans from a gang of Opiri," Isis said quickly.

"I have no doubt," Athena said, meeting Daniel's gaze again.

"You believe it was self-defense?" he asked.

"Isis would not have brought you here if she didn't believe in your innocence. It was courageous of you, Daniel, considering the odds."

"You might say that I acted in a way that is impulsively human," Daniel said.

Athena laughed, turning her head aside so that her teeth were not clearly visible. "Impulsivity is not only a human trait, though some of us prefer to believe we are wiser."

"We all prefer to believe the best of ourselves," Daniel said. "Human or Opir."

"Indeed." Athena looked at Isis. "I see why you wished to guide Daniel yourself. He would be a most excellent addition to our city's populace."

Isis winced inwardly. Athena didn't mean it, but speaking of Daniel in the third person instead of addressing him directly wasn't likely to make him feel comfortable. But, again, he only smiled and inclined his head.

"Thank you, Lady Athena," he said.

"Hasn't Isis told you that there are no lords and ladies here?" Athena asked. "You must not think that the Opiri who attacked the humans are typical of our people."

"I appreciate your perspective, Athena," Daniel said, his voice betraying no emotion at all.

"Then perhaps you would like to meet some of my friends," she said. She rose and strode to another room, returning a few moments later with several Opiri, all dressed simply in tunics, pants and soft boots.

Daniel got to his feet. Isis rose with him, ready to take his arm if he reacted with hostility. But she did him a disservice; he simply waited, and when the Opiri settled onto the couches on either side of Athena's, he sat, as well.

"Daniel," Athena said, "these are my companions—Damokles, Loukas, Homer, Dionysia, and Ianthe." She smiled at her friends. "Daniel is new to our city. He has many questions."

Isis prepared herself for more awkwardness, but the conversation went smoothly. Athena's companions were among the most enlightened Opiri in Tanis, and Daniel seemed more interested in listening to them speak than in questioning them as he had Athena. They made polite conversation about the attractions of the city, particularly the gardens Daniel hadn't yet seen, and the new architecture where the human sector was being expanded.

To Isis's ongoing surprise, Daniel spoke to them as if he'd dealt with Opiri as equals on many occasions. Still, Isis was relieved that none of them asked about Daniel's past, or the incident with the Opir gang. When the Opiri finally left, Athena accompanied Daniel to the door.

"Much has yet to be done," she said, "but I believe, as Isis does, that we will become a guidepost for the world, not only a place of sanctuary but an example for humans and Opiri to follow."

"I hope that Tanis fulfills your hopes," Daniel said.

"You are skeptical," Athena said.

"Isis brought me here to meet Opiri who shared her optimism," Daniel said.

"And did you find what you expected?" she asked.

"My good opinion is hardly essential to your success."

Athena laughed softly. "Apparently Isis believes it might be."

With a pointed glare at Athena, Isis rose. "It has been very kind of you to welcome us."

"Yes," Daniel said. He offered his hand. Athena gripped it firmly.

"I hope the remainder of your visit is a pleasant one," she said. She paused. "If it is of any use to you, I will speak on your behalf."

Daniel thanked her, and he and Isis walked into the lobby.

"That went very well," Isis said when the door had closed. "One would never know you had been a—" She flushed. "I'm sorry."

"I've had a little practice," Daniel said drily. "Where now?"

"To Hermes," she said. "He represents the half-bloods of Tanis, the Lawkeepers."

"Then he's the chief of police."

"No. He is merely their representative."

Daniel nodded and followed her back to the elevator. It took them up two levels to Hermes's door.

A smiling dhampir opened the door to Isis's knock. His age was impossible to determine, as was also true of most Darketans and, of course, Opiri. He ushered Daniel and Isis into the antechamber, which featured a mural of rams, tortoises and hawks in a field, topped by a caduceus.

The attendant disappeared and a moment later Hermes arrived to greet them. Like Bes, he smiled frequently, though he was Bes's opposite in almost every other way: tall, slender, agile and red haired.

He was also no less blunt than Athena. He looked Daniel up and down with a grin.

"The human who defeated three Opiri. Congratulations." He thumped Daniel's shoulder in a friendly gesture, but Isis could see Daniel freeze at the touch.

Hermes was oblivious. "Come in, come in. I want to

hear all about it from your own lips, Daniel. The towers are buzzing with the story."

Isis would have intervened, but Daniel returned Hermes's smile with a flash of his teeth. "Buzzing like an angry hornet's nest?" he asked.

"Oh," Hermes said in an offhand manner, "some Opiri took it a little to heart. They'll get over it." He looked into Daniel's eyes. "Perhaps you had an advantage they didn't expect."

Isis wondered what advantage Hermes was referring to. Daniel's speed and strength, so unexpected in a human?

"It was no pleasure for Daniel," she said, setting the thought aside. "But he knows that those who attacked the humans are in the minority."

"Of course, of course." Hermes almost skipped ahead, gesturing them to follow him into the reception room. It was vastly different than Athena's, cluttered with trinkets collected in ancient times from the area of the world extending from Italy to North Africa.

Daniel was fully alert as he scanned the room. His gaze came to rest, not on one of the objects on display, but on the narrow, nearly hidden door at the far left side of the room.

Isis knew what it was: the door to the serfs' quarters downstairs. They were no longer used as such, of course, but she could imagine what was going through Daniel's mind.

Again, Hermes seemed oblivious. He guided Daniel and Isis around the room, pointing out this or that object he had collected over his long years of wandering.

"I am particularly fond of this," he said, pointing out a small sculpture of a curly-haired man with a small ram slung over his shoulders. "The good old days."

"When you ruled as a god," Daniel said, a note of challenge in his voice.

Hermes flashed a glance at him. "I always enjoyed

being a god. I had a great fondness for humanity, and they made me into a trickster, which was even more amusing."

"Whom do you trick now?"

"Alas, nobody. Your average Opir is rather humorless, and humans are unlikely to appreciate a joke coming from one of us."

"Even in a city where humans and Opiri live as equals?"

"One can't expect perfection in a few years. Isis is an idealist, but I am more pragmatic."

"I share your pragmatism."

Hermes glanced at Isis, who was desperately trying not to interrupt, and then back to Daniel. "You were a serf, were you not?"

Daniel's face went blank. "Yes," he said.

"Then of course you'd have your reservations. I'm sure Isis has already shown you the good that has been achieved in this city."

Unexpectedly, Daniel smiled at Isis. "She's done her best."

It should have felt like a slap to the face, but Isis recognized his words as blistering honesty. Honesty she had every reason to respect.

Daniel's smile faded. "I'm sorry," he said. "Isis had no obligation to bring me to your tower."

"And it's hard for you to be beholden to an Opir," Hermes said airily, as if the words were of no consequence. "My worshippers were never particularly devout, and that was why I liked them so much."

"But now you deal with the half-bloods."

"The old humans said I was of two worlds—the half-bloods are, too, which is why I appreciate them. It is a difficult balancing act, but we are very good at balancing." He clapped Daniel's shoulder again, and Isis could almost feel Daniel's scars burning under his shirt.

Daniel backed away. "I have one more question," he said. "Did you meet Ares?"

"Ares? Why do you ask?"

"I met him elsewhere. He was a good man. I was told that he was here for a while, and left after seeing the city."

"I did not witness his departure, but we spoke a little of the old days. He had changed a great deal since I knew him millennia ago."

"You don't know anything else?"

"He was actively interested in all aspects of life in the city. He asked many questions…like you." Hermes arched his brows. "In some odd way, you remind me of him."

Daniel laughed briefly, as if the idea was preposterous. But Isis continued to wonder about his interest in Ares. His questions didn't seem like those of a former serf seeking the whereabouts of a Bloodlord he could hardly have known well.

"Thank you," Daniel said. He offered his hand to Hermes, and the Opir took it without hesitation.

"If you have more questions, I am at your service," Hermes said. His brief solemnity vanished, and he grinned again. "Good luck."

He saw them to the door with a merry wave. Isis waited until she and Daniel were alone again.

"What did you think of him?" she asked.

"I believe he means well for humanity, as you do. But according to human myth, he always had that reputation. As you did."

"Why did you ask him about Ares?"

It was as if a wall had come between the two of them. "It's not important," he said.

"You have not been honest with me," she said, torn between sadness and anger. "Ares was not merely a Bloodmaster you briefly observed in Vikos, was he? Your interest in him is far from casual."

Daniel lowered his head and stared at the floor. "Ares saved my life when my owner would have beaten me to death," he said calmly. "He defeated my owner in a challenge and demanded that he treat his serfs less brutally. My owner didn't keep his word, and I escaped soon after that."

"And you want to find him again, to thank him?"

"If he believes as you do, I can show my gratitude as an equal."

Daniel's words made sense to Isis, and yet she knew that something had been left out of his story. "I wondered why you were so at ease with Athena and her guests," she said. "You said you dealt with rogue Freebloods after your escape, but you must have met Opiri who had no interest in enslaving you or draining your blood. You did not need to be shown that such Opiri exist." She paused to swallow the knot in her throat. "Why did you lie to me?"

Chapter 10

"It was not a lie," Daniel said, meeting her gaze. "I did withhold some information from you, and for that I apologize. I should have told you as soon as I realized that you could be trusted," Daniel said to her with a sigh.

Isis saw the real regret in his eyes, and a little of her hurt dissolved. "What is the truth?" she asked.

"I did meet Opiri who believe as you do, living in a small community in the wilderness," he said. "They wanted peace with humanity and had an arrangement with a nearby human colony to trade blood for other goods."

Isis was shocked by his admission. "You allowed me to believe—"

"This was a very small group of Opiri, and they lived apart from humans." He looked into her eyes. "The circumstances in Tanis are completely different. This is a city inhabited by Opiri *and* humans, where the temptation to relapse into the old ways would be far greater."

"You mean where Opiri might simply decide one day to turn all the free humans back into serfs."

"I needed to know, Isis," he said, his voice husky with sincerity.

"And have you reached a conclusion?"

"It's too soon to tell. I need more time."

All at once Isis was afraid of what might happen if they continued their tour of the tower. Athena and Hermes were personable enough, but Anu was more of an enigma. She had known that all along, of course, but now she felt the full weight of Daniel's judgment.

If Daniel was as blunt with Anu as he'd been with Athena and Hermes, he might not receive such a warm reception. And Isis would be putting Daniel on display as if he were a serf in the Claiming Hall.

"I think this has been enough for one day," she said, taking Daniel's arm. "Let us go down, and I'll show you the gardens and the—"

"We came here so that I could meet Anu," he said, his eyes very grave. He cupped his hand around her cheek in a deeply intimate and tender gesture. "You were right before. If I've been accused of breaking the law, I'd prefer to defend myself personally."

She took his hand and kissed his palm. That intensely physical awareness flared between them again.

"Isis," a female voice called.

She and Daniel turned as a tall, handsome, dark-haired woman emerged from one of the other two elevators. She wore a Greek chiton, a long draped tunic, embroidered along the hems and sleeves with peacocks, their eyes glowing with jewels.

"Hera," Isis said coolly.

The former goddess blinked slowly and looked at Daniel. "Surely you cannot be thinking of leaving already?" she asked.

Daniel stared at her, the hard lines of his face revealing his dislike. Isis knew he was remembering the poor state of Hera's ward, as *she* was. His opinion of her had already been set.

"We are just on our way to see Anu," Isis said.

"Of course," Hera said, gazing at Daniel through half-lidded eyes. "Anu has invited you both to his Household." She smiled with a show of teeth. "This human has already gained quite the reputation in the towers."

"Perhaps," Isis said. "But as no judgment has yet been made—"

"We accept Anu's invitation," Daniel said, holding Hera's lazy stare.

Hera looked at Isis in surprise, as if she couldn't imagine why Isis would let a human speak for her. "Anu is waiting," she said.

She moved ahead of them into the elevator and stood near the control panel. As she pushed the button for the eleventh floor, Isis drew Daniel aside.

"There will be a few humans there," she said, "hired servants, like the one you saw in Athena's suite. But they receive compensation for their work, as they would for any other profession in Tanis."

"They are privileged to have such employment," Hera said.

"I'm sure they're aware of the honor," Daniel said. "But the humans in your ward, Lady Hera...*they* don't have many privileges, do they?"

Hera looked at him sharply, the indifference gone from her eyes. "What do you mean?" she demanded.

"I've seen how they live. It isn't pretty."

"He visited three wards," Isis said. "Yours was the last."

Hera clucked her tongue. "And you do not approve, Daniel?"

"It was in very poor condition," Isis said, holding Hera's gaze.

"If the humans cannot see to their own welfare, it is none of my concern. Not one of my humans has asked for an audience with me nor informed me of any problems."

Say nothing more, Isis begged Daniel silently. But he

was quiet until they reached the eleventh floor and Anu's quarters.

Of all the Nine, he had done the least to alter his living space from the Bloodmaster's Household it had been before the fall of the Citadel. It was twice as large as the suites claimed by the other Nine, with a foyer and wide entrance hall leading to a spacious reception room, pillared and draped with rich fabrics and furnishings humans and ordinary Opiri would have considered luxurious. Decorative tiles paved the floor, and a wide, curving stairway led to another floor above.

Daniel paused in the doorway, and Isis heard him take a deep breath. She touched his hand and felt his skin jump like that of a stallion beset by flies.

Respect is not obeisance, she reminded him silently.

"Isis," Anu called from across the room. Daniel's gaze snapped to the former god. Anu sat on his chair, a bejeweled king with dark hair and golden skin, dressed in elaborate robes. He was surrounded by a small crowd of his favored Opir courtiers, a small cadre of ceremonial Opir guards and his closest companions among the Nine. The courtiers were dressed like princes themselves, and the guards were armed with real rifles as well as shock sticks.

Bes stood apart, speaking with several former Bloodlords and Freebloods. A good dozen plainly dressed human servants wove among Anu's guests and courtiers, serving food and drink.

Every face turned toward Isis and Daniel as Hera walked by them to join Anu. Conversation stopped, and then resumed at a low murmur.

"Come," Anu said in his deep, resounding voice, handing his glass to the human servant standing behind him. "Let us see the human who defeated three Opiri."

His strides long and almost defiant, Daniel walked into the reception room. Ishtar rose from her couch with a slightly strained smile, and Isis felt a disturbing sensation of triumph. Ereshkigal, former goddess of the underworld, remained reclining where she was, studying Daniel through hooded eyes, and broad-chested Hephaestus, standing beside Anu's chair, examined Daniel as if he were weighing the capabilities of a possible challenger.

Of course he wouldn't think that of Daniel, Isis thought. None of them would.

Isis felt the desperate instinct to move ahead of Daniel, but she repressed it and followed him across the richly carpeted floor, passing through the outer circle of Anu's courtiers and stopping a few feet from his chair. Isis was keenly aware of the proximity of the attending Opiri, their stares, the weight of their silence.

And of Anu's inborn, unmistakable power. Power he projected without thought.

Power Daniel could surely feel.

"Daniel," Anu said. "Welcome to my Household."

A pair of human servants appeared with refreshments. Anu waved them away and gestured to a chair beside him. "Isis," he said.

With a quick glance at Daniel, Isis remained where she was. Anu smiled and nodded to one of the seated Opiri, who swiftly rose from his own chair.

"Please," Anu said. "Both of you, sit."

After a moment's hesitation, Daniel gestured for Isis to precede him and took the second chair. The dislodged Opiri showed no resentment, and Isis exhaled softly. There was no overt hostility here, only curiosity and calculation.

"Daniel," Anu said, "you look strangely familiar. Have we met before?"

"I don't think that's possible," Daniel said coolly.

"I know that you came to us to learn if Tanis was the place it was reputed to be," he said. "What are your thoughts?"

Daniel held Anu's imposing gaze. "I can see that much effort has been put into the project," he said.

Anu laughed. "A diplomatic answer," he said. He leaned forward. "You are fortunate to have had Lady Isis as a personal guide. No doubt the incident in Bes's ward has swayed your opinion."

"It showed me that some here are not fully committed to the ideal of peaceful coexistence."

Anu's eyes narrowed, and Isis held herself very still. "I have heard more than one account of this conflict," Anu said. "It is not permitted for any human or Opir to prevent another citizen from entering any other ward."

"Nobody was prevented," Daniel said. "And I assume that the law doesn't apply when the visitors intend to make trouble."

The Opiri murmured among themselves. Isis rose.

"I brought Daniel here so that you could see for yourself that he is not a troublemaker," she said.

"Isn't he?" Anu said, stroking his chin.

"He tried to defend—"

"Tried, and apparently succeeded," Anu said. "How does a human have the strength and speed to fight an Opir on equal terms?"

"Practice," Daniel said, walking the fine line between frankness and insolence.

"You were a serf," Anu said. "Where did this 'practice' take place?"

"During the year after I escaped from Vikos."

"A year?" Ishtar murmured.

"Remarkable," Anu said. "Which Opiri did you practice with? Rogue Freebloods, perhaps?"

"I stayed some time with a human colony between here and Vikos. They gave me the benefit of their experience."

"Did you come on their behalf, to learn if *we* were a threat to them?"

"I came only for myself," Daniel said.

"Very brave," Anu said. He leaned back and rested his chin on his fist. "I would like to see these fighting skills."

Daniel froze. "Why?" he asked.

Bes, along with several of the Opiri to whom he'd been speaking, stepped forward. "It is my fault that such a thing happened in my ward," he said. "Daniel's case has not yet reached the Council."

"I assure you he will come to no harm," Anu said.

Daniel shot a glance at Isis, and a chill passed through her veins. Every muscle in his face and body seemed to form a shield around emotions he didn't dare express. Or couldn't.

"I do not understand this request, Anu," Isis said, more sharply than she would have dared in the past.

"There was a time," Anu said, "when men fought each other to determine who was innocent and who was guilty. They left it up to the gods to decide."

"These are not those times, and we are no longer gods," Isis said.

"But some of the old traditions still have use," Anu said.

"I thought the Nine didn't enforce the laws or pass judgment," Daniel said.

"Yet we *can* make recommendations to the Council." He stroked his beard. "The choice is yours."

"Then I agree to fight."

Anu signaled to one of the human servants. Two Opiri came through a back door, young men Isis didn't recognize. They homed in on Daniel as if they were starved for blood.

"I forbid this," Isis said to Anu. "Daniel, we will go."

Daniel met her gaze. "You don't own me, Isis," he said. "If this will help prove my innocence, I'll take my chances."

Isis saw the wildness behind the apparent calm in his

eyes and knew he had traveled back into a part of his past he had shared with her only in bits and pieces. He would not back down. He had something to prove to the watching Opiri, even though it might backfire on him.

"You recognize these Opiri?" Anu asked Daniel. "They have accused you of attacking them without provocation."

"Where is the third I fought?" Daniel asked with a cold smile.

"He is unable to join us today." Anu nodded to the two Opiri. "Choose which one of you will face Daniel first."

Isis kept her focus on Daniel, noting the tiny changes in his body. He was preparing—breathing with long, slow breaths, subtly shaking his muscles loose, briefly closing his eyes.

When he opened them again, one of the Opiri had stepped forward. Hatred blazed in his purple eyes.

"I will step in if this goes too far," she warned Daniel softly.

"Stay out of it, Isis. Please."

The Opir courtiers in the room gathered close, avid interest in their eyes. Isis was sickened by their greedy anticipation of coming bloodshed. Daniel assumed an alert but deceptively relaxed stance, slightly crouched, hands held loosely in front of him. As if from a great distance, Isis heard Anu tell him and his opponent to begin.

The Opir attacked first, in the way of most of their kind: relying on superior strength and speed to take down human prey. Daniel was ready for him. The Opir dived at Daniel, teeth bared, and Daniel was flung back, only to roll with the attack and kick the Opir over his shoulders.

Then there was a blur of motion, both human and Opir moving so fast that Isis could scarcely detect each individual strike and parry. The memories of ancient battles filled her mind...battles she had hoped never to see again.

A cry of startled pain brought her back to the present.

Daniel stood over the Opir, holding the man's arm twisted behind his back as his knee pinned the Opir to the floor. Daniel's sleeve and collar were torn and there was blood on his neck, but Isis could see no serious injuries. She felt her knees shaking beneath her gown.

Anu began to applaud. His courtiers joined him, some more enthusiastically than others. Isis could plainly see the shock on several faces, including Hera's and Bes's.

"What do the gods say now?" Daniel asked, licking a trickle of blood from his lip. "Or do you want me to fight the other one?"

The second Opir had somehow become much smaller, clearly of no mind to fight Daniel again.

Isis raised her voice. "The Nine find you innocent," she said without looking at Anu.

Daniel straightened and released the Opir, who staggered away. When he seemed ready to come at Daniel again, Anu raised his hand and four of his guards escorted Daniel's opponents out of the room.

"It was *their* idea," Anu remarked. "They wanted another chance to kill you, if possible. I told them that if you were to beat one of them, they would confess their guilt in attacking Bes's humans. Now it is done."

"And you had your entertainment," Daniel said, pulling the collar closed around his bleeding neck.

Anu chose to ignore Daniel's insolence. "I will have someone look after your wounds," he said.

"That is not necessary," Isis said. "I will do it myself."

"Very well," Anu said. He looked at Daniel. "The Council must, of course, agree with our decision, but I believe they will accept the aggressor's confession and deal with them appropriately. I advise that the next time you find yourself in a similar situation, you contact the Lawkeepers instead of taking matters into your own hands."

"Do you expect there to be a next time?" Daniel asked.

He held Anu's gaze for a moment, and then turned to Isis. "If you have no objection, I think it's time we left."

"By all means," Anu said, his voice indifferent, though Isis could still feel the raw edge of his power. And anger. "Isis, please stay for a moment."

Firmly dismissed, Daniel strode out the door. Isis heard it close and turned back to Anu.

"You treated him little better than a serf," she said.

"But he acted with courage and dignity," Anu said. "That is much to be admired in a human. And his innocence in that matter has been established." He stroked the arm of his chair. "Have you learned anything more of his time in Vikos?"

Isis thought of Ares, but said nothing. "No more than I knew when we last spoke."

"He is a most unusual human. See that he remains in Tanis until the Games and the Festival are over. That should not be difficult for you, since you have chosen him as your consort."

"I have *not*," Isis said. "It is merely that…he and I—"

"Find any excuse," Anu said, "but keep him by your side. If he has not attempted to escape by then, and has taken no action against us, we will know our suspicions are unfounded."

"Your suspicions *are* unfounded," Isis said. "There are no spies in Tanis. But I shall do what you ask."

"It will surely not be too great a sacrifice," Ishtar said with a throaty chuckle. "Send him to me if you tire of him, and I will keep him for you for a little while."

Isis didn't bother to answer. She left without another word. When she reached the door, she knew that something was wrong.

She opened it carefully to find Daniel facing a prosperous-looking and strikingly handsome Opir. Daniel was very still, the pulse beating hard in his throat. Man and

Opir stared at each other with bitter recognition. Daniel's fists clenched. The Opir smiled.

"It has been a long time, has it not?" the Opir said. He inclined his head to Isis. "Don't bother with introductions, Daniel. Of course I know the Lady Isis."

"Hannibal," Isis said.

"I am flattered to have attracted the lady's notice. Perhaps Daniel has told you that he and I are old...acquaintances."

Chapter 11

Daniel's fury burned so hot that Isis almost recoiled. "Be careful, Hannibal," he said to the Opir before him. "I am not what I used to be."

"That is obvious. But then you had Ares to help you." He smiled. "Odd that he visited us and then vanished so suddenly. Are you looking for him?"

Daniel took an aggressive step forward. "Where did he go?"

Hannibal shrugged and nodded to Isis again. "Good-bye, Lady."

He pushed past Daniel and entered Anu's suite. When Isis touched Daniel's arm, she found that he was shaking.

"Come," she said. "Let us leave this place."

Like an automaton, he went with her, his eyes blank and the muscles of his jaw standing out in harsh relief. It wasn't until they'd left the tower that the tension began to go out of his body. She could hear the sound of his teeth unclenching.

When they were at the base of the tower, she put her arms around him and pressed her cheek to his chest, trying to ignore the smell of his blood.

"I thought you would die," she whispered.

He touched her hair. "I wasn't so sure about it myself," he said, his voice unsteady.

"I am so sorry, Daniel. I do not know why Anu behaved as he did. I have never seen anything like it before."

He set her back to study her face. "It isn't your fault."

"If I had known something like this could happen…"

"It's all right."

"It is not," she said. "I thought you would see that he was a just Opir."

"You've known him for years, and you obviously didn't doubt him before."

"I knew he was arrogant," she said, "but I believed he would be fair."

"I felt what Anu was throwing out into the room."

"Yes," she said. "I am sorry. I know he turned his influence against you, but I do not understand—"

"I've known only a handful of Opiri with so much charismatic power. You're one of them."

"I told you before that I did not intend—"

"I know. You aren't like him at all. He could probably convince anyone, even other Opiri, to see only what he wanted them to see."

"He did not compel you to fight?"

He curled a lock of her black hair around his fingers. "Knowing what he was, I was prepared. He couldn't force me to do anything. But he was willing to try."

"And this gives you good cause to dislike him."

"I don't trust him, Isis."

"Because of this incident?" she asked, looking up.

"Because he reminds me too much of the Bloodmasters in the Citadel," he said.

Isis framed one side of his face with her hand. "Why *did* you agree to fight? Was it only to defend your innocence, or to prove something to yourself?"

His hand dropped to his side, and she knew he wouldn't answer. Not now.

"I apologize for attempting to command you," she said, changing the subject.

He smiled crookedly. "Habit," he said. "We're all at its mercy." He met her gaze with the warmth that had been missing since they'd come to the tower. "You didn't make a mistake in bringing me here."

"We must see to your injuries," she said, turning toward the ramp leading down to street level. "There is a human medical center—"

"No doctors, Isis."

"Then I shall do my best to help you myself."

Isis's best proved to be good enough. Once they reached her apartment in the administratve district, Daniel expected her to do the obvious and offer to use the chemicals in her own saliva to help heal him. But she obviously remembered his reaction to the prospect of her bite, and set to work with a needle instead.

Working quickly, she stitched up the lacerations Daniel's opponent's teeth had left on his arm. She offered him wine before the makeshift surgery, but he refused, grateful to be reminded that he could bear pain without flinching, even though his brief time in the tower had nearly broken all his defenses.

At least Isis knew only what she had observed. She hadn't felt the worst of it. She didn't know how he had frozen inside when he'd been among Anu's company, how he'd snapped back to the old days as if those years of freedom had never happened. She didn't realize that his rage had almost overcome his promises to her, how close he had come to turning on Anu when he had been asked to fight.

There had been such fights in Erebus, before Ares. It

had amused Palemon to pit his serfs against each other, and when Daniel had refused to kill, he had paid for it.

Since then Daniel had become adept at every kind of combat against humans, half-bloods and Opiri. But only when it was necessary, and never for the amusement of an audience.

No, Isis could only guess what had driven him. And she didn't know that Hannibal could easily refute many of Daniel's claims about his past. He would have to decide whether or not to tell Isis that he'd never been to Vikos in his life, and why he'd lied to her.

Deep in thought, he hardly noticed when Isis peeled back his collar and examined his neck, gently touching the bruises, shallow punctures and smaller cuts.

"He never got a firm grip," she said, dabbing at the wounds with a herb-infused cloth.

"If he had," Daniel said, "I wouldn't be here."

Her teeth pressed into her lower lip, and he knew she still felt guilt that he had no power to assuage.

An Opir who could feel real guilt was rare enough. A woman like Isis was one in a million. She claimed responsibility for him, but he felt the same for her.

He had no right to keep her in ignorance.

Isis leaned over him, her lightly covered breasts brushing his bare chest. Daniel came to full arousal, but Isis seemed unaware..

Still, she clearly wasn't indifferent to their intimate situation. She seemed to be trying to avoid touching any part of him that she wasn't stitching or bandaging, twisting her body into positions that would have been awkward if not impossible for a human.

Self-disgust formed a knot in Daniel's chest. Isis was afraid to start anything, and he couldn't blame her after the way he'd acted the previous times.

"Isis," he said, gently pushing her away. "I'll heal."

Her dark eyes reproached him. "You bear enough scars already," she said.

Daniel reached up to touch his neck, the ridges of old bite marks that striped his skin. "They don't bother me," he said.

"The vicious Opiri who did this to you...why would they not heal you after they took your blood?"

"Some of them did," he said lightly. "There'd be nothing left of my throat if they hadn't."

He regretted his words immediately; Isis gazed at him, appalled, and placed a herbal plaster over his neck. He caught her wrist gently and kissed the underside.

"There's another way you can heal me," he said.

She pulled free and rose from the chair beside the bed. "You should take food and drink," she said. "You cannot recover if you do not—"

"Come here," Daniel said.

"I will send for—"

He grabbed the trailing end of her robes. "Isis," he said. "I'm asking for your help."

Spinning around, she jerked the robes from his hands, pulling the wide straps of her gown halfway off her shoulders. "Do not tempt me!" she cried. "I will not do to you what those others did."

"You won't." He sat up, willing her to look at him. "I know what I said before. I regret it, Isis. I'm sorry."

"Daniel—" She looked at him with exasperated bewilderment and sat down again. "I do not blame you for your reluctance to give your blood. You may tell yourself that those scars don't matter anymore, as it doesn't matter that you had to fight for your life at Anu's bidding. But you can never convince me that the past is gone, Daniel. Not for you."

Taking her hands in his, he said, "You have no part of that past, Isis. Maybe you don't want any complications between us. But if it's because you think you'll remind me of bad times, I can set your mind at rest. You can never do to me what the others did, because you're nothing like them. You could never be."

Her eyes were like deep twilight, complex and beautiful. "I want it too much," she said.

Daniel's pulse rose. "I've done this willingly before, Isis. But I would never give my blood out of obligation. It's what I want, too."

"You trust me so much?"

He let go of her hands and lay back on the bed, pulling her down across his chest.

"Are you certain?" she whispered.

"Take only what you want from me, Isis. I won't demand more of you."

Closing her eyes, she bent over him, her breath warm and soft on his torn skin, her lips brushing old scars. She tasted his neck with the tip of her tongue. He stiffened and then quickly relaxed before she could register his instinctive response.

When her teeth grazed him, not yet breaking the skin, he cupped his hand behind her neck and gently urged her on. Her teeth pierced his flesh, and he expelled his breath slowly. A moment later she was drinking, lapping at his blood with her tongue, sucking so lightly that he barely felt it.

He let himself drift, keeping his mind blank, and so he wasn't fully prepared when her fingers found his fly and released him. She stroked his length with the very tips of her nails, sending wild shivers through his body. She continued to drink as she pushed her robes apart and straddled him, eased her wet heat over him and took him inside her.

Moving in a steady, firm rhythm, he filled her up, holding her in place with his hands on her hips. Her breasts, nipples erect, pressed into his chest. She moaned as he moved his hands to her bottom and caressed it, massaging the firm, rounded shapes with his fingers.

Abruptly she stopped drinking and reared up over him, her breasts swaying. He pulled her down and took one nipple into his mouth, rolling his tongue around the firm bud and withdrawing slowly to flick the tip with his tongue. Isis gasped as he did the same with the other breast, welcoming the way she slowed her movements to make the most of his ministrations. He wanted it to last, to give her all the pleasure he could. And to fully realize for himself just how much he had rejected because of his pride.

After he had given full attention to each delectable breast, he lifted her off him, to her faint protests, and laid her on her back. He stretched out just below her parted thighs and dipped between them, putting his tongue to work again. Her breath came fast as he ran the tip of his tongue between the delicate folds, tasting the honeyed nectar that emerged from her glistening lips. He pushed deeper, seeking the center, and found it. He pushed his tongue inside her and withdrew quickly, giving her a preview of what he had denied her a few moments before.

Isis began to squirm, clearly unwilling to let herself come. When she made another low protest, he worked his way up her body, licking and kissing her belly and just beneath her ribs, lingering over her breasts again as he moved into position. Her thighs came up around his hips, welcoming him. She gave a little cry as he entered her, urgently, pushed to the edge of his own endurance by her honeyed warmth and her moisture on his lips.

She arched to meet him just as urgently, and after a moment her teeth closed on his neck again. A kind of ecstasy came over him, and some faraway part of him wondered if she was using her body's natural aphrodisiacs to enhance his experience.

At the moment, he didn't care if she was manipulating

him. He reveled in the feel of her body gripping his, the smooth glide of flesh in flesh, the rhythm growing faster and faster.

Isis reached her completion before he did, but he wasn't long behind her. He moved hard for a few seconds and then slowed and stopped, letting her cradle him within her as the urgency passed into glorious lassitude. He sought her lips and kissed her gently, moving his mouth against hers and skimming the inside of her lips with his tongue. He tasted a little blood, and something else that filled him with quiet joy.

Slowly he rolled over, carrying her with him so that her body was half-sprawled across his. Isis kissed his chest and his throat and his mouth. She kissed the wound on his neck again…but there was no wound. She had healed his flesh. And, for a moment, she had healed something else.

"Will you tell me now?" she murmured.

"Tell you what?" he said, stroking her damp hair away from her face.

"What it is about Hannibal that you hide from me."

Daniel slid into a sitting position, moving the pillows so that he and Isis could remain as close as possible.

"I have to ask you something first," he said, kissing the corner of her mouth. "What I say has to stay between us. Can you agree to that?"

Gazing into his eyes, she ran her delicate forefinger over his lips. "I promise you that I will keep any secret you share with me. I will never betray you."

Daniel sighed and pulled her closer. "I didn't come from Vikos," he said, "but from a place much farther west, in California. A place called Avalon."

Chapter 12

Isis's warm breath spilled out of her mouth as if she'd been holding it back, anticipating the worst. Daniel knew what she was about to ask.

"What is this place you call Avalon?" she asked.

"I told you that I had come across peaceful but separate human and Opir colonies after I escaped from Vikos," he said. "But I traveled here from a colony where humans and Opiri live in cooperation and to their mutual benefit."

Isis sat up, the sheets bunching around her waist. "Such colonies *do* exist?"

"Yes. In several places along the Pacific seaboard. Some have been more successful than others. But we have learned that it *is* possible to have peaceful coexistence."

"We?"

"The humans and Opiri who founded the colony." He shifted to look into her eyes. "I did serve in a Citadel, Isis. But it was Erebus, not Vikos. And I was not the only one to escape. With the help of other Opiri and humans, we founded our own mixed colony, and fought for its survival."

She moved sideways, putting a clear space between herself and Daniel. "You lied to me," she said, "claiming that you needed to find out if such a thing was possible by observing Tanis. You already *knew* it was."

"Yes."

"How many other lies have you told me?"

He caught her wrist as she rolled away from him and began to climb out of bed. "Listen to me, Isis. I was sent here to gather information without revealing myself, in case Tanis proved to be hostile."

"Hostile?"

"We had little information to go on. I needed to learn if Tanis was a potential threat to us in the west."

"How could we be a danger to you?"

"If you were not what you were rumored to be—if Tanis was run by ambitious Opiri—you might send raiders west to attack the colonies as some of the Citadels do."

"Do you now think that is possible, Daniel?"

Daniel sighed. "When I talked about cooperation within Opir and human colonies I found on the way from Avalon, I told you that I wondered if that kind of life could be maintained on a larger scale."

"I remember. You thought a city such as ours would relapse to the old ways," she accused.

"That's not all," he said. He released her wrist. "Our colonies in the west cannot stay small forever. Tanis is an experiment that, to our knowledge, had never been tried before."

"So you worry about the future of your own colony."

"Yes." He met her gaze, willing her to understand. "Our people are divided on how to deal with a growing population of free humans and Opiri who want to live in such colonies. Some believe we can continue to expand into cities like this one."

"But you disagree."

"I believe it's wiser to divide the larger colonies rather

than lose the intimacy and personal knowledge of fellow colonists."

"And of course you do not believe we have that here."

"I see the distance between most Opiri and humans in Tanis. I fought Opiri whose only desire was to cause trouble for humans. I observed the way Hera and Anu and Ishtar behaved, and I know—"

He broke off, unsure about Isis's ability to accept what Hugh and the other humans had told him.

Isis slumped back on the bed. "Your judgment will determine your colony's attitude toward us," she said, "and even affect the future of Avalon? If you were so badly treated as a serf, how could you be objective?"

"I wasn't the first observer to be sent here, Isis. Ares and his wife came first. They never returned to Avalon."

Her eyes widened as she realized what he meant. "Then Ares was *not* a Bloodmaster you knew in Vikos."

"I knew him in Erebus." The memories pushed their way into his mind, and he shut them out. "When I was younger, it was every bit as bad as Vikos is rumored to be. Ares joined our colony when he saw that his work in Erebus could not be successful."

"His work?"

"To convince the ruling Council and the Bloodmasters that the way of the Citadels was not sustainable. He began by trying to get better treatment for the serfs. But he was badly outnumbered, and he had to leave to protect his wife."

"Trinity."

"A dhampir originally sent to Erebus as a spy from the San Francisco Enclave. She posed as a serf and was claimed by Ares, but she found the good in him and stayed by his side to help him."

"And now you—" Isis inhaled sharply. "You think something happened to him *here*."

He threaded his fingers through hers. "I have no proof, no clear reason to believe it. But I can't discount it, either. Anu still thinks of himself as a god. Ares was...*is* powerful, possibly a rival to Anu."

"You think Anu would have—"

"I didn't say that. But I have to know what happened."

"But not only out of duty or gratitude. You care for him."

"Yes," he said, swallowing the tightness in his throat. "He *did* save my life."

"And Hannibal?"

"Just what I said he was, a close ally of my owner. He and Ares were always enemies. He was exiled from Erebus when—" He stopped at the look of sympathy in Isis's eyes, rolled away from her and swung his legs over the side of the bed.

"Daniel," she said, rising behind him. She touched his shoulder, tracing a scar with utmost gentleness. "How long were you a serf?"

He couldn't look at her. "All my life, until I escaped from Erebus."

Her hand stilled on his shoulder. "But Opiri never take infants or young children."

"They took my mother when she was pregnant," he said. "I was born in Erebus. I stayed with her for six years before I was separated from her."

"I am sorry," Isis whispered.

"Don't feel sorry for me. I survived."

"And how *did* Ares save your life?" she asked softly.

"He bought me from Palemon when I was a very young man."

Firm, slim arms wrapped around his waist from behind. "Now I understand," she said. "None of these scars came from him, did they? Ares treated you well, as you had never been treated before."

Daniel gently detached her hands, turned and held her back. "Now you know the truth," he said roughly. "Most serfs in the Citadels are sent as convicts from the human Enclaves. I was never free until Ares came to understand that keeping serfs was wrong, and his allies got dozens of serfs out of Erebus. Once I was away from the Citadel, I had to learn to be what I am now. Do you understand?" He lowered his voice. "I had to learn how *not* to be a slave. And you're a goddess. Do you regret becoming my caretaker now?"

She freed her arms and took his hands in hers. "You have given me more than the truth I asked for. You did not lie to me about your primary purpose here, or your desire to find Ares or Hannibal's identity. You merely changed the details and concealed your origin because you didn't know how much you could trust me. Now I know how much you *do*."

"Then let me tell you the rest, Isis," he said with brutal directness. "When you slept with me, you shared a bed with a man who was used as breeding stock."

"Daniel," she gasped.

"It was illegal in Erebus, as a condition of the Armistice, but some Bloodlords did it anyway. Palemon and those like him, including Hannibal, used…extreme measures to get our cooperation. We always tried to refuse, but—" He turned away. "I don't know what happened to the children, if there were any."

Isis gathered her robes, rose, and left the bed, moving with uncharacteristic awkwardness, and he closed his eyes. Had he told her so much in order to push her away, when only a short while ago he had reveled in their joining and given her his blood? Had he said it to protect himself from making the mistake of growing closer to her, when he still had no idea what drove the Nine and the Opiri in the towers…or where her ultimate loyalty lay?

"You mean to shock me," Isis said, turning back to him. "I am shocked at the cruelty you suffered, but I will not be driven away because of these terrible things you were forced to endure."

"I have killed," he said. "I learned how to be a weapon when I left Erebus. I've taken Opiri and human lives to defend two colonies."

"We have made our own defenses strong so that we will never be put in the position of killing in order to protect ourselves."

"It isn't always that easy," he said. "I want you to understand. If I have to, in the defense of my colony or the people I care for, I will kill again."

"But not because of your hatred?" she asked. "Never out of revenge? Would you kill Hannibal?"

"Hannibal," Daniel said heavily. "He knows things about me, Isis…everything that happened in Erebus before and after Ares's rebellion against the Citadel's rulers. He knows I'm not from Vikos, and I still don't have any idea how much information he has about my life afterward."

"He could already have told Anu what he knows," Isis said, folding her arms across her chest. "If they realize that you have lied about your origins, you could be arrested as a spy, after all."

"But I haven't been, so far. And I know Hannibal is not here in good faith, as an Opiri looking for a new way of life. He wants something from Tanis, and he thinks he can get it."

"He might be a spy himself, from Vikos, or one of the other Citadels who might see us as a threat."

"If he is, Anu clearly doesn't know it." Daniel rose to stand with Isis, his hands hovering above her shoulders. "I still need your help to learn the truth about what's going on here, and I'm betting that you want to know that as much as I do. If there's a problem with Tanis, you wouldn't let it continue."

"No," she said, lifting her chin. "I would not. But I think it is time for you to leave the city."

"Why?" he said, dropping his hands. "If you're afraid for me—"

"Tanis is my city, as you said. Mine to protect. But your secrets are secrets no longer, if they ever were. I do not know why Anu would try to control you, unless Hannibal saw you in the city and has told tales about you. If I were to have to choose between defending you or taking action to save Tanis—"

"You would never have to make that choice," Daniel said. "I wouldn't let you."

"It would not be your decision." She pulled her robes close around her body. "But you will not leave, will you?"

"I can't, Isis. Not until I find Ares."

She shivered as if invisible hands were shaking her. "What do you want me to do?"

Daniel released his breath. "If you think *you'll* be in danger—"

"From whom?" She turned around to face him. "The Opiri I have known for millennia? I am not afraid of them, and they would do me no harm."

"I don't think that Anu likes you," Daniel said, feeling his way. "Who is the second eldest of the Nine, Isis?"

"I am."

"Could you be leader if you chose?"

"Only if I were to challenge him, and win. And we no longer engage in such barbaric activities, even if I had any desire to take his place."

"It's enough that he knows you have power, too, even if you don't intend to use it."

"I have never defied him," she said. "I have had no reason to."

"Except when you tried to keep me from fighting."

She made an inelegant noise. "I am no serf, Daniel." Her cheeks flushed. "I am sorry. I will help you, if you will help me."

Daniel badly wanted to take her in his arms, but he knew better. There was only one way to make this work, to maintain some vestige of objectivity. For both of them. He should have realized that from the moment Isis had given herself to him in his visitor's quarters the night he'd arrived.

He'd wanted her too much then, as he did now.

"What is my status in Tanis?" he asked.

"You are still considered a visitor, with the option of becoming a citizen of Tanis if you are found acceptable. I can arrange for a provisional citizenship, but you must take a job and help support the city."

"That won't be a problem. I'll take whatever work is offered."

"I believe they need more workers on the construction crews in the expanding human sector," she said. "I will look into it." She hesitated. "There is one other duty you will be expected to perform."

"I know. I'll do whatever is necessary." He gazed at her for a long moment of silence, memorizing the soft lines of her face, her eyes, her lips, as if he were about to lose her forever. "Under the circumstances," he said, "it would be better if we break off any personal relationship. If you're to remain my sponsor, we can't be seen as lovers."

Chapter 13

"Yes," Isis said quickly. "I agree." She tied her robe at the neck and waist, hiding herself from him. "It may be too late to maintain even the pretense of objectivity. But we must try."

She seemed, Daniel thought, almost relieved at his suggestion. It was no surprise to him that the things he'd told her had overwhelmed her. In spite of her reassurances, he knew he'd shaken her faith in him...and in herself.

He almost decided then to tell her the most important secret he had kept from her: that he wasn't human at all. But she might treat him differently if she knew, even without meaning to, and that secret might stand him in good stead if it caused potential enemies to underestimate him as a "mere human."

"We'll start over from the beginning," he said, though the words stuck in his throat. "You're my guide, nothing more. And I don't want you to do anything that will lead anyone to believe that *you* have a particular interest in Ares."

"How, then, are we to learn anything?" she asked, giving him a wide berth.

"It's still possible that the friendlier members of the

Nine may have more to say about Ares's visit here. Athena, Hermes, Bes—"

"Anu will almost certainly learn of anything you say and do in Tanis. He will know you are looking for Ares."

"That won't be a problem, unless he has something to hide. I'm still only a human."

"A human who defeated several Opiri in combat, and treated Anu like a peer instead of a lord of the city."

"If he finds *me* dangerous, that will tell us a great deal. But I may be getting ahead of myself in suspecting Anu at all."

She flashed a glance in his direction, and her shoulders relaxed. "You will get another chance to speak to my peers, and we can further investigate the incident in Bes's ward. And the Games are in three weeks, followed immediately by the Festival. That will be an excellent chance to speak to many different people, for it is a time when humans and Opiri mingle freely, wearing masks to dissolve the barriers between them."

Daniel was careful not to say what he thought about "dissolving barriers."

"Where can I find a mask?" he asked.

"That will be no problem. I will show you mine." Isis moved to a pair of doors that opened to a closet hung with gowns of various colors and patterns. She withdrew a half mask molded in the shape of a stylized lioness with kohl painted around the eyeholes and an ancient Egyptian headdress falling back to cover the wearer's head and shoulders.

"Sekhmet, the goddess of war and healing. Wearing this, I can move among the people unrecognized." She fingered the mask and hung it in the closet again. "Perhaps you can introduce me to those humans you spoke to when the Opiri gang attacked. They will be less suspicious if they do not recognize me."

"They'll know you're Opir."

"Not if I am careful."

Careful not to let her natural charisma escape her control, Daniel thought. But he couldn't believe that Hugh or his friends would ever agree to speak frankly with a stranger, even if they attended the Festival.

Still, he didn't have the heart to discourage Isis now. He could try approaching Hugh beforehand, but he'd have to be certain not to attract any notice.

"I will find an appropriate mask for you," Isis said, "and have it delivered to your quarters the day before the Games." She turned back to him. "I will also acquire a good seat for you at the Games. They take place by day, so I will be sitting among the Nine under a canopy in the top row of seats."

"In other words, the Nine won't be mingling with the humans of their wards."

"It is best that we remain separate during the actual competitions."

"And the ordinary Opiri citizens?" he asked. "Will they be in the upper seats, as well?"

"Relatively few come to observe," she said, with an uneasy shrug of her shoulders.

"They might be more enthusiastic if the Games featured actual fighting."

Isis began to walk around the room, graceful in spite of her agitation. "I have told you that such competitions are not part of the Games."

But he knew that she, like he, was thinking of his own fight in front of Anu's court, and how eagerly the Opiri had watched.

Daniel glanced at the door to Isis's apartment and back to her nearly expressionless face. Less than an hour ago, they had shared blood and bodies with abandon and joy.

Now it was as if that time were a dream, and Isis was a vision of perfection he could never reach again.

"I'll go," he said. "You'll let me know when you find me a job?"

"Yes. And tomorrow I will finish our tour with the library, the arena and the formal gardens."

He matched her brisk, professional tone. "Thank you," he said. "I look forward to it."

With those last, formal words between them, Daniel left her apartment. The space beneath his ribs felt hollow, but the more distance he put between himself and Isis the less he noticed it, until finally he felt nothing at all.

Daniel spent the next three weeks settling into the rhythm of life in Tanis. After his tours with Isis, he was given a job with the construction crews building additional human residences on the north side of the city. It was hard physical labor, which suited Daniel very well; it kept his mind off Isis and gave him a chance to speak with the other men and women on the crew.

Isis was unable to arrange further sit-downs with Hermes or Athena, but during Daniel's brief meetings with her she assured him that she was spending more time in the towers and keeping her ear to the ground. On the construction site, there was a constant low buzz about the Games and Festival; a large portion of the workers seemed to look forward to both, and there was even a spirit of relatively peaceful rivalry between humans who wore the various emblems of their wards and sponsors.

There were a few workers who wore no emblems and maintained a stubborn silence about the coming events, but though Daniel tried to learn if they shared the tavern folks' disdain, the quiet ones remained elusive and seemed to vanish whenever Daniel went looking for them.

Still, he was left with the sense that there was a group of workers who met in secret, like members of the human Underground had done in Erebus. Once, he heard grumbling about the hardest labor in Tanis going to humans, while Opiri never sullied their white hands.

As if to confirm the workers' concerns, Opiri in clean and elegant clothing occasionally stopped by the site, observing from some elevated position as if they were enjoying the antics of animals in a zoo. They consulted with the architects and supervisor in a way that suggested that the Opiri were the ones in charge of the construction. Each time they came, the grumbling grew louder.

During the second week, Daniel had observed another incident that suggested all wasn't well in Tanis.

He became aware of the commotion when the crew's supervisor rushed to the construction area's entrance, drawing a dozen men and women with him. Daniel climbed down from his perch on the scaffolding and caught sight of a familiar face moving among the humans: Hephaestus, visiting with the supervisor and the almost fawning human residents of his ward, all of whom wore the Opir lord's emblem on their shirts. Daniel could feel the Bloodmaster's influence from across the yard.

He moved closer to hear what was being said, and saw several other well-dressed Opiri clustered around Hephaestus, acting as his entourage. They seemed grossly out of place on the site and avoided touching the humans.

Some of the humans noticed. They jostled the Opiri with false smiles and bows of apology. Other humans, wearing competing emblems, stood apart as all work ceased.

But that wasn't the end of it. A few minutes later there was another commotion at the gates, and Hera—followed by her own Opir entourage—made a grand entrance, projecting her own power before her. Her human followers flocked around her as she steadfastly ignored Hephaestus, her regal bearing making her fellow "god" seem ordinary.

Only when both members of the Nine drifted away did silence fall over the site. The supervisor urged everyone to return to work, but the atmosphere had changed. A group of Hephaestus's men and women blocked the path of Hera's followers as they tried to return to their work stations. The two factions stared at each in silence for a moment, and then the jeering and taunting began. Real hostility rang in the voices on both sides, claims of the superiority of one ward's sponsor over the other.

Even when the shouts turned to scuffling, the supervisor didn't interfere. Daniel waded in and tried to separate the fighters, who flailed at him with fists and feet. He managed to break up two fights and force the opponents to return to their own sides.

"What's wrong with you?" he demanded, standing between the two groups. "Are you children fighting over a ball?"

The leaders of each faction stared at Daniel sullenly. "What's it to you?" one of them said. "You're only a newcomer. You don't support a team."

"You have no right to interfere with our customs!" shouted the leader of the other faction.

"I want no part of these so-called customs," Daniel retorted. "The Games are another week away. Are you incapable of waiting that long to squabble with each other?"

Daniel was well accustomed to governing large groups of people, humans and Opiri, and gradually the antagonists began to back down. Belatedly, a pair of Lawkeepers arrived, but by then the two groups had begun to scatter and drift away, though not without a few curses thrown over their shoulders.

That evening, Daniel met with Isis in her apartment. He pretended not to notice her warm, velvety scent or the way she moved about the room from one random point to another. She wore a heavier gown that should have concealed her figure but only emphasized what it was meant to hide.

We're here to do a job, he reminded himself. *There's no room for mistakes.*

"What I saw wasn't ordinary rivalry," he said, when both he and Isis had settled in their seats on either side of the living room table. "Their sponsors' visits primed these people to go at each other to prove their superiority over their opponents. It was almost as if Hera and Hephaestus meant to cause a fight."

"That would be extremely foolish," Isis said, not quite meeting his gaze. "I have never heard of such a thing happening before."

"Are you sure, Isis? Or do you prefer not to notice?"

Daniel regretted his harshness immediately, but there was nothing he could do to assuage Isis's obvious distress without getting much too close to her.

"What you describe," she said in a level voice, "is merely another aberration."

"Is it an aberration that hardly any Opiri seem to be involved in hard physical labor, and that they seem to have better access to resources than the human citizens?"

Isis started. "Who told you such things?"

Daniel was silent for a long while, wondering how to explain the other facts he had withheld from her. "That time at the tavern, before the Opiri gang arrived in Bes's ward," he said, "I overheard humans talking about the Games. They felt the Games were only a distraction for humans who might otherwise notice that Tanis has not been wholly successful in enacting its ideals of complete equality."

Isis blinked. "You said nothing of this before."

"I swore that I wouldn't expose them."

"To what?"

"To anyone who might object to their complaints."

Isis squeezed her hands together. "What else did they say?"

"After the fight with the Opir gang, they claimed that humans would never be anything but peons to the Opiri in Tanis, and that the justice system was rigged against them. They were sure I'd be considered the guilty party. You were afraid of the same thing, Isis."

"Was there anything else you neglected to tell me?" she asked coldly.

"Only that the humans clearly feel there's something wrong in Tanis, and that the Opiri are the favored class under the Nine and the Council."

"But these humans have not seen how our Opiri live!"

"Whose fault is that, Isis?" He sighed. "I saw more than a few Opiri in the tower, dressed like lords. And acting like them."

"They were Anu's favored—"

"Courtiers, yes."

"You cannot make a judgment of all Opiri citizens based upon what you saw in Anu's quarters."

"No," he said, "but the only Opiri I've seen working at all are a few in your ward and outside in the fields at night."

"Just because their jobs are not visible to you does not mean that they do not exist."

"Would humans be given these 'invisible' jobs if they asked for them?"

Isis flushed with anger. "Humans have free will here," she said. "They *can* speak freely, whatever Bes's humans may fear."

"Then show them their options, Isis. I know humans are discouraged from entering the towers, even if freedom of movement is part of your law. Let them *see* how the Opiri live."

She averted her eyes. "It is a…fair observation," she said, her hands worrying the trailing ends of her golden sash. "I will bring it up with the Nine."

"Your suggestion will probably be unpopular with some of them. I don't think Anu will be pleased."

"Then let him be displeased." She started, as if her own words surprised her. "He must listen."

Daniel took a deep breath. "Have you learned anything about Ares?"

"No," she said, with real feeling. "I am sorry. Perhaps I have been too cautious."

"I asked you to be. I'm grateful for your help."

She only looked away, and Daniel left before he could feel tempted to comfort her.

Isis looked over the rows of seats from her position above the crowd, searching for Daniel. It was no simple thing to pick out one human from among the hundreds gathered for the Games, but something drew her eyes to him almost at once, as if a thread of emotion connected them across the distance.

His face turned toward her, and she felt his eyes on her. He didn't raise his hand to acknowledge her, but he didn't need to.

She thought of that last, painful exchange about the Opiri of Tanis. She hadn't been able to stop thinking about it, though they had met twice in the past week and he had said nothing more about it.

There was truth in what he had said. She knew it, though she realized now that she had never permitted herself to dwell on this issue. Her own innate prejudices shamed her.

Now that the crowds had gathered and the Nine, along with their closest attendants, were ensconced in their canopied seats high above the arena, Isis felt the vast chasm between her peers and their human charges. She was intensely aware of the ordinary Opiri assembled on the slightly lower, covered platforms to either side. They had set themselves above the humans as if they were masters, not equals.

She studied the arena, where the various teams were assembled in athletic clothes bearing the emblems of their sponsors. They stood in columns, each team separated by several yards from the next: Hera's team, wearing the peacock; Hephaestus's, the flame; Bes's, the sheaf of wheat; Ishtar's star; and Athena's owl. They stared up at the Nine's box with a kind of fixed fascination that sent a chill up Isis's spine. It was as if they were, indeed, supplicants standing before their gods.

Her gaze drifted back to the human audience. Most faces were alert with anticipation, but for the first time she noted a few that held darker expressions. Why, she thought, would they attend the Games if they didn't enjoy them?

She wondered if news of the conflict at the construction site had reached Anu. He had certainly not brought it up with the others. Neither had Hera or Hephaestus.

She glanced at Anu. Hannibal had the privilege of sitting close to him, and they were speaking to each other in an undertone. Isis had tried to learn if he had told Anu the truth about Daniel's origins, but she'd seen no indication that Anu was overly concerned about Daniel.

And Anu had said that if Daniel had not attempted to escape by the time of the Games, he would admit that his suspicions were unfounded.

"You look pensive," Athena said, taking a seat beside her. "Are you well?"

"Yes," Isis said with a faint smile. "Your team seems very competent."

"I have been seeing more of my people of late," Athena said, a note of pride in her voice. "They are eager to make a good showing."

"What do they say of the other teams?"

Athena looked surprised at the question. "Nothing,"

she said. "What would they have said?" She chuckled. "I remember the first Olympic Games in Greece. They always generated much excitement."

So, Isis thought, either Athena hadn't heard of the fighting at the construction site, or she thought nothing of it. Perhaps she wouldn't understand Isis's new concerns about the Games.

"Isis," Anu said behind her. She turned as he loomed over her, smiling, and invited her to sit beside him. Hannibal was gone.

"A pity you have no team in the Games," Anu said as he sat and adjusted his heavily embroidered robes around him.

"I find I have nothing to prove," Isis said without thinking.

Anu looked at her sharply. "Would you care to explain that remark, Isis?" he asked.

Chapter 14

Isis was spared the need to answer by Daniel's arrival. He stood just to the side of her, his expression neutral.

"I invited our prospective citizen to join us here," Anu said, gesturing at Daniel. "I thought you might enjoy his company since I know you have seen little of him for the past several weeks."

Of course he would know, Isis thought. He had wanted her to keep Daniel close until the Games, and she'd failed to carry out his instructions. He was reminding her of her failure.

"He has been working with the construction crews," Isis said. "And performing admirably, according to his supervisor's report."

"I am glad to see that he is settling in so well," Anu said. He gestured for Daniel to take the empty seat next to Isis and abruptly withdrew. Athena took Anu's chair, her small coterie of familiar Opiri behind her.

"Welcome, Daniel," Athena said. "You remember my companions, Ianthe and Homer."

"Of course," Daniel said, nodding to the two Opiri.

"This is your first time at the Games, is it not?" Ianthe asked.

"Yes," Daniel said. "I understand that few Opiri attend."

Ianthe blinked. "That is true," she said, "but some of us enjoy sharing our fellow citizens' enthusiasm."

"And it is always a pleasure to observe the skills of others," Homer said.

A noisy group of Opiri arrived on the platform just below the box, and Isis heard them laying bets on the teams with intense concentration. They joked about various humans and spoke of the contestants' rumored strengths and weaknesses as if they were arguing over horses in a race.

"*They* seem to be very enthusiastic," Daniel said, cocking his head toward the bettors.

Athena shook her head. Ianthe sighed. "They make fools of themselves," she said.

"What they do is wrong," Homer said. "The Games were not established for their private amusement."

Isis glanced at Daniel to see if the Opir's assertion had registered with him. But he was still staring at the other Opiri with an icy expression that seemed to dismiss the goodwill of Athena's companions. Isis could almost feel his anger. Justified anger, an emotion she shared.

Anu returned, and Athena quickly vacated his seat. Her Opiri moved well away from him. Isis determined to take the betting up with Anu after the Games.

But she had no chance to talk to Daniel again, for the sound of trumpets and drums announced the beginning of the Games. The teams marched around the arena bearing their sponsors' banners, and the audience cried out approval in a roar that, for the first time, seemed to Isis like beasts aroused by the scent of blood.

"The races are first," she said, resisting the urge to reach for his hand. As the field cleared, officials took their various positions beside the track that ran around the inner wall of the arena. The Opir bettors fell silent. Anu rose again and descended to the front of the box.

"Let the Games begin," he said, and a group of five contestants, one for each human ward, approached the starting line. The first race was a one-hundred-meter sprint; when the drum sounded, the contestants set off at breakneck speeds.

Hephaestus's team won, and Isis was immediately aware of shouts of disapproval and resentment mingled with the happy cries of victory. The negative reactions seemed far more volatile than she'd observed at previous Games. Athena, too, seemed to notice the differences and frowned as she leaned toward one of her favorites. None of the other Nine reacted except Hephaestus himself, who limped down the stairs to the lower box to bequeath the award to the winner. The victorious human looked up at his sponsor with shining eyes, and Isis almost expected him to fall to his knees in reverence.

A warm hand gripped Isis's under the concealment of her chair. Daniel laced his fingers through hers when the next event began...and ended with the same show of mingled approval and derision from the audience when Hera's human claimed victory. This time, even Anu seemed to take notice of the clamor.

Before the third event could begin, there was a ripple of movement in the crowd closest to the starting line. The ripple grew into an obvious disturbance, and humans spilled out into the arena, some flooding the track, others jostling each other with deliberate hostility. Isis heard the names of Hera, Bes, Athena, Hephaestus and Ishtar shouted in hoarse voices, and saw several banners ripped apart. Lawkeepers began to converge on the scene.

Without warning, Daniel was up and out of his seat, descending from the box and vaulting over the wall into the arena. He ran toward the disturbance as if he intended to stop it himself. Isis rose to follow him, but Anu held her back with a hand on her shoulder.

"I shall be most curious to see what he does," Anu said, a hard note in his voice.

Shaking him off, Isis ran after Daniel. She reached the arena floor after he had already disappeared into the crowd, and she felt the heat and anger of the closely packed humans from some distance away. She calmed herself as she approached the mob, gathering her dignity, highly aware of her own power to influence the mood of the angry humans.

Something she truly didn't wish to do.

The humans who noticed her quickly stepped out of her way, their eyes glazed with confusion. Daniel was at the center of the crowd, speaking firmly to the humans closest to him. "You gain nothing by this," he was saying, commanding attention with firm authority. "If you want to prove some Opiri's belief that we're little better than animals, this is the way to do it."

Resentful murmurs followed his words, but when Isis showed herself the protesters grew quiet. Some actually bowed their heads, filling Isis with a sense of shame.

"Please listen to Daniel," she said, moving up beside him. "There is no reason for such anger. The Games are not yet over."

"The Games are rigged," said a man sporting Athena's owl. "*We* should have won the race."

"Your man was too slow," one of Hera's followers said loudly.

Arguments started up again, but Daniel raised his voice above the noise. "Calm yourselves," he said. "If you have issues with the Games, there are better ways to present them."

"And who will listen to us?" a big, burly man asked.

Daniel looked at the man with recognition in his eyes, and Isis wondered if they'd met on the construction site. She spoke up.

"You will be heard," she said. "I promise this. If you have complaints, come to me, and I will see that they are brought before the Council."

"Nobody has listened before," the big man said. "The Council has no power or will to help us."

"Be patient, and I will act on this information."

Slowly the crowd began to settle, and the arguments and anger subsided. Daniel took Isis's arm and smiled with warmth and approval, his grimness melting away. Isis smiled back at him, unable to contain her happiness at his approval. She had tried not to use her influence, and he knew it.

People began to scatter, not without a few final mutters, and gradually found their seats. Lawkeepers approached with shock sticks at the ready. Isis wondered if Anu had told them to use the weapons on the crowd.

"There is no need for your intervention," she told the half-bloods. They exchanged glances and retreated as Isis and Daniel started back for the box.

"Very impressive," Anu said as they reached their seats. "I commend you, Daniel, for calming your people so effectively. And, Isis…" He smiled, showing his teeth. "The humans seemed inclined to listen to you. But then again, they always have." His smile faded. "What was the cause of this disturbance?"

"Concerns that I will present when the Nine next meet," Isis said.

"Some of them thought the Games were rigged," Daniel said, staring at Anu in a way that made Isis very uneasy.

Anu laughed. "I see that you have not lost your candor," he said. "Whatever the cause, we must question the troublemakers in order to discourage such incidents from occurring again."

"You'll arrest more than a hundred people?" Daniel asked, his jaw clenching.

"If their concerns are heard, this will *not* happen again," Isis said.

"You are truly their champion," Anu said, mockery in his voice. "Perhaps I will put this affair into your hands, if you allow *your* champion to compete on your behalf."

Isis knew immediately what he meant, and so did Daniel. "Another challenge to be decided by the gods?" he asked. "What did you have in mind?"

"Simply a race," Anu said. "Surely you are capable of that."

Daniel glanced at Isis with a reassuring nod. "You'll let Isis deal with this incident if I win one of your competitions?"

"A child's dare," Isis said, not bothering to hide her derision from Anu. "You would not make this offer unless you expected Daniel to lose."

"But he defeated Opiri in hand-to-hand combat," Anu said. "He may have a great advantage over the average human contestant. We will impose an appropriate handicap."

"What handicap?" Daniel asked.

"The next event is the four-hundred-meter race. You will leave the starting line after the other contestants have reached the halfway point."

"This is not amusing, Anu," Isis said coldly.

"I'll do it," Daniel said, "as long as there are no penalties against Isis if I lose."

"Penalties?" Anu said with a raised brow. "The only issue at stake is whether or not Isis takes charge of the human troublemakers."

He stared at Daniel so intently that Isis immediately knew that he was attempting to use his influence again, though for what purpose Isis couldn't guess. Isis pushed her way between Anu and Daniel, knocking Anu aside.

For a moment, Anu was the startled one. He blinked

clearly astonished that Isis would dare to interfere, let alone challenge him so openly.

"The contestants are waiting," Isis said, keeping her eyes on Anu.

His expression taut with anger, Anu signaled to one of his Opir attendants, who left the box. "By the time you reach the starting line, it will be arranged," he said to Daniel. He turned his back on Isis and resumed his seat.

"I do not trust this bargain," Isis whispered, moving closer to Daniel. "Anu had no reason to make it."

"He wants to humiliate you," Daniel said. "I was right. He sees you as a rival, even if you don't know the reason."

Isis closed her ears to his warning. She longed to touch Daniel, but kept her hands at her sides. "Can you win?" she asked.

"I don't know. But if I can rub his face in it, I will."

The other contestants were watching as Daniel joined them at the starting line. It was obvious to Daniel that they resented his sudden appearance, though it was also clear they had been informed that they had no choice in the matter.

The men and women were to run barefoot, and so Daniel removed his soft boots. He looked up in the box for Isis, and caught a flash of her white gown and gold sash.

"The Lady Isis sends this cup to you," a young human attendant said, offering Daniel a crystal goblet of water. Daniel stared at it for a moment, wondering what message Isis meant to send, and then drank the water. He took his place at the starting line and waited, listening to the deep breathing of the contestants.

The sharp rap of a drum sent the runners sprinting off along the track. Daniel watched them reach the two-hundred-meter mark and heard the young attendant give him the signal. He burst into a run, focusing only on the track ahead.

The shouts of the human audience formed a background drone as he caught up with the trailing runner and surged past him. One by one he shot by the contestants, and reached the finish line ahead of the others by a good fifty meters.

He stopped to catch his breath, the blood throbbing behind his ears. Dizziness overcame him, and he nearly lost his balance. His stomach roiled with sickness. He was barely aware when a dozen humans crowded around him, their voices so much meaningless noise.

"Daniel?"

That voice was familiar, and Daniel tried to listen. She asked if he was ill, and instructed others to take him off the field. He stumbled, his legs giving out from under him, but somehow his helpers kept him on his feet until they were clear of the seething crowd and in a clear space where the voices faded to a hum. They eased him down onto a hard surface while the blood continued to pound in his veins.

"I will take him now," Isis said, and the others disappeared.

"You are ill," Isis said, her cool hand on his forehead. "What has happened?"

"The water," he said, the word hoarse and grating.

"Water?" she echoed.

"Wasn't from you." He coughed uncontrollably. "Poison."

"Then there is no time to get you to the hospital," she said.

Daniel hardly moved when her teeth pierced his skin. Almost at once Isis drew back and spat out the blood, her breath catching hard.

"There is a taint in your blood," she said, "but I can draw it out of you."

"No," he said, his vision clearing just enough to let him see her face. "Might...hurt you."

"It was clearly meant for a human," she said softly. "It will do me no harm."

Before he could respond, she bit him again. He was lost in another kind of limbo, aware of her scent, the softness of her skin, the soothing warmth where her lips met his neck. Several times he heard her spit out the blood. He tried to push her away, but his arms and legs had lost all sensation and he felt himself losing consciousness.

He woke in Isis's bed, her silken sheets pulled up to his chest, her pillow under his head. She paced beside the bed, turning when she heard him stir.

"Isis?" he croaked, trying to sit up. She pushed him back down and sat on the bed beside him.

"Try to rest," she said. "Your body has suffered a great shock."

"You saved my life," he said, finding his voice again.

"I could not have done it unless you were strong enough to help me fight the poison." Her lips tightened. "I did not send that water to you. Someone gave you a substance meant to kill you."

Chapter 15

Isis's revelation could mean only one thing. "Anu," Daniel said.

"He may not like you," Isis said, "but I cannot believe he would attempt to murder a man who was proved innocent of any charges laid against him."

"Any open charges."

She placed her hand on Daniel's forehead. He felt each of her fingers, the texture of her palm; saw the lingering fear in her eyes, the faint lines around her mouth. "I remember what you said," she murmured. "But we do no *know* it was Anu."

"I know he tried to control me in the box," Daniel said. "He failed a second time. I've openly defied him more than once, and that makes him look bad in front of the Opir and his peers."

"He is very proud," Isis said with obvious reluctance. "But is that enough?" She stroked the bedcovers with nervous hands. "Perhaps our fears were correct, and Hanniba convinced him that you are a spy for one of the Enclaves." She pushed her long, glossy hair behind her ear. "There is another possibility, but it rests on theories I…still find difficult to accept."

"The inequalities in Tanis."

"If the situation is as bad as you surmise, Anu may suspect that you, as an outsider, see what others do not."

"Or that I listen to what discontented humans say."

"Anu may find it troubling that a newcomer with your skills proved to be so effective in influencing the mob at the Games," she said. "Your qualities as a leader are obvious."

"Which would suggest that he doesn't really want to see any human influencing other humans in Tanis, even to keep them from rioting. He wants full mastery, for himself and his Opiri."

"It is difficult—" Isis began. She drew a deep breath. "I am sorry, Daniel. I am not yet prepared... I cannot believe it. And even if these things were true, still he would not kill you. He would want to extract all your knowledge and experiences here in Tanis first." Her fingers fluttered like butterfly wings. "If it was not Anu, who else? Hannibal?"

"He has a place here," Daniel said. "He wouldn't risk it just to kill the serf of a former ally." He frowned. "Unless *he* is a spy for some Citadel, and thinks I know it."

"How could you?"

"I only know that destroying Tanis and its ideals would suit him far better than reforming a lifetime's habits and beliefs."

Abruptly Isis sat up. "Daniel, I should speak to Anu again. It may be possible to learn more without directly questioning him."

"You've become his enemy, Isis." He touched her cheek with his fingertips. "Whether or not he meant to kill me, I know he sees you as biased in favor of humans. They listen to you. You threaten his mastery, whether you challenge him outwardly or not."

She gazed at him, and all he could think of was the softness of her lips, the glory of her dark hair, the sleek curves of her body fitted against his. He remembered telling her

that they had to remain apart if she were to prove her ob
jectivity, remembered how he had thought that he coul
stop wanting her. He laughed softly.

"We will learn the truth, Daniel," Isis said earnestly
misinterpreting his amusement. "The Festival begins i
five hours. Even though you are too ill to attend, I—"

Throwing the sheets and blankets away from his legs
Daniel sat on the edge of the bed and did a mental survey o
his body. It felt a little weak, and there was some lighthead
edness, but he knew he wasn't sick enough to stay behind

"I'm completely able to attend the Festival," he said.

"Daniel—"

"I should be asking if *you're* all right," he said, lookin
her over carefully. "Getting rid of the poison could hav
weakened you."

"I am well."

"Would taking my blood now help you?"

"You must fully recover before you can donate blood,
she said. She lifted her chin. "I have visited the depository.

"Good," Daniel said. "But if you're even a little un
sure…"

"You worry about me," Isis said, "but spare no concer
for yourself."

"I know we're likely to be separated at the Festival," h
said, holding her gaze. "You swear to me, Isis, that you'
find me if you sense a threat from anyone, human or Opi
The seams of this city are starting to come undone."

Isis frowned, and Daniel saw the storm of the goddes
in her eyes. But her expression relaxed, and after a mo
ment she laughed, too.

"You were a fool to come to Tanis," she said, "and
became a fool when I learned to care about your fate. I
seems we must be fools together."

"Do you have a fool's mask for me?" he asked.

"No," she said, her eyes bright, "but I hope you will not find the one I chose for you unsuitable."

The plaza was loud with shouts and laughter and music. Both human and Opiri bodies jostled and bumped each other with no regard for sex or species.

On the surface, the revels seemed rowdy but peaceful. Lawkeepers moved quietly among the citizens, but they didn't seem to be expecting trouble. Daniel scanned the ever-shifting crowd but saw no signs of conflict, though the Games had ended only a few hours before.

Now it was night, the open sky a gem-spangled swath of deep blue silk. Daniel felt his mask again to make sure it was secure.

Isis had delivered a disguise as lovingly crafted as hers. She had chosen for him the face of another Egyptian god: Osiris, god of the dead and ruler of the underworld, a man with the green skin of growing things and a tall feathered crown. Daniel had learned enough of Egyptian mythology to understand the mask's significance: according to legend, Osiris had been Isis's husband and mate.

It seemed a strange choice, given that they had decided to return to the roles of guide and prospective citizen. But such a pretense seemed pointless after the events of the Games. *That* masquerade would be increasingly difficult, if not impossible, to maintain.

As they moved through the square a little distance apart, Isis in her lioness mask, Daniel noticed that wood stalls had been constructed around the square. Some were selling food grown in personal gardens, others small hand-crafted items both functional and decorative. Someone had created something like a beer garden with lantern-draped canopies overhead, and one large, closed booth on a side street advertised itself in both the Opir language and English as a "blood exchange" location.

Daniel signaled to Isis. "Another depository?" he asked.

She leaned close. "There are several such booths at the Festival," she said, "where humans and Opir can make private transactions to give and take blood."

"If it's already legal in Tanis, why hide it in a side street?"

"I see that I never fully explained," she said, her voice not quite its usual rich timber. "At the Festival, such transactions can be highly intimate. They sometimes involve other physical acts."

"Sex," Daniel said. "Is it the humans or Opiri who want to keep it so private during such a public event?"

"Often both," Isis said. "Though every kind of non-harmful act is permitted during Festival, there are still some who do not wish others to know of their proclivities."

"The perverse proclivities of humans and Opiri sharing more than blood?"

He couldn't see Isis's face, but he could almost feel her blush. "I have already told you that it is not unknown for Opiri and humans to bear children together in Tanis."

"But it still isn't common."

"That is why the Festival aims to break down such barriers."

Daniel would have liked nothing better than to break down a few barriers with Isis then and there, but he reminded himself that he had to keep a clear head in order to be an effective observer. He was still hoping for news of Ares as well as more signs of rebelliousness on the part of the humans and misbehavior by Opiri.

And if any others of the Nine put in an appearance, he might be able to talk to them. Any information he could gather now was valuable.

A burst of laughter caught his attention, and he noticed a number of anonymously robed and masked people gathered around a small band of human musicians: a drum-

mer, a flautist, a guitar player, a fiddler and a pianist with
a slightly battered instrument.

"A concert?" Daniel asked Isis.

"A dance, I believe," she said.

"You disapprove?"

"Opiri do not dance," she said. "It is a human pastime."

"And that makes it beneath you?"

Her head swung toward him. "I have seen a thousand
different dances over many centuries," she said, "from
the simplest to the most complex. I have never learned
any of them."

"Then maybe it's time for you to try."

"I would look ridiculous."

"Nobody knows who you are. They won't even know
you're Opir."

"Daniel, do not be—"

The music began with a flourish of drum, flute and
fiddle, quickly joined by the piano and guitar. Daniel immediately recognized a waltz.

"Come on," he said, taking Isis's hand.

She dragged her feet. "Do *you* know how to dance?"
she demanded.

"I learned a few steps in Avalon," he said. "This is a
simple one. All you need to do is follow my lead."

Obviously reluctant to draw attention to herself, Isis allowed Daniel to lead her onto the cleared area where the
dancers had gathered. Daniel presumed that most if not
all the dancers were human, but they came in all shapes
and sizes, and he and Isis didn't significantly stand out
from the others.

Clasping Isis's hand, Daniel showed her the few easy
steps of the dance. Her natural Opiri grace overcame her
uncertainty, and in moments they were moving in perfect
accord, Isis's hand on his shoulder and his at her waist.
He lost himself in the supple movements of her body; the

subtle scents that rose from her body beneath its flowing, high-waisted gown; the steady rhythm of her breathing. She looked up into his mask—the face of her ancient lover—and smiled.

The music moved faster, and he swept her into a flying step. It was almost like making love to her; their bodies became one in glorious motion—hearts speeding, pulses pounding. They spun around the circle of dancers, and it was only when the music stopped that Daniel realized they were the last couple on the floor. The watchers surrounding them began to applaud, and he quickly released Isis before she could pull away.

By the time he'd given the musicians a tip in thanks for their work, Isis was gone. He pushed his way through a line of people carrying narrow, sparkling torches and searched for her swirling robes and cat's head.

When he found her, she was talking with a group wearing masks of animals, mythological figures and abstract designs. Daniel sensed at once that they were Opiri, though their bodies, hands and heads were completely covered. He hung back to listen.

"Perhaps I should learn to dance as humans do," said a man wearing a tiger mask.

A woman with the beak and feathers of a raven laughed and tilted her head toward Isis. "Ah, Isis," she said. "It was a shock to see you dancing with your Osiris."

"Who is he?" tiger mask said.

"Can you not guess?" said a woman in a sun mask. "Have you not been keeping company with a particular human, Isis? I heard that at the Games—"

"I must go," Isis said. She strode off while the Opiri stared after her. Daniel followed by an indirect route and caught up with her.

"I thought your plan was for us to remain anonymous,"

he said when they were alone again. "They guessed who I was because of the mask I'm wearing."

"It could not be helped," Isis said, agitation in the nervous sweep of her hands as they adjusted her mask.

"You could have chosen another mask."

She wrapped her arms around her chest. "I do not know what was in my mind when I selected it," she said.

Daniel was half-afraid to imagine. His heart thought it knew the answer, but he stifled its voice.

"The old stories about you and Osiris are true, aren't they?" he asked. "He was one of the most powerful Elders, like you. The two of you guided the people of Egypt when they were still learning the ways of civilization."

"Yes."

"Not many Opiri make lifetime partnerships. How long were you together?"

"Two millennia," she said.

"You…loved him very much."

She wouldn't meet his eyes. "It was long ago. He died."

Death did not come easily to Opiri, particularly the Bloodmasters, Bloodmistresses and Elders. Daniel could only imagine her grief.

"I'm sorry," he said quietly. "I shouldn't have asked you to dance with me."

"That does not mean that everyone will recognize you."

"Or you." Daniel looked for the beer garden. "Still, the more quickly we move, the better. I need to find humans who were involved with or knew about the protest at the Games. A drinking establishment is a good place to start." He gazed at Isis through the eyeholes of the mask. "I want you with me, Isis, if you think it's worth the risk."

"Humans are far less likely to know the old stories than Opiri."

"Then just do your best to pretend you're human. If we need to split up, we'll meet by the food stalls in four hours."

He turned toward the beer garden, but she grasped his loose black shirt and held him back.

"Why *did* you ask me to dance?" she asked.

"Because I knew it would be like holding a feather in my arms."

"Once, my people believed," Isis said, "I had wings."

"You still do," he said, touching her mask as gently as if it were her most tender skin. "Let's go."

Nearly every table in the beer garden was occupied, and the noise of many loud conversations hurt Isis's ears.

She took comfort from Daniel's nearness and his sure movements as he pushed his way through the tight clusters of humans. Alcohol flowed freely, and there was much laughter and jesting and the music of simple instruments.

If there were Opiri here, she thought, they were well hidden behind their masks, and she could not sense them. Daniel found a table with room for two more, and made a space for Isis between him and a tall, thin man with the mask of a god she recognized: Apollo, deity of music and healing, a beautiful male with stylized sun rays springing from his curly hair.

"Osiris," Daniel introduced himself, "and the Lady Sekhmet."

A woman in a silver, almost featureless mask peered at Isis curiously. "Sekhmet was an Egyptian goddess like Isis, wasn't she?"

"Surely not the same Isis as ours?" Apollo asked.

"I don't know," Isis said. "I just thought it was a pretty mask."

"Isis is pretty, too," a second man said in a slurred voice, his face half-covered with a mask of a bull's head. "But I woul'n't trust her no more than that lion thing if it came to life right now."

"Are you afraid of Isis?" Isis asked with real surprise.

"Lundquist," Apollo said. "You're drunk."

The bull swung his head toward Isis. "They say all the Nine c'n control people."

"Who says this?" she asked.

With a sharp jerk of his broad shoulders, Lundquist shrugged. "I listen."

"I've never seen Isis try to control anybody," the woman said.

"How'd *you* know?" Lundquist said. "Everyone seems to love 'er, but issat because she makes 'em?"

"Where did you get that idea?" Apollo asked, so quickly that he nearly tripped over Lundquist's final words. "I was here at the beginning, and she was always the one who spent the most time with us. I don't care what she was or is. *I* trust her."

Bull Mask snorted. "She sure got to them protesters at the Games."

"It was that newcomer who quieted them down," the woman said.

"The one they say Isis keeps as a lover?"

Daniel shot Isis a swift glance. "I've been hearing things, too," he said, lowering his voice, "about an Opir gang attacking humans in Bes's ward."

"Some say there've been other attacks," Lundquist said eagerly. "*They* keep it quiet. *They* won't do anything about it."

"The Council?" Daniel asked.

Lundquist ducked his head. "The Nine," he said. "Are you stupid enough t'think the Council would do anything without the Nine backing 'em?"

"Lundquist!" Apollo snapped. "That's stupid talk."

"Why wouldn't the Nine stop such attacks?" Daniel asked. "What about the Lawkeepers?"

"They don' care about us. Never did." Lundquist took a hearty swig of beer. "What about th' people gone missing? Huh?" He swept his arm across the table, nearly up-setting the other glasses. "Disappearing right unner the noses of their friends 'n' families, taken away by *them*, and nobody knows where—"

"People missing?" Isis said.

"Don't pay any attention to him, Sekhmet," Apollo said with an uneven smile. "Lundquist, talk sense for once."

But Lundquist had apparently reached his limit. His head sank toward the tabletop, and when it came to rest he fell into a stupor.

Chapter 16

Isis could hardly believe what she'd heard. Humans disappearing? Not once had she encountered such a rumor, not from her own peers or anyone who passed through her ward.

The human's accusation about her *making* humans love her closely echoed Daniel's early allegations, the ones she had denied. Who had put such thoughts into the man's head? And his claim that there might have been other gang attacks...

"He's drunk," Apollo said, a little too loudly. "He rambles about his crazy theories all the time. Crazy conspiracies." He tilted his mug at Isis. "Buy you a drink?"

"It's on me," Daniel said. He flagged down a server. "Drinks for everyone!"

Still afraid to move, Isis waited until she was presented with her drink and sipped it cautiously. It tasted sour, but not unbearably so. Soon the others were drinking, and she heard their voices begin to slur. She heard talk of the action by the mob at the Games. They spoke of Daniel with a kind of grudging admiration and speculation as to his origins. He came from another Citadel, they said. He had lived in the wilderness for years, they said. He had fought off a dozen Opiri thugs.

But he wasn't one of *them*.

Daniel listened without comment. But the others said no more about the disappearances or the Nine abusing their powers.

When Daniel had finished his drink, he got up from the table and exchanged a few final words with the others, subtly taking Isis's arm. They made their way out of the beer garden and into the crowd outside, which was, if anything, even thicker than before.

Isis stumbled, and Daniel grabbed her. "Is it the alcohol?" he asked.

"No," she said, a little breathless. "I cannot become inebriated."

"Maybe we should find a place for you to rest."

"I am fine." She straightened with effort. "Had you ever heard that humans were disappearing?"

"No." He gripped her arm, and at that moment she was glad for his support.

"Did Lundquist not say that his fellows were being taken away?"

"By someone he wouldn't or couldn't name," Daniel said with a quick glance around.

"Surely it is just because he was drunk, as his companion said," Isis said. "He spoke of conspiracy theories—"

"You mean the companion who seemed so eager to shut Lundquist up and blame his accusations on alcohol?"

Isis pulled away. She remembered how anxious Apollo had seemed to excuse Lundquist's words...and not, she thought, merely because he thought they were ridiculous.

"Even if there was any truth in the man's claims," she said, "he must be mistaken about the cause. Anyone is free to leave Tanis when they wish. Perhaps these humans simply chose to seek another life outside."

"People don't just vanish from their homes and work and families."

"We still have only the word of one drunken man," she said, "and no details. Would their loved ones not approach the Lawkeepers if such a thing were to happen?"

Daniel drew her away from the nearest booths to the side of the avenue, where there was little activity. "We discussed this, Isis. You heard Lundquist. The humans in Bes's ward had no faith in the Lawkeepers or in Tanisian justice. Is it so surprising that other humans share their opinion?"

"Do you suggest that the Lawkeepers are corrupt?" Isis asked. "There could be no peace here at all if they did not do their jobs." She caught her breath. "Anyone aware of these supposed disappearances could have come to *me*, and I would have—"

"You've already given reassurances to people with similar doubts, but Lundquist certainly doesn't trust you, either."

"It was as if he had been coached to say what he did."

"I agree. But who was coaching him?" He paused and began again. "Let's assume that Lundquist was telling the truth and Apollo knew it. Could these people who disappeared have been found guilty of some crime without public knowledge and been exiled in secret?"

"I would know."

"Who else could be responsible?"

"Do you truly think the Nine have something to do with such actions? It is far more likely that the humans themselves are responsible."

"How?"

"You witnessed them quarreling among themselves," she said. "At the construction site some became violent. Perhaps, if one of them commits a crime, the others might—"

"Take the law into their own hands? Exile or even kill their fellow humans?"

Isis felt sick. "None of this makes sense," she said. "Is it not far more likely that Lundquist said these things to arouse ill feelings?"

"But why? What would be his motive?"

"If he shares other humans' resentment of Opiri, justified or not, would that not be motive enough to invent stories of further perfidy on our part?"

Daniel shook his head, less in denial than in bemusement. "What about these other Opir gangs he mentioned? Could there have been further attacks without our hearing of it?"

"There must be a way to find out. Other humans at the Festival—"

"And the Nine," Daniel said.

"If any among the Nine are aware of these things," Isis said, "I will find out."

"You'll have to be very careful," Daniel said. "If some of them know and haven't told you, there's a reason they're keeping it from you."

"You claimed that Anu was not my friend, but there is still no reason to believe that the others—"

"Isis," Daniel said, resting his hands on her shoulders, "maybe you should return to your apartment. If anyone suspects what or who you are, I'll lose any chance of gaining the trust of the humans who might know more about this."

"You have forgotten that someone tried to poison you. I will not leave the Festival without you."

"And I'm not leaving." He squeezed her shoulders gently. "We'd better split up. Find other Opiri, and see if you can learn anything from them. Rumors, gossip, it doesn't matter so long as it points us in the right direction."

Isis longed to hold him, to remind herself that he was not a dream who would suddenly vanish like the humans in Lundquist's story. "I am afraid," she whispered. "Afraid for Tanis. For you."

"Isis," he said. Only the one word, but it held a wealth of meaning: understanding, concern, encouragement. Affection.

And perhaps even...

"Do you believe that I force humans to love me?" she asked, though it took all her courage to speak the words.

"I don't think you have to force anyone, Isis."

Her throat tightened. "You will be careful?" she asked.

"I will, if you promise to do the same."

"I do." She backed away quickly, before she could change her mind. "I will see you in four hours."

Daniel had almost reached the beer garden when he heard the muffled scream. He ran down the nearest alley to find two shadowed figures struggling, the larger holding the smaller up against the wall as his mouth clamped on her neck.

Sprinting deeper into the alley, Daniel hit the Opir with the full weight of his body, forcing him to let loose of the young woman's throat. At once the Opir turned on Daniel, his face barely covered by the mask of some grotesque animal, and counterattacked.

Within seconds, Daniel knew that this Opir would be far harder to defeat than the gang members in Bes's ward. He was strong and fast and experienced, and he knew how to overpower humans; he knocked Daniel's mask off and went straight for his jugular.

"Run!" Daniel shouted to the girl just before the Opir made contact. He felt sharp teeth grazing his throat, and blood spattered his skin as he dodged the worst of the attack. He twisted his body, crouching and spinning to knock his opponent's legs out from under him. The Opir leaped out of reach and snarled, scarcely hesitating before he launched his next assault.

Daniel had braced himself, but the Opir still bore him down to the ground, pinning Daniel's arms and snapping at his neck. Daniel slammed his knee into the Opir's groin, and bought just enough time to roll out from under him. Panting hard, he considered his limited options.

There was one trick that worked on overconfident Opiri who were accustomed to the crippling effects of human fear. Daniel pressed himself against the wall, frozen, and then suddenly burst into a run toward the front of the alley. The Opir easily intercepted him, and Daniel put up a weak struggle as the Nightsider slammed him back into the wall and sank his teeth into Daniel's throat.

For a moment, Daniel was truly frozen. He relived his life before Ares, the feeling of utter helplessness, the inability to fight back because Palemon almost always kept him chained. The Opir drank deep, obviously intending to drain him into a coma or death.

It was madness for an Opir of Tanis to openly kill a human citizen, but clearly this one didn't fear the consequences. Daniel thought of leaving Isis alone, and all at once his strength and will returned to him. While the Opir fed, believing his prey to be helpless, Daniel struck without warning and grabbed the Nightsider by the hair, jerking his head back. He groped with his other hand for the knife hidden under his belt and jammed it into the Opir's shoulder close to the base of his neck.

With a cry of pain and surprise, the Opir staggered backward. Daniel followed with several kicks and rapid-fire punches, and the Nightsider began to retreat.

Snarling like a panther, Daniel flung himself on the Opir, who fell to his knees with Daniel's knife still in his shoulder. Daniel grabbed at the knife's grip, but the Nightsider twisted away and staggered toward the mouth of the alley, leaving the knife in Daniel's hand. The Opir lurched onto the main street, where a dozen masked revelers caught and held him for a moment before he broke free and lumbered away. A few in the crowd started after him, but the rest huddled around a weeping young woman, comforting her with touches and soft voices.

Daniel wiped his knife on the inside of his shirt, sheathed it and limped toward the mouth of the alley. Several people looked up as Daniel approached, and a pair broke free of the group to meet him. Daniel paused to pick up his mask and held it loose in his hand.

"We saw it," a young man said in a breathless voice. "You got that bloodsucker away from the girl just in time." He removed his mask to reveal a freckled, wide-eyed face. "If I hadn't seen it, I'd never've believed it."

"Is the girl all right?" Daniel asked, wiping the blood away from his throat.

"Scared out of her mind, but okay." The young man glanced over his shoulder. "She'll want to thank you."

"That isn't important," Daniel said. "What *is* important is that an Opir attacked a human with the intent to take blood against her will, or possibly to kill her."

The boy's companion, an older woman with a deeply weathered face, removed her mask, as well. "Yes," she said. "I have been here since the beginning of Tanis, and this has never happened before."

"The Opir escaped," Daniel said. "He could do this again."

"I know." The woman's face became distorted with anger. "If they think for one moment that they can get away with this…"

"Who?" Daniel asked.

Her expression became guarded. "Others like him. The ones that still look on us as slaves." She clamped her lips together as if to stop herself from saying more. "What you did was very brave. We'll report this to the Lawkeepers, but we won't tell them about your part in this. I'd leave now, if I were you."

It was just like the gang attack all over again, Daniel thought. "Take care of the girl?" he asked.

"Of course we will."

"Thank you," he said.

She smiled, her teeth white and even. "Good luck," she said, and turned back to the people gathered around the girl. The young man lingered.

"We saw what you did at the Games," he said, his eyes shining. "We won't forget."

Daniel knew he didn't deserve praise for what he'd done, either at the Games or tonight. He was ashamed. Ashamed for freezing during the fight, for remembering too much, for letting the Opir win, if only for a few seconds. His years as a fighter and scout for Avalon, his time at Delos had made no difference.

Isis was right. *You may tell yourself that those scars don't matter anymore,* she had said. *But you can never convince me that the past is gone, Daniel. Not for you.*

Oblivious to Daniel's dark thoughts, the boy pulled his mask back on and ran after the woman. Daniel thought he caught a glimpse of a Lawkeeper beyond the throng, and turned in the opposite direction. The blood on his neck was already coagulating, though the Opir must have healed the wound out of reflex rather than because he wanted to preserve Daniel from exsanguination.

It took several seconds before Daniel realized that someone was applauding. The Opir standing in front of him wore no mask. His long, handsome face was cast in shadow, and he was smiling.

"Bravo," Hannibal said. "Daniel of Erebus. Brave defender of helpless females, victor over the evil bloodsucker."

Daniel strode toward him. "Did you have something to do with this, Hannibal?" he growled.

"I only happened to catch the fight while I was passing by the alley," Hannibal said. "You were very good, except that one moment when you froze and let him take a bite out of your neck. It must have required considerable effort on his part to pierce the scar tissue."

Barely containing his contempt and anger, Daniel balled his fists. "If you intend to report me for fighting, you'll find there are plenty of witnesses who'll be happy to mention that the Opir attacked the girl first."

"If I'd witnessed such an attack, I would have interfered immediately." He cocked his head. "I can hardly fathom the change in you. Except for those few moments in the alley, no one would mistake you for a former serf. And I've heard you did more than thrive in the wilderness after your escape."

"What have you been doing since you were cast out of Erebus?" Daniel asked. "Visiting other Citadels? Vikos, perhaps?"

"What do you imply, Daniel? That I might be a spy?"

"I know you have no interest in the ideals of this city."

"Ah, yes. The ideals, as expressed so recently in the alley." He showed the tips of his teeth. "Have you heard anything more about Ares?"

"Have you?"

"I think of him often. What a pity his dreams for Erebus failed, and he was himself cast out."

"And survived," Daniel said.

"Unfortunately. Why do you think he is in Tanis?"

"I looked for him in a colony in the West. They told me he'd come here to learn about Tanis."

"And you followed him?" Hannibal shook his head. "You are too late. They determined that he was a spy, and had him killed along with his half-blood bitch."

A hard knot formed in Daniel's throat. "Did you witness their deaths?"

"Of course."

"And I am supposed to believe you?"

"Believe or not, as you choose. Your decision will not affect my plan to destroy you."

"I'm honored to be ranked so high among your priorities," Daniel said with a mocking bow. "Why?"

"Because Ares valued you, and you believe yourself to be the equal of your Opir masters. Since I didn't have the pleasure of directly taking his life, I will have yours."

"Ares won't be here to see your revenge."

"It will amuse me, nevertheless."

A kind of numbness settled the tension in Daniel's body. "Did you send the water to me at the Games?" he asked.

"Why? Is that significant?"

"It was poisoned. That's an easy and cowardly method of killing."

"But most unsatisfying. Perhaps you have more than one enemy here, Daniel."

"Maybe it would 'amuse' you to tell me who they are."

"Oh, no. Just as I didn't tell them that you lied about being from Vikos, or about what you are. That would be too easy. I don't need to expose your dishonesty to make them believe that you are leading human troublemakers to undermine Tanis, and that Isis is fully engaged in encouraging them to flout the law."

"Even if you could convince them of the first," Daniel said, "Isis is one of the Nine. They won't take your word over hers."

"Are you so sure?"

Daniel moved as fast as his Opir blood allowed, fast enough to take Hannibal by surprise. He grabbed the Nightsider by the throat and squeezed.

"If you do anything to threaten her, I'll kill you," he said.

Hannibal jerked free. "You think you can protect her?" he asked, rubbing his throat. "She cannot even protect *you*. I could report that you attacked me, and you would be thrown out of the city with nothing but—"

A burst of laughter sounded behind Hannibal. He edged away from Daniel, turning just enough to see who had joined them.

A scantily clad young woman, accompanied by a man in clothes almost as revealing, looked from Hannibal to Daniel with curiosity and surprise.

"Look, Dustin," she said from behind her flower mask. "Two of our fine citizens with nothing to do!" She reached for Daniel's hand. "You're missing all the fun!"

"By all means, go with her," Hannibal said with a contemptuous smile. "Enjoy yourself while you can."

Daniel almost stayed behind, but he reminded himself that it was Hannibal's intent to provoke him into doing something stupid. He let the young woman pull him away from the alley.

"Come along," she said when he stopped in the street.

"Who are you?" he asked.

"A friend," she said, as the young man slipped away.

Daniel pulled his hand from hers. "There's someone I have to find."

"Perhaps you will find her where I am taking you." She tilted back her mask for a few seconds, and Daniel recognized her as Hugh's redheaded friend from the tavern in Bes's ward.

"You remember me?" she asked, pulling the mask in place over her face. "I'm Greta. We know what you want. I can take you to the right people."

"Hugh?" Daniel whispered as she tugged on his hand again.

She didn't answer. Very much on his guard, Daniel let her lead him through the crowd and along several alleys to a very ordinary building that might have been some kind of community hall. Greta directed him toward a side door and tapped on it lightly.

The door opened. The man behind it nodded to Greta and looked hard at Daniel.

"He's with me," Greta said.

The doorman nodded, and Greta pulled Daniel into the main corridor. The first room they entered was furnished with at least twenty couches, the floors obscured by dozens of cushions. Men and women in various states of undress were kissing and fondling each other: the white hands of Opiri on human skin, humans of all skin tones caressing other humans or very enthusiastic Nightsiders. Opiri were taking blood from willing humans of both sexes.

Daniel stopped. Greta took his hand.

"Almost everything is permitted here, as long as it is consensual and does no harm," she said. "We must blend in with the others."

"No," Daniel said, thinking of Isis.

"I don't expect you to do anything," she whispered. "Just play along."

Chapter 17

Before Daniel could protest again, Greta was unbuttoning his shirt. Without hesitation, she shed her own filmy robes to reveal a nearly transparent sheath dress.

"Take your shirt off," she said. "Pretend you're interested."

Realizing that he could either choose to trust her or walk out, Daniel removed his shirt and draped it over his shoulder. Greta spread her hands across his chest and kissed him. He pretended to respond, and she dragged him deeper into the room, where hands reached for Daniel and plucked at his pants and boots.

"You would be very popular here," Greta said, dodging the grasp of a male Opir. "There are private rooms in the back."

By the time he and Greta reached the rear of the room and another door, Daniel had turned down seven offers from men and women, and helped Greta disentangle herself from a threesome hoping to add another to their private party. She reached the back door and pushed him through.

It opened onto another corridor with many doors, most of them closed. In the corridor itself, a man and woman were making love against the wall.

"Where are these people I should talk to?" Daniel asked, turning his face away.

"In here." She reached one of the closed doors, knocked, and walked into the room.

Several men and women occupied the room, some half-dressed but none engaged in anything but conversation. Their masks lay at their feet. Hugh stood up as Daniel entered, nodded to Greta and instructed Daniel to sit.

"We know you've been trying to gather certain information," Hugh said without preamble. "Whatever I tell you can't go beyond this room."

Daniel glanced around at the serious, almost grim faces of Hugh's associates. He recognized Apollo from the beer garden. "I have no intention of betraying you," he said.

"If we thought you would, you wouldn't be here," Hugh said. He nodded to each of his companions. "Marcel, Chaya, Jessica, Fernando, Kevin. If you meet them again outside this room, you don't know them."

"Understood," Daniel said. He took an empty chair. "I presume you have something to tell me."

"We've heard enough to know that you've come from outside, looking for answers to certain questions."

"You're a spy from some colony in the west," Fernando said.

"Who told you that?" Daniel asked, beginning to rise.

"Maybe *spy* isn't the right word," Hugh said.

Daniel decided to take a chance and trust, as these people had done. "My colony has both human and Opiri members, living as equals," he said. "I came here to learn if an entire city could maintain the same way of life."

"That's all?" Hugh asked with a skeptical frown.

"I also needed to be sure that Tanis wasn't a threat to us, which it might be if it wasn't what rumor claimed."

"And now?" Chaya asked.

"I've seen and heard enough to doubt that Tanis is as devoted to equality and peace as it seems on the surface."

"Then you know enough to leave Tanis and make your report to your colony," Greta said.

"Not yet," Daniel said. "There's too much I don't understand."

"How did you manage to escape the consequences of fighting the Opiri in the first gang attack?" Kevin asked abruptly.

"I went to the Nine. I convinced them of my innocence."

Glances were exchanged. "How?" Hugh asked.

"Anu decided that guilt or innocence could be determined by combat with the Opiri involved."

"More corruption," Kevin muttered. "Are you sure your friendship with Isis didn't have anything to do with it?"

So his and Isis's relationship was common knowledge even among humans, Daniel thought. "Isis helped me get in to see Anu," he said. "She never believed in my guilt."

People shifted in their seats. Kevin continued to glower.

"You and Isis tried to stop the protest at the Games," Hugh said. "Was it for Anu?"

"I didn't want to see anyone hurt. Neither did Isis."

"So you acted entirely on our behalf."

"If you thought I was working for the Nine, would I be here now?"

"You said there were better ways to present our issues to the Nine."

"And Isis agreed to help you." Suddenly, Daniel felt like an idiot. "Were *you* behind the protest?"

"There has been evidence that Opiri were bribing the contestants to throw the Games, as well as gambling at the competitions."

"And after all your concern about the public exposure of your grievances, you thought a protest conducted by fighting among yourselves would get the Nine's attention. Or wasn't it completely under your control?"

Hugh had the grace to look embarrassed. "It was a mistake."

"Did you expect so many people to be arrested?"

"No," Greta admitted. "But we know that Isis was given charge of them, and that they were released."

"You can thank her for that."

Kevin muttered something that brought Daniel to his feet. Greta glared at Kevin. Hugh smoothed his beard.

"Kevin," he said.

The younger man clenched his fists and stared at the floor. Daniel sat down again.

"You know that discontent is growing, Daniel," Hugh said. "Tanis's original charter claims that free speech is a necessary part of true civilization. But we know the difference between what is and what should be. And we know that hypocrisy reigns in Tanis."

"We," Daniel said, his pulse drumming in his ears. "How many of you are there?"

"Not nearly enough," Greta said. "Too many humans here are mesmerized by the Nine and are blind to the problems."

"Why don't you leave?" Daniel asked. "You're free to go."

"Are we?" Kevin asked.

"Not all of us were originally serfs," Hugh said. "We came here believing in the dream Tanis promised. Why should we be driven away?"

"You know about the Opir who attacked a human woman a short time ago?" Daniel asked.

"I saw it," Greta said. "I also saw what you did."

"It's crazy," Marcel said. "A public assault, with the obvious intent to kill. And then there's the gang raids on the wards."

"Lundquist was telling the truth? There've been more of them?"

"He's a drunk, but he's not a liar," Greta said. "The gangs taunt us about human weakness, how we can't be trusted to run our own lives. It's as if they want to provoke us."

"You think these are organized attacks?"

"You heard what Lundquist said."

"So did everyone else in the beer garden," Daniel said. "He thinks the Nine control people. He also said that humans have gone missing."

"It's true," Hugh said. "About fifty in the past six months."

Eight a month, Daniel thought. "And there's been no public outcry?" he asked.

"There's fear," Kevin said.

"Do the victims have anything in common?" Daniel asked. "Age, sex, profession?"

"Adult men and women," Greta said, "mostly young. The disappearances seem to occur randomly, and sometimes nobody knows the people are gone until they don't show up for days on end."

"We did our own investigation," Hugh said. "None of them planned to leave Tanis or went on patrols with the rangers outside the city. No one held a grudge against any of them, as far as we know."

"You believe Opiri are responsible."

"Who else?" Hugh asked.

"And you all think that the Nine know about this?"

"There is a rot in Tanis," Hugh said, "and it can only have begun in one place. With the founders."

Daniel massaged his shoulder, which the Opir had nearly pulled out of its socket, thinking of his conversation with Isis. "What motive would they have?" he asked.

"We don't know," Greta said. "But they could stop all these problems if they wanted to."

"Negligence," Daniel said, playing devil's advocate. "Detachment. Why do you assume their purpose is malicious?"

Nobody offered a further explanation. But Daniel couldn't shake the impact of their certainty…or his own strong doubts about the Nine, especially Anu.

"I'm still an outsider," he said. "What can I do to help you?"

"Isis," Hugh said. "Of all the Nine, she is most sympathetic to humanity and yet strong enough to hold her own among the others." Hugh cleared his throat. "We want you to approach her, Daniel. She's our only direct connection to the true rulers of the city. We need her to be completely on our side."

"You want her to betray her own kind?"

"We need her to listen to the Nine and inform us of their next move against us. We need to know what they're trying to achieve."

"Isis isn't in Anu's confidence."

"She's the only hope we have," Hugh said.

Pacing across the room, Daniel considered the man's request. Isis had already agreed to try to learn if the Nine were aware of further Opir attacks on the wards as well as the supposed disappearances. Yet for all that had happened, in spite of what he and Isis had heard, he didn't know if she was willing to turn against her peers, the "gods" who had shared her dream. She would have to acknowledge, at last, that there was a deadly chasm in Tanis that might soon rip it apart.

And that the humans were on the right side.

"Lundquist doesn't trust her," he said, facing Hugh again. "Obviously Kevin doesn't, either. Are you so sure she won't turn against you?"

"You know the answer to that, Daniel," Isis said, walking into the room. She removed her mask and met his gaze steadily.

At once all the humans were on their feet. Daniel moved between them and Isis. She shifted to stand beside him.

"Do not fear," she said to Hugh's people. "Nobody else knows I have come."

"How did you find us, Lady Isis?" Hugh asked, his voice gruff with suspicion he couldn't conceal.

"I was not followed," she said, avoiding his question.

Daniel looked her over carefully. "You went through the main room?" he asked.

"It was an interesting experience." She took the nearest seat. "Please," she said. "Continue your discussion."

No one spoke. Daniel stood beside her chair and stared at Hugh and his comrades.

"You wanted her help," he said. "Have you changed your minds?"

"We did not expect to meet you today, Lady Isis," Hugh said.

"No. You would have left Daniel to convince me to help you." She swept her gaze over the gathering. "If you will not trust me now that I am here, I will go. I will neither hinder nor report you."

There was a long, uneasy silence. It was evident to Daniel that, for all their defiance, Hugh's people were a little in awe of Isis.

"How much did you overhear?" Hugh asked quietly.

"You wish me to report on the future activities of the Nine," she said. She glanced at Daniel. "I have heard several wild theories and speculation without proof. Nevertheless, I am prepared to take whatever steps are necessary to heal our city."

"And if healing isn't possible?" Hugh asked.

Isis didn't reply. When Daniel touched her shoulder, he felt her muscles tense as if she suspected imminent attack.

"Will you help us?" Greta asked.

"If you will accept my assistance, now and in the future, without doubt or hesitation. You must avoid calling attention to yourselves, and advise other humans to do the same. No more protests at the depository, the Games or elsewhere."

"Nobody leads all the humans in Tanis," Hugh said, "and no one person has the ability to prevent future protests."

"Talk to as many as you can," Daniel said. "Explain that incidents like the one at the Games aren't going to help them now."

"And what about defending ourselves from the Opir gangs?" Kevin asked. "Are we just supposed to let them attack us?"

"I will approach Hermes and see that his officers station more Lawkeepers in the human wards," Isis said. "I will make certain he understands that they must do their work for *all* Tanisians."

"Will he agree?" Greta asked.

"He will listen to *me*," she said.

Kevin snorted in exasperation. "What if he's in on all this with the rest?"

"In on the conspiracy?" Isis asked. "I do not believe that Hermes would ever wish ill upon humanity. But I thank you for your concern." She flashed Daniel an enigmatic glance. "How will we arrange to meet again?"

"You can find me at the tavern, when it's safe to approach," Hugh said.

"Safe for the lady as well as for yourselves," Daniel added.

"Of course." Hugh addressed Isis. "Is there anything you want us to—"

Without warning, she broke for the door and stepped out into the corridor. Daniel followed her.

"I'm sorry," Daniel said, closing the door behind them. "I know how hard this must be for you. But we have to get at the truth, no matter how difficult—"

She snatched up her mask, charged through the door to the main room and stopped, her gaze sweeping the tableau of couples and groups engaged in unashamed lovemaking. Her chest rose and fell rapidly. Then she turned around, clasped Daniel's shoulders and kissed him.

At first, Daniel was too startled to respond. The wild, almost desperate nature of the kiss convinced him that Isis wanted to escape all the terrible implications of the conversation with Hugh and his people. She wanted to lose herself in passion, like every other person in the room.

As did Daniel. Even if it meant breaking the last threads of his commitment to keep his distance from her. Isis was a creature of pure sensuality now, indifferent to her surroundings, lacking all inhibition. If he'd let her, she would have dragged him down to the cushions then and there, opened up to him and pulled him inside her with no thought to the others around them.

Daniel had to maintain his reason. He took her hand, drew her back into the corridor and led her from door to door while she kissed his neck and pulled at his clothing. The first two rooms were occupied; the third was not, and Daniel had barely closed the door before Isis was shedding her robes. She stood before him, panting, her eyes almost as black as a moonless night.

Chapter 18

Daniel began to unbutton his shirt, but Isis was unable to wait. She dragged the shirt over his head and kissed his chest, her tongue running over his nipple. He shuddered as she unbuttoned his pants and grasped him with her slender hands. She began to stroke him, running her fingers up and down his erection, teasing him with the tips of her nails.

Then she took him into her mouth. He moaned, startled by the almost violent rush of sensation, and she caressed him with her tongue as well as her hands and fingers, scarcely brushing him with the tips of her teeth.

But he couldn't accept so much pleasure without giving it in return. He pulled her up and over him, his erection resting between her thighs, and kissed her. Her kiss was almost savage in response, tongue and lips dueling with his, and he rolled over with her, bracing himself on his forearms. She clawed at him again, her nails trailing across the scars on his back, and he kissed her neck, sucking her skin as if he could draw her blood by sheer strength of will.

This was not merely an Opir he held in his arms or even a Bloodmistress. She gave herself to him like a goddess of ecstasy, whimpering as he trailed kisses from her jaw to her breasts. She arched against him, offering him her breasts as she wrapped her thighs around his waist.

He took what she gave, sucking on her nipples with hungry force, urged on by her gasps and moans of excitement. He devoured her, rolling his tongue around the peaks of her nipples, running his hand down the length of her body to stroke the junction of her thighs.

She was moist and warm, and when his fingers slid between her lips, she moved so that they slipped inside her. She pushed against him, but she was so wet that his fingers alone couldn't fill her.

"Take me," she whispered hoarsely.

Daniel wanted to give her more pleasure, to lick the wetness and tease her to the edge of orgasm. But she continued to move and slide until his cock was poised at her entrance, its tip skimming her heat until he couldn't stand another second's delay.

He plunged into her with one hard thrust, and she cried out. He had never felt so hungry to be one with her, to brand her, to make himself hers. Ferocity overcame him, the need to prove that she could never find anywhere else what she had with him, that she would remember him all her life, long after they had parted.

But the thought of parting was more than he could bear. He thrust again and again, surging deep, and she took sharp little breaths every time he entered her.

Still his hunger wasn't satisfied. He sat up, lifting her with him, and parted from her just long enough to turn her onto her hands and knees. Her bottom was firm and full, her lips pink and swollen, and she looked over her shoulder with eyes heavy lidded with heated desire.

Taking her hips between his hands, he entered her again. She rocked forward, and he held her still to thrust deeper, his own breath coming short and harsh. He stroked her back and continued without slowing, all animal instinct now, beyond anything but need.

He hesitated only once, when her moans became a cry. But she pushed back against him, taking him in again, her hot juices bathing him with liquid fire. He reached beneath them and stroked her near the junction of their bodies, finding the little nub and rubbing it until her cries grew more insistent.

A moment later she came, trembling violently. He followed, flinging his head back and finishing with a few final, glorious thrusts.

Panting, her body damp with perspiration, Isis went still as if she were savoring the final joining of their bodies. Then she jerked away without warning, scrambling onto her back and drawing her legs close to her chest. Her eyes were wide behind the veil of her hair.

Daniel didn't understand her reaction, but he let her go as she climbed off the couch, pulled on her mask, snatched up her robes and flung them on, leaving the fastenings half undone as she fled the room. Daniel dressed hastily and followed her, but by the time he entered the corridor, she was gone. He ran out of the building, searching for her, worried about her strange state of mind and what she might do .

But she had vanished among the Festival crowds, and Daniel had no idea where to look for her. He made certain that his own mask was firmly in place and began to search. The revelers spun around him, a blur of masks that seemed more and more like grotesque caricatures.

Forcing himself to act calmly and rationally, he became more methodical and careful in his search. Isis had clearly been under tremendous pressure, forced to accept facts that stood in direct opposition to her beliefs and experience. She'd given herself over to unrestrained passion, and he'd accepted that without question, instinctively understanding that she needed those heady minutes of escape.

But she hadn't really escaped at all. Had she been so ashamed of the act, when she'd never shown the slightest restraint before? Or was she angry with herself for helping to end the hope that they could maintain any kind of distance from one another?

Daniel had no answers. He gave up scanning the crowds and began looking into the side alleys, hoping she hadn't actually left the plaza area.

He was on his last side street when he finally found her. She was stumbling out of the deeper shadows, her clothing torn, her mask gone.

Daniel raced toward her and took her in his arms. "Isis," he said. "Are you hurt?"

She shuddered and wrapped her arms around his waist. "I am all right," she said.

"What happened to you?"

"They…attacked me," she said, her voice shaking.

"Who?"

"Humans." She sucked in a sharp breath and let it out slowly. "Four or five. They came at me…suddenly, and grabbed me."

Daniel's worry turned to rage. "Who were they?" he demanded, stroking her loosened hair.

"I don't know." She pulled away just enough to study Daniel's face. "I am all right. Daniel, look at me."

He met her gaze. She shook her head almost wildly.

"I see what you want to do," she said. "But there is no one to punish. They all wore masks, and I am sure they have discarded them by now."

"*Why* would they attack you?" Daniel said through clenched teeth.

"I do not know." She shuddered again and relaxed into his arms. "I did not sense them before they came at me, so

I was not prepared to fight. They were only able to hold me for a short time."

"Your clothes—"

"They grabbed at whatever they could reach. I do not think they were attempting to—"

"You would have killed them if they tried."

"I fought," she said. "They ran, but I fell." She scraped at her smudged cheek with the back of her hand. "I am well, Daniel."

"No, you're not." He picked her up and cradled her in his arms. "I'm taking you somewhere quiet, where you can rest. You tell me anything you can remember, and I'll find your attackers."

"But I *have* told you," she said, gripping him around the shoulders. "Daniel, you will not find them."

"Then we'll get help."

"From whom? We cannot give the Lawkeepers any excuse to turn against humans now. If someone among the Opiri or the Nine is responsible for the disappearances and the attacks on our human citizens, they have made sure that these incidents are ignored. Would they ignore this, as well?"

"This was clearly an act of revenge. If these humans lost family members and believe as Hugh and his companions do, they may feel they have the right—"

"Perhaps they *are* right, Daniel."

"You'd let them go because you think they're justified in attacking you? If you'd been hurt, every human in Tanis would be questioned."

"And I do not wish that." She sighed into his shoulder. "Put me down, Daniel. I can walk."

But they had already drawn attention from the Festivalgoers, who gaped at them and began to murmur and chatter over the maskless appearance of one of the Nine, carried in a human's arms. Daniel set Isis down, keeping her close, and took off his mask. He dropped it onto the ground.

As if they had heard what had happened even before Daniel had found Isis, a group of five Lawkeepers, shock sticks in hand and led by Anu himself, plowed into the throng. Revelers jumped out of their path, and there were cries of astonishment. Anu never appeared among humans.

Instinctively, Daniel put himself between Anu and Isis, but Isis moved around him before he could stop her.

"What has happened here?" Anu demanded, striding ahead of the Lawkeepers. "Isis?"

She faced him, chin up. "All is well, Anu," she said. "Why are you here?"

Anu glared at Daniel over her shoulder. "Who did this to you?" he demanded.

Tidying her robes with nervous sweeps of her hand, Isis smiled. "I am fine," she said. "I merely stumbled and fell. Daniel was taking me to a place where I might rest a little."

"You fell?" Anu asked. "*You*, Isis?"

It sounded ridiculous, Daniel thought, given her natural grace. But now that he had the chance to tell the truth and possibly find her attackers, he couldn't bring himself to do it. As Isis had so wisely pointed out, every human in Tanis could suffer for it.

But he was to have no say in the matter. "You were assaulted by humans," Anu said to Isis. "The state of your clothing is not the result of a fall, and it is humans who are rampaging on the streets of our city."

"I do not know who they were," Isis said, no longer attempting to lie.

"I believe that you would do almost anything to defend humans, even if they were to harm you."

"What are you suggesting?" Isis said, rising anger in her voice. "That any human could actually *hurt* me?"

"There are new reports of violence done by humans

throughout the wards," Anu said. "Destruction of property, rioting, even assaulting Opiri who venture too near. Lawkeepers are searching for any citizens exhibiting hostile behavior."

"Does that include Opiri?" Daniel asked.

Anu ignored him and moved closer to Isis. "You will come with me, Isis."

She began to protest, but a moment later Athena appeared, her mask hanging from her neck. "Isis!" she said, coming up beside Anu. "What—"

"Take her back to the tower," Anu said. "She was accosted by humans."

"Accosted?" Athena said in disbelief.

"You should go back to your apartment," Daniel said softly to Isis. "I don't want you in the tower now. Not with Anu."

She nodded slightly and stared Anu down. "I have the right and duty to see what is happening in this city," she said. "If humans are behaving out of character—"

"You can say that, after the Games?" Anu said. He glanced around at the Festival-goers, many of whom had quietly slipped away. "Today's events have provoked activity we could not have anticipated, but considering the nature of hu—" He broke off. "It is not necessary for you to become involved unless you have specific information to give us."

"What are you planning to do about the Opir who took blood from a human woman by force?" Daniel asked, made reckless by his fear for Isis. "Maybe it wasn't an isolated incident. Maybe humans are fighting back against the gangs that have been harassing their wards."

Isis stepped between Daniel and Anu. "Have you heard the reports of Opir attacks?" she asked the Bloodmaster.

"None except for the one involving..." He waved dismissively toward Daniel.

Daniel knew that he was lying, and he was sure Isis knew, as well. "I can tell you they *are* happening," she said. "Humans have been provoked."

"If they have been, we will determine the truth," Anu said.

"If Lawkeepers sweep the human wards," Daniel said, "no one will talk to them."

"I think they will," Anu said.

"They'll lie if they feel threatened," Daniel said. "But they'll listen to Isis." He met Anu's gaze. "Of course, if you're more interested in punishing humans than keeping the peace..."

"Daniel!" Isis snapped. "Anu," she said, "he is disturbed. Someone attempted to poison him during the Games."

"You saw this?"

"I saw the effects," she said. "But we have not been able to determine why it was done, or by whom."

"Almost certainly one of his opponents in the Games," Anu said. "This incident, too, will be examined." He stared at Daniel. "Since you have also been threatened, Lawkeepers will escort you back to your quarters."

"That will not be necessary," Daniel said.

But Anu simply moved away, leaving two of the Lawkeepers behind with Daniel and Isis. Athena lingered, hovering anxiously over Isis.

"It would be better for you to go back," Isis said, for Daniel's ears alone. "I will observe these sweeps myself, and try to determine the cause of the disturbances."

"You're in danger," Daniel whispered. "If humans attacked you once, it could happen again. Go back to your apartment, Isis." He frowned at the rebellion in her expression. "Promise me."

"And you?" she asked. "If you resist the Lawkeepers..."

"Tell them you need their escort, and that I'll do as Anu commanded."

He saw the disbelief in her eyes, but she approached the Lawkeepers and evidently convinced them. Athena left a few minutes later, though not without a long backward glance at Daniel.

Without acknowledging Isis again, Daniel headed in the direction of his quarters. Soon after he'd cleared the plaza and was nearly home, he circled back.

The plaza, bathed in the wan sunlight of breaking dawn, was empty of revelers and littered with discarded masks. Daniel returned to the building where he'd spoken to Hugh, and found it empty, as well.

Choosing a route along minor streets, Daniel jogged toward Bes's ward. He saw immediately that Anu's claims had been true. There were groups of humans fighting in the streets, almost mindlessly, and not all wore opposing emblems from the Games. Lawkeepers were rounding up some of the fighters, but they were clearly outnumbered.

Daniel pushed his way between two small groups of brawling humans and kept them apart with a combination of strength and sheer will.

"Why are you fighting?" he demanded as the leaders of the two groups panted and glared at each other.

"Who in hell are you?" one of the men said, curling his fists.

"They're traitors!" said a woman on the other side. "They're working for the Nightsiders against their own kind!"

"Lies!" the first man said.

"Stop," Daniel ordered. "What do you mean, working for the Nightsiders?"

"Stealing people for the bloodsuckers!" the woman yelled.

Nausea built in Daniel's throat. He had denied that humans were involved in the disappearances, and Isis had agreed with him.

"What proof do you have?" Daniel asked. "How do you know the Opiri are taking humans?"

"Rumors," the leader of the accused group said. "That's all they have."

"Is that what's behind this violence?" Daniel asked. "Rumors? You turn on each other and give the Lawkeepers good reason for cracking down on the human wards?"

Just as he finished speaking, a boy threw a rock into a window across the street. Everyone turned to stare.

"This isn't about the disappearances," Daniel said. "Something else is going on."

"How do *you* know?" the first leader said.

"He's Isis's favorite," the woman shouted. "*He's* with them, too!"

"Isis is with *you*," Daniel said, holding out his hands as several of the humans lunged toward him. "If you have a grudge against the Opiri, you'd be wise not to reject your allies."

"They still rule," a man said. "We've never been full equals to them."

"If the Opiri are the problem, giving them reason to judge you as savages doesn't help your cause."

"Don't listen to him," the first leader said. "He's been corrupted by—"

He broke off as three Lawkeepers armed with shock sticks appeared and began moving in their direction. The humans scattered, each group ignoring the other.

Turning on his heel, Daniel set out for Hugh's tavern.

Chapter 19

At first it seemed as if the tavern was securely locked up for the night, windows latched, still as a fortress anticipating a deadly attack. The neighborhood was just as quiet, human citizens hiding in their homes or out roaming with the angry mobs in the thin predawn light. Daniel moved cautiously to the door and pressed his ears against the heavy wood.

The place was far from deserted. He could hear murmuring voices…one, two, four. Six in all, urgently discussing the problems outside in tense whispers.

Daniel knew they were closer to the back kitchen door than the front, so he circled the building and paused until he heard the voices drift into silence.

"It's Daniel," he said, his mouth close to the door. "Let me in, Hugh."

He knew they heard him; a chair scuffed against the floor, and two voices argued in soft tones. After a long moment, Daniel heard footsteps moving up to the door. The latch clicked, and Hugh stood framed in the doorway, his shoulders squared and his expression far from welcoming.

"What do you want?" he said.

"I didn't think we should wait for another meeting," Daniel said.

"You walked out on us before."

"Isis promised to work with you," Daniel said. "Was there something I missed?"

Hugh threw a glance over his shoulder. "Come in," he said, "before the Lawkeepers see you."

Slipping through the door, Daniel faced the nervous stares of Hugh's companions, three he had met before and two he didn't recognize.

"Do you expect the Lawkeepers to come hunting you?" he asked, standing by the door. "Are you suspected of inciting the protests out there?"

"We had nothing to do with it," Hugh said, leaning against the counter with his arms folded across his chest.

"Apparently," Daniel said, "the news of human disappearances is all over the city. Humans are accusing other humans of being behind them."

"We have no control over that," Hugh said, glancing at his companions.

"You might try to stop it."

"How can we, if the Opiri are provoking all this?" Hugh set his jaw. "Where is Isis?"

"She's in her apartment," Daniel said. "Someone tried to kill her."

A muffled gasp emerged from the four men and women sitting at the table by the counter. "Who?" Hugh asked.

"Humans."

"What did they do to her?" Greta asked.

"They ambushed her in an alley when she was alone. She fought back, and they ran."

"She didn't scare them into attacking her?" Kevin asked.

Daniel took one long step, standing toe-to-toe with the younger man. "I don't care what you think of the rest of the Opiri," he said, "but you'll show respect to Isis."

"If someone attacked her, it had to be part of the plot

against humans," one of the strangers said. "Did she report them?"

"Anu was there right after it happened. If she wanted those humans caught, she could have seen to it easily. But she was more concerned about the consequences if she insisted on finding her assailants…what it could mean for every human in the city." He laughed humorlessly. "Right now, humans are doing themselves enough damage. If a real rebellion breaks out—"

"It will never get that far," Hugh said, his words more certain than his tone.

"We have to get people to calm down until we find out what's really going on." Daniel moved for the door. "I didn't take you for a coward, Hugh. You wanted acknowledgment of what you believe is going on in Tanis. You're getting it now, but it's out of hand. Take responsibility."

"Who are you to give orders?" Kevin demanded.

Daniel gave him a hard look. "Someone has to," he said, and stepped through the door, closing it firmly behind him.

Isis changed quickly, ignoring the slight ache in her shoulder and the quickly healing scratches on her arms, and quietly left her apartment. She knew that Daniel hadn't gone home as Anu had advised, but she had no idea where he'd head next. Even if he tried to stop the fighting Anu had described, he was only one man, and he'd be looking for explanations.

Just as *she* would.

She stepped into the apartment elevator before she realized it was already occupied. The doors closed, and she was left alone with a tall Opir whose face and eyes were invisible under his cowl. Instinctively, she felt he was dangerous, and also had the strong feeling that she'd met him before.

She was trying to analyze his scent when he spoke.

"Anu and his chosen companions mean ill for the humans of Tanis," he said in a low, hoarse voice. "The missing humans are part of it. There are records. Find them."

"Who are you? Why did you come to me?"

The elevator reached the first floor, and the Opir strode through the open doors without answering. Isis tried to follow, but he had vanished like an illusion.

He could have been anyone, she thought: one of the Nine in disguise, an Opir living in any one of the towers. The fact that he knew she was looking for something— even *what* she was looking for—unnerved her greatly. She had no reason to trust a ghost who appeared and disappeared within seconds.

It could even be a trap, if someone was attempting to prove that she was acting against the Nine. The strange Opir's words ran through her head again and again: Anu, the missing humans, records. Records of what? And where would she find them?

She hesitated just outside the building, considering her next move carefully. There was, of course, the public Hall of Records. The records included the names and ranks of every Opir who had lived in the old Tartaros: those who had chosen to remain as equals to humans and those who had left. They also held the names of every human serf and current citizen: those who had stayed and those who had chosen to take their chances at a life outside the protection of a Citadel. The name of every immigrant was carefully noted, along with the date of immigration. The same was true for those who left Tanis for any reason.

But the Hall was not the only place where information of that kind was stored. Isis knew that Anu kept his own records in the tower, a duplicate set meant to be a backup should anything happen to the public records.

It seemed highly unlikely that Anu would keep anything

incriminating in either set of records. But the only way to be sure was to return to the tower and look.

The tower was quiet, as it usually was, but Isis could also sense an emptiness that reassured her. She paused at each floor and listened carefully at the doors. She heard servants moving about inside, but no indication that the suites' owners were in residence.

All dealing with the problems below, she thought. At least some, like Athena and Bes, would be working *with* the humans to find a solution. She didn't want to think about what Ereshkigal and Hera—and Anu himself— might be up to.

She had to take a chance. She rode the elevator to Anu's suite. He had left no guards—he would hardly have a reason to, unless he believed humans would dare to invade the tower—and Isis listened again, her heart pounding in her chest. She could hear one of Anu's several servants moving within. She concocted a strange but somewhat plausible story and knocked on the door.

As much as she had come to despise her abilities, she made use of her influence to "suggest" to the servant that he had no reason to question her claim that Anu had sent her to fetch a book on Tanisian law. He let her in, and she made her way quickly to Anu's private office.

The room was as big as any other in his suite, the shelves filled with antique books and bound writings from before and after the War. There were also polished wooden file cabinets along one long wall, all locked, though not beyond her ability to break into.

Just to be thorough, she searched his desk first. He and the Nine left most of the administrative paperwork to the Council, but Anu often used pen and paper to communicate with them.

She found nothing of interest, and continued to the file cabinets. Most of the cabinets were labeled by contents, some alphabetically, but she had absolutely no idea where to start.

She returned to Anu's desk, looking for a key. She found it without much difficulty, and unlocked the cabinets one by one.

The duplicate records were there, as she had assumed, but nothing seemed suspicious or out of place, let alone incriminating.

Until she found a folder labeled "Hannibal," completely empty. Isis's neck prickled. There must be a reason there was nothing in the folder.

She quickly locked all the cabinets and hurried out of the library with the appropriate book. The servant wished her a good day without showing the slightest curiosity about why she'd been in Anu's office so long. She asked him casually where Hannibal lived, assuming he resided with the other Opiri in one of the other towers.

The servant surprised her by telling her that Hannibal had his own rooms on the lower level of the Household, once the realm of human serfs. Gritting her teeth, Isis worked her influence again, this time sending the servant out on an errand and making certain that he would forget she had ever been there.

Once he had gone, she rushed down the stairs into the former serfs' quarters. There were many narrow halls and small rooms set aside for the higher-ranked serfs, but Isis knew that Hannibal would never stay in one of those simple rooms. She continued into the common area, and found that Hannibal had transformed it into a combination of general living quarters and bedchamber, using a creative placement of drapes and furniture, all of the finest quality.

There was a desk with many drawers, and they were locked. Unable to find a key, she pried the top drawer open as gently as she could.

The drawer was virtually empty. She opened the second drawer and then the third. There was a thin stack of papers there, loosely bound. Isis pulled out the bundle and laid it on the desktop.

Names. Lists of human names, with ages and dates written next to them. The humans were of both sexes, primarily in their late teens to midtwenties, and the dates went back almost exactly six months.

Isis knew without question that these must be the missing humans. She was nearly as certain that these records were meant to be accessed by Anu as well as Hannibal.

There was no information at all about what had become of the humans. Isis searched the desk again but could find no further data.

Regardless of how careful she had been, she knew that Hannibal would see that the desk had been broken into and would surely report it to Anu. She had been careful in touching the papers, but her scent might give her away if Hannibal returned too soon.

That was the least of her concerns. Anu wouldn't dare hurt her in such a way that he or any of the Nine would be connected with it. Not when any conflict among them would eventually be noticed.

What she needed was proof as to why these humans had been taken, and why Anu, as the strange Opir had said, held such ill-will toward the humans of Tanis.

Leaving the drawers as they were, she ascended the stairs back to the main floor, making certain that the servant hadn't returned, and left the suite. She made it to the base of the tower without meeting anyone else, but as soon as she stepped into the ground floor lobby, she found herself facing four Opir guards, armed with stunners and shock sticks.

"Lady Isis," one of them said, inclining his head. "We are to escort you to Anu."

"Not if the Lady doesn't want to go," Daniel said, appearing in one of the three arched doorways at the base of the tower. The guards swung around to face him, raising their stunners.

Daniel moved before Isis did. He kicked the stunner out of one Opir's hand and turned on the guard already coming for him. Isis darted in to grab the third Opir's shock stick and turned it on him. It only immobilized him for a moment, but she used that second to remove his other weapon and toss it through the nearest archway. He came at her, and she wrestled with him, calling upon her most ancient strength to push him into the wall. Out of the corner of her eye she could see that Daniel was still occupied with the first two Opiri, and the fourth was almost right behind her.

She banged the third Opir's head against the wall, dazing him, and whirled about to kick the fourth Opir's feet out from under him. After that, she gave herself wholly to the battle, and the individual moves no longer had any meaning except as part of the dance.

When it was over, all four Opiri lay on the ground, disarmed, two unconscious and two barely moving. Daniel strode toward her, caught her around the waist, and kissed her. She responded instantly, but the moment lasted only a few seconds before Daniel set her back.

"We can't stay here," he said, collecting the weapons and tossing them out of the archway as far as he could throw them. "Anu didn't send four guards without a reason."

"How did you know I was here?"

"You weren't in your apartment and this seemed the next place that you would be. I won't ask you what you've been doing until we're somewhere safe."

"Anu would not dare hurt me."

"He's underestimated you," Daniel said. "He won't do that again."

"And he has gravely underestimated *you*," Isis said, staring at the fallen Opiri.

"What do we do with them?" Daniel asked, touching a fresh laceration over his cheekbone. "The minute they wake up…"

With a sigh of deep regret, Isis knelt beside the nearest semiconscious Opir. "I have used this ability too many times already," she said. "This will be the last time, Daniel."

He nodded, seeming as conflicted as she felt. "Do what you have to do," he said.

Isis touched the Opir's face, stroking his cheek. His eyes opened. She smiled.

"Look at me, Opir," she said gently. "You were never able to find me, as Anu commanded. You will not remember the fight that followed. You will conceal your injuries and keep them covered until they heal, and tell Anu that you saw no one but a few Opiri at the tower while you waited. Do you understand?"

The Opir nodded once, his mouth slack and his eyes glazed. Isis rose, took a long breath, and moved to the next guard.

The last two required a little more effort, but Isis finished with confidence that the guards would follow her instructions. She met Daniel's gaze.

"I have done what I could," she said.

"Then we need to go," Daniel said. He waited for her to pull her cowl over her head, grabbed her hand, and pulled her down the ramp.

"There is much I must tell you," she said, a little breathless. "How are matters in the human wards?"

"Improving," he said. "Wiser heads are beginning to prevail."

At least nobody had tried to storm the towers, Isis

thought. Given the anger she had felt among the humans, it would not have shocked her.

"We must find Hannibal," she said.

He looked at her as if she'd gone mad. "Why?"

"Because he is connected to the disappearance of the humans. We must know why they've been taken, and to what extent Anu is involved."

"It's too dangerous now."

"Trust me, Daniel."

"I wish I could trust you to take care of yourself."

As they began to slow their pace, Isis checked her hood to make sure it covered most of her face. "Is there any reason that someone might be after you?" she asked.

"I went to talk to Hugh and his band, trying to get them to help," Daniel said. "I've avoided everyone else on my way here."

"Then we must keep a very low profile until we can find a way to get Hannibal alone."

"And if he answers our questions? What do you think Anu will do once Hannibal tells him that we interrogated him?"

"We cannot let him go, Daniel."

He cast a sharp glance at her. "You mean we'll have to kill him?"

"I don't know."

"You aren't a murderer, Isis."

"I hope we can find another way." With a quick glance left and right, Isis took the back lanes through Hera's ward, where she and Daniel found only small groups of humans huddled in their doorways or watching nervously from shelter. In Bes's ward there was more commotion, but Daniel had been correct; it seemed quieter than it had been when Isis had left for her apartment, and she caught sight of Bes himself talking with a small group of humans who looked as though they had been in a fight.

Avoiding Bes, Isis led Daniel in a roundabout search for Hannibal. They reached her ward and found Anu and several of the Nine addressing a crowd of humans from the steps of the Hall of Justice. Hannibal stood slightly behind Anu, staring down into the crowd. The people moved restlessly as if a breeze were blowing them this way and that.

"It isn't over," Daniel whispered close to Isis's ear as they crouched at the corner of one of the administrative buildings. "Anu has these people under his spell."

Chapter 20

Isis didn't want to admit it, but she, too, felt the pull of Anu's power. He could not control the entire city, whatever some humans might believe, but a throng of this size was not beyond his skill. When the humans began to disperse, their expressions relaxed in spite of scratched and dirty faces, Isis and Daniel remained still and watched to see what Anu would do next.

He exchanged a few words with Ishtar, Hera and Hermes, who had been standing with him, and quickly walked down the steps. The other members of the Nine lingered a moment longer and then separated, leaving Hannibal standing on the steps alone.

Daniel hissed through his teeth. "We have him," he said.

"Now we have to catch him," Isis said.

"I'll follow him. You stay here. If you aren't with me, no one can claim you were threatening him."

"And nobody will be with you to help keep him quiet and restrained once he's caught."

"Damn it," Daniel breathed. "Isis, you—" He broke off. "Hannibal's moving." He jumped up from his crouch and ran back through the small strip of garden between their building and the one beside it. Isis ran after him into the alley behind, and they remained parallel to Hannibal as he strode in the direction of the main tower.

Apparently there were no shuttles running, because Isis knew that an Opir as proud as Hannibal would never walk if he could ride. Still they had to wait for the right moment to catch him alone and out of sight of observers—just as he was approaching the ramp to the causeway.

"Hannibal!" Isis called, emerging from her hiding place. "I have been looking for you."

The Opir stared at her. "What are you doing here?" he asked. "Why are you not in your rooms?"

"Why was I excluded from Anu's meeting with the citizens at the Hall of Justice?" she countered.

Hannibal blinked. "Anu is concerned for you," he said. "You were attacked—"

"But he's not interested in protecting her," Daniel said, striding out of the shadows. He pushed Hannibal into the slight recess under the ramp. "What *does* he want with her?"

Hannibal tried to shove his way past Daniel, but Daniel knocked the Opir's cowl aside and pinned him to the wall by his throat. "Anu is afraid of Isis, isn't he?" he asked. "Why? Because she's his only true equal in Tanis?"

"That isn't important now," Isis said. She addressed Hannibal. "I want to know about the humans who have disappeared, and why you keep a list of them in your quarters."

Eyes widening, Hannibal looked genuinely shocked for a moment, and then broke into a laugh. "You entered Anu's Household without permission?"

"He doesn't even bother to deny it," Daniel said. He grabbed a handful of Hannibal's collar and twisted it in his fist. "We're betting that Anu doesn't want this getting out to the entire city after what's gone on today. Tell us the truth, and you won't meet with any unfortunate accidents."

Once again Hannibal fought to escape, using brute Opir strength, but Daniel held him where he was.

"You cannot do this," he gasped, and Isis sensed that he meant Daniel's unusual capabilities as well as his right to hold and question Hannibal.

"Why was that list of humans in your office?" Daniel asked.

It was not a long interrogation. For all his bluster, Hannibal seemed frightened of Daniel, and Isis could see why. There was a ruthlessness in the human's face and eyes she had never seen before, an absolute commitment to getting answers at any price.

"You will be executed," Hannibal said in a strangled whisper.

Daniel didn't react. He repeated the question. Hannibal answered—hesitantly, his pale face tinged with green.

When he had finished, Isis felt sick, and Daniel was grimly silent. *Anu and his chosen companions mean ill for the humans of Tanis*, the stranger in the elevator had told her. Isis didn't know what she had expected, but it wasn't this.

"What do we do with him?" Daniel asked, his voice as cold as winter sweeping down from the mountains.

That was the ugly question, Isis thought. They could simply remove his cowl and expose him to the sunlight in the lower city, where the shadow of the dome didn't reach.

But she wasn't ready to kill, despite her hatred. "Where is Anu now?" she asked him.

"He said he was…gathering his worshippers," Hannibal said, choking and coughing.

Daniel looked at Isis. "His worshippers?" he echoed. "The people he mesmerized at the Hall of Justice?"

"I do not believe so," Isis said, her gaze turned inward. "That is not worship."

"What do you mean?" Daniel asked Hannibal.

"He's a god," Hannibal whispered. "He has...never been satisfied with anything less."

"I think I understand," Isis said. "Where does he assemble these worshippers?"

"In an abandoned part of the city," Hannibal said.

"You're going to show us," Daniel said.

"If Anu sees you, he will kill you both."

"And if you don't take us, I'll shove you out into the sun."

There was no doubt that Hannibal believed Daniel. Isis pulled the Opir's hood over his head, made certain that there were no observers, and gestured for Daniel to bring Hannibal out from under the shadow of the ramp.

Keeping to the less traveled streets between largely abandoned buildings under the dome, Isis and Daniel forced Hannibal to lead them, Daniel's hand locked like a vise around Hannibal's wrist. After a fifteen-minute walk they reached the completely deserted east side of the city, deep under the dome and far from the nearest two towers. Hannibal became very quiet. With Daniel's less-than gentle encouragement, he led them along a street almost directly under the causeway. The street passed between two cracked pillars, and beyond the pillars was a heavy gate, firmly closed. The gate did not look old.

"There," Hannibal said under his breath. "That is where he summons them."

"What is this place?" Daniel asked, scanning the door.

"The old arena," Isis said, shivering. "The previous Bloodlords and Bloodmasters, the ones we cast out, used to pit humans against each other in combat."

"Is there another way in?" Daniel asked Hannibal, his eyes glittering with rage.

"We must wait a little," Hannibal said.

"For what?" Daniel asked.

"For Anu to set the stage. Only then will you understand."

"If you're tricking us—"

"Listen," Isis said. They all held their breaths as the sound of approaching feet broke the silence. The three of them hurried away from the gate and rounded the corner of the wall to hide and watch. Human men and women carrying strange regalia entered the gate. Isis counted over a hundred people. After ten minutes, the last humans entered and barred the door behind them.

Still, Hannibal made it clear that they should wait until it was obvious no more visitors would arrive. Only then did he lead Isis and Daniel along a passageway between an outer wall and the inner one enclosing the arena, stopping at a smaller side door only wide enough for a single man to pass through at a time. It was unlocked. A stairway set into the wall led to some higher level.

"The mezzanine," Hannibal said.

Shoving the Opir ahead, Daniel began to climb the stairs. Isis followed. She became aware of a droning sound like that of many voices humming or chanting, and when they reached the balcony and peered over the edge, she saw what made the noise.

More than a hundred humans crouched on the ground facing the balcony on the other side of the arena. Anu sat on a richly upholstered throne while, just below him, men wearing sun and demon masks acted out some kind of ritual on the arena floor. They spoke words of praise and awe, bowing to Anu again and again, while the other humans bent their heads to the ground.

"Worship," Isis murmured. "It *is* what he wants."

"These people can't be here of their own free will," Daniel said. "It's no better than slavery."

"And this is only the beginning," Hannibal said. "Do

you believe Anu will be content with only a hundred worshippers?"

"Do you think any of the other Nine know about this?" Daniel asked.

Certainly not Athena, Bes or Hermes, Isis thought. "If Anu has taken such great pains to hide this," she said, "they must not."

"Then either he believes something bad will happen if his extracurricular activities become common knowledge," Daniel said, "or he's not ready to reveal what he's done." He stared at the ground. "It all makes sense now. If Anu can provoke humans to fight and then sends the Lawkeepers to arrest them, he can take more humans for himself." He turned on Hannibal. "You've been part of this from the beginning."

"Daniel," Isis said, touching his arm, "we must not remain here any longer."

His gaze met hers, hard and ruthless. "You're right. Anu knows you'll oppose him with all your strength. I'm going to get you out of Tanis."

She shook her head. "Few Opiri in Tanis will be sanguine about Anu setting himself up as a true god. They will see—"

"But will they act?" Daniel asked. "Or will they simply let themselves fall back into the old patterns?"

As Isis began to answer, Hannibal jerked free of Daniel's hold and darted away. Daniel made a move to follow, but Isis held him back.

"You will never catch him now," she said. "And he has betrayed Anu by showing all this to us. I think he will hide until he knows what will come of this."

"And what *will* come of this, Isis?" Daniel asked.

"You are wrong about the Opiri here. They will not accept what Anu has done. You have met Bes, Athena and her companions, and you know they are not—"

"I've also met the Opir who tried to kill that girl."

Isis and Daniel stared at each other, painfully at odds in a way Isis could hardly bear.

"I believe that Anu will kill you without hesitation as soon as he learns that you know about the missing humans," Daniel said. "I can hide among Hugh's Underground. *You* can't."

"And will you tell the rebels about the disappearances?" Isis asked. "You will only create more chaos that could play right into Anu's hands."

"They have to know, Isis."

"Then we must agree on a strategy that will not make things worse."

Isis touched Daniel's fisted hand, sick with regret and grief. "You must go, Daniel. But I *must* stay." She stopped his protest with a fingertip against his lips. "Listen to me. I will determine a safe time to approach my allies and explain the circumstances. If it comes to a direct confrontation, some of the Nine will stand with me."

All Daniel's feelings were in his eyes. "You know I can't leave you," he said.

"I fear for *you*, Daniel."

"I can't let you do it. Your life is the most important one in this city. You know it."

Isis was silent, realizing that she would never convince Daniel to change his mind. She had to play along, see him to safety and then do whatever must be done.

"There is a way out of the city which only a few know of," she said, "a small, unguarded gate within my ward, off one of the lanes behind the Immigrant Center. That does not mean that it will be easy to access. But it will be simpler than confronting guards who may have been instructed not to let us leave Tanis." She paused. "We will wait until dusk."

"We'd better find a place to hide until then," Daniel said.

Though it wasn't much of a plan, they made their cautious way toward the front of the city. There, in Bes's ward, they found an empty building to wait out the remainder of the day. The streets were quiet now, and no one disturbed them. A little before dusk they emerged and walked with casual confidence toward the Immigrant Center.

Shouts arrested them in their progress, and Isis turned to look toward the depository. Another protest was in progress, but this time a much larger one, attended by fifty or more men and women with signs, chanting slogans and harassing the few Opiri who emerged from the building. One of the Opiri paused to argue, and a human struck him in the face. Other humans dragged the Opir down, crying out with animal-like voices.

Immediately the other Opiri came to his aid, and there were cries of pain and terror. Isis smelled blood. She knew she had to intervene, even at the risk of compromising her plan to get Daniel to safety.

"Wait here," she said to Daniel before she ran toward the melee. She heard Daniel curse behind her, his low voice gradually lost amid the angry howls of the mob.

A mob that had become a monster. Other Opiri had found their way to the fight, and their greater strength was beginning to leave its mark on the struggling humans.

A few moments later Daniel was there beside her, speaking to the humans in the calm voice of authority she had heard him use before.

This time the humans didn't listen. Isis knew that her influence might stop them. But Anu had demonstrated how easily that power could be turned to evil. If she gave way again…

She had no time to think. As Daniel tried to intervene, Isis fought to save human lives from Opiri whose predatory instincts had been fully aroused, even placing herself physically between one of her people and his prey. More humans arrived, greatly outnumbering the Opiri, and the tide turned again. Opiri's cowls were pulled from their heads, exposing vulnerable skin to the open sky overhead.

Before Isis could move to their aid, a dozen Lawkeepers were surrounding the roiling crowd, grabbing Daniel as they stunned the other humans. Isis cried out for them to stop, but they ignored her, bound the humans—including Daniel—and herded the dazed captives toward the Hall of Justice.

"He had nothing to do with this!" Isis shouted, striding alongside them.

Once again they ignored her, and she had no choice but to follow them to the jail at the rear of the hall. The Lawkeepers blocked her from entering, and she considered her options. She could rely on her authority as one of the Nine, but that might provoke unwanted attention from Anu.

If Daniel faced only the relatively minor charge of participating in the protest, he might simply be ejected from the city. Then, Isis thought, he would be safe. But she couldn't be sure what would happen after a long night and day of protests and fighting. Anu might see this as a perfect opportunity to be rid of a potential troublemaker and rebel once and for all.

There had not been an execution in Tanis since the day it was founded, but if Anu wished to arrange it…

Her stomach churning with dread, Isis set out for the tower.

Chapter 21

Three hours later, Isis stood before the Nine in their meeting hall, fighting a battle she was very much afraid she would lose.

"Daniel must be permitted a jury of his peers," she insisted.

The Nine gazed at her with expressions ranging from distaste to sympathy, but Isis knew the odds were against her. She felt extremely lucky that Hannibal, whatever had become of him, had not appeared at Anu's side again, and nobody knew of her searching his apartments.

Anu didn't bother to conceal his suspicion of Isis. *Somehow he knows I have guessed that he is the cause behind the trouble in the city*, she thought.

"Why should we change our customs for this newcomer?" Ereshkigal asked, her fringed robes draped over her chair. "He was caught with the protesters, infringing upon the rights of Opir citizens. He has been seen among other humans involved in the fighting—"

"Trying to stop them," Isis said, pressing her hands flat to the table. "And I was there during the protest at the depository. He was only speaking to the humans, attempting to calm them, when—"

"So you have told us," Anu said, his voice heavy in its

softness. "But you have favored this human since the beginning. You would claim anything to save him."

"If you will not accept my word, then give him a chance to defend himself. You can surely find enough trustworthy humans to—"

"Humans will not judge one of their own fairly," Hephaestus said. "If any are sympathetic to these troublemakers, they will favor him."

"Hephaestus is right," Ishtar said. "Humans are incapable of objectivity. A jury such as you suggest is a human invention, and no part of Tanisian law."

"But you believe the Council will be objective, when they have already condemned a dozen humans to expulsion from Tanis?" She tried to gather her wits. "Can you blame the humans for doubting the way we dispense justice?"

"Expulsion is not death," Hermes said, not meeting her eyes. "Your human was resilient enough to survive in the wild, and he can do so again."

Isis sensed that she had come to the end of her argument. To push it further would be to provoke Anu to radical action.

Still, when the meeting was over, she risked stealing an antique dagger from among the displays and hiding it in her robes. After she left the tower, she made an attempt to see Daniel, but the human prisoners were locked away from visitors. There were no protesters on the steps of the Council building or Hall of Justice; Lawkeepers stood guard, discouraging anyone from approaching.

But they could not stop the tension from growing in the city. Even those humans who'd had no part in the protests were beginning to react, if very quietly. In her own ward, men and women slipped away when they saw her. Any sense of trust was gone.

Isis made many attempts to visit Athena and Bes in their suites or their wards to discuss what they had seen in the arena, but they were either absent or fully occupied in monitoring and reassuring their humans. She had no better luck with Hermes, though his words at the meeting had aroused her doubts about him. It was almost as if they feared to speak with her.

Anu continued to leave her alone, but she knew she couldn't afford to attract his attention. Instinct told her that he was watching to see what she would do; he still didn't seem to know about her presence at the arena, and whatever his suspicions about her, he had no proof to lay before the other Nine. Even his power could not guarantee that the others wouldn't turn on him if he exposed himself while speaking against Isis.

The following day, at the hour of Daniel's hearing, she sat apart from those of the Nine who were present. Athena and Bes were missing. She tried to catch Daniel's eyes, but he stared straight ahead in the witness box facing the Council's table, his expression coldly defiant and as far from humble as any human's could be.

There was never any question in her mind that he would be found guilty. He was sentenced to permanent exile from Tanis.

On the morning of the prisoners' departure—and after several more unsuccessful attempts to speak with her allies among the Nine—Isis was finally able to see Daniel, though the Lawkeepers guarding the prison were reluctant to let her into the holding area. She had prepared to accompany him part of the way out of the city, and wore a loose day coat over practical traveling clothes. She also carried a hidden bundle that included food and a change of clothes for him.

Daniel was pacing slowly back and forth in his cell, his hands clenched behind his back. He paused when he saw her.

"You shouldn't have come here," he said. "Associating with me now could be deadly for you, Isis."

"Are you well?" she asked anxiously.

"They don't let us starve," he said. "Though it's not as if they'll be feeding us much longer." He moved up to the bars. "What about you?"

"I spoke to the Nine on your behalf. I tried to convince them to show mercy, but Anu—"

"You should never have tried," he said, resting his clenched fists against the bars. "Anu had you right where he wanted you."

"But he did nothing to me. There have been no threats. He has not even attempted to speak with me alone."

"And Hannibal?"

"Still no sign." She lowered her voice. "I have been thwarted in every attempt to tell my allies about Anu and his worshippers. But I have no intention of—"

The barred door to the corridor swung open behind them, and two Lawkeepers in day coats respectfully asked Isis to step aside while they opened Daniel's cell, cuffed him and took him out of the holding area. Sunlight shone into the city, and Isis was surprised that the humans had been given the benefit of being released during the day.

She was glad that she'd made preparations to travel when she saw that the escort would include not only Lawkeepers, but Opir guards armed with both shock sticks and actual firearms.

She followed Daniel to the main gate, where heavy rope barred the human onlookers from approaching the prisoners. Protest emerged as a low hum, no one daring to speak out and call attention to themselves.

Isis remained as close to Daniel as possible while he and the other convicted prisoners were given bundles of supplies and clothing. They had no weapons with which to defend themselves from rogue Freebloods.

Head high, Isis boldly walked out with the humans. The

gates remained open behind her. The Lawkeepers wouldn't close them on one of the Nine.

She and Daniel gazed at each other, not daring to touch. His blue eyes seemed to catch the sunlight and reflect it under her hood, giving her nowhere to hide.

"I don't want you to deal with this alone, Isis," he said.

She moved closer, slipping the knife and her secret bundle of clothes and food into his hand. "You cannot protect me," she said, backing away. "Daniel, listen to reason. You must go, or you will distract me with worry for you. You will hinder every action I take to counter Anu's ambitions. If I could find a way for us to stay together without endangering your life or my duty to Tanis, I would gladly take it."

"I'll be sticking close to Tanis, so you can find me again when it's safe for you."

She swallowed. "Do you remember the location of the nearest human colony? You can warn them of what is occurring in Tanis. Or you can carry out your duty and return to your own colony to bring them the information you were sent to gather."

"Not without you," he said.

"Lady Isis," the captain of the Lawkeepers said, edging between her and Daniel. "We will leave shortly. Will you go back inside?"

"I will accompany you to the final location," she said, "and return with you to Tanis."

The captain opened his mouth, on the verge of argument before closing it again without speaking. The other eleven Lawkeepers gathered the prisoners and herded them away from the gates.

The group walked northwest throughout the day, crossing over prairie, forest and the ruins of old towns, passing gradually into the foothills. Isis felt pity for the fearful men and women, and even for those who concealed their fear.

Daniel strode ahead of them all, his head up, stopping only if one of his fellow humans needed his help or support. He seemed to give the other humans courage and purpose.

He will see them to safety first, Isis thought with relief. *He will not abandon them in the wilderness.* She knew he would inevitably attempt to return to Tanis, no matter what she said. But she would have some time to see what she could accomplish within the city, whether she decided to work only with those of the Nine she trusted or also with the humans under Hugh's leadership.

The group of exiles reached their goal just before sunset: a large, rocky outcrop near a woodland that provided shelter and potential hiding places from any threats they might face on their first night of exile. The prisoners' hands were freed, and as the Lawkeepers prepared to return to Tanis, Daniel took Isis's arm and led her around to the back of the outcrop.

He kissed her, and she returned the kiss with a desperate fear.

"It's all right," he said, gathering a handful of her hair and pressing it to his face. "We will find a way, Isis."

"I believe you," she said. And she did, in spite of all the obstacles they faced.

"I'm going to get these people to the nearest human colony," he said. "After that..."

She took his rough hands and kissed his knuckles. "I depend upon you to be sensible, Daniel," she said.

He only kissed her again. The other humans joined them, crowding close, and she and Daniel stepped apart.

"If you are ready, Lady Isis," the captain of the Lawkeepers said with a slight bow.

Somehow, Isis managed to break away from Daniel, though it seemed as if her heart were tearing in two. She turned twice to look back at him, and each time he met her gaze directly and with reassuring confidence.

When she and the Lawkeepers moved out of sight of the prisoners, Isis drifted in an inner space filled only with loneliness and longing. She couldn't bring herself to think of what her next act in Tanis should be; the city was as unreal to her as the woods through which they passed and the stars in the indigo sky overhead. She hardly noticed when they stopped to rest, and two of the Opir guards left to hunt for game. When they returned, she took her share of the blood with indifference, though she noticed that it seemed slightly off in taste and texture.

After that, her dream-state took on a new life of its own, and she lost track of time and place. Only gradually did she begin to realize that they had been traveling too long, and that Tanis was nowhere in sight. Still she was unable to focus, and the Lawkeepers didn't seem to hear her questions, even when the sun began to rise again and they pulled their hoods up over their heads.

They stopped again in a place she didn't recognize, and one of the Opir guards, his face a blur in the light, urged her to lie down and rest. Some remnant of self-preservation made her refuse, and the others pushed her to the ground, one of them forcing the mouth of a blood-flask against her lips. She choked on the stream of foul-tasting liquid, her body aware that it was tainted even before her mind recognized that she had been betrayed.

The sun blinded her as the Lawkeepers dragged off her day coat and left her in the open grassland, the altered blood curdling in her stomach. The sky seemed made up of a hundred colors she didn't recognize, and her skin felt scalded.

Isis rolled over onto her stomach and breathed in the scent of dry earth. She knew that her betrayers had counted on her sickness from the blood preventing her from reaching shelter soon enough, but she was not about to grant them victory.

Her legs and arms like rubber, Isis dragged herself to

the west, toward a stand of battered trees along some minor watercourse. Her attempts to rise met with utter failure. Still, she remembered Daniel's face and continued to fight, inch by inch, reaching out to gather handfuls of golden grass to pull herself forward.

She had gone no more than a hundred feet when the boots appeared—one pair directly in front of her face, a dozen more surrounding her. She froze, waiting for a strike to her heart or the removal of her head from her body.

"Here," a man said, holding his hand down to her. Several others moved closer, helping her to her feet, supporting her weight as she swayed and began to fall. They covered her with a day coat, and one of them put a water flask to her mouth. She drank greedily, though her stomach fought to reject what she swallowed.

"Easy," the first man said. "We've come to take you to safety."

The sky was too bright for her to see his hooded face. "Who...are you?" she whispered.

"My name is Cassius. We've been following you, but we had to wait until the others were gone." He spoke softly to his comrades. "We have horses. If you can hold on for a few hours, we'll get to a place where you can rest. Whatever they gave you obviously wasn't a fatal dose."

A dose of what? she wondered. But she couldn't keep the question in her head. Cassius and the others lifted her onto the back of a horse, already occupied by an Opir woman who supported Isis against her chest.

When they started moving, Isis drifted into semiconsciousness again, feeling the horse's movements but unable to make sense of them. She heard voices like the grumbling of badgers. Occasionally someone put water to her mouth, and her body insisted that she drink.

At sunset, she ejected everything she had swallowed, including the tainted blood. Her thoughts became more lucid, and when they reached their destination, she could see the details of what appeared to be a military camp in a clearing among tall pines, complete with uniformed, well-armed Opiri and tents in precise rows. Large pens held cattle as an obvious source of blood. She saw no humans at all.

A tall, imposing Opir met her as the others helped her dismount, his black hair swept behind his shoulders. She felt the force of his will immediately, a fierce and dangerous determination, and realized who he was even before she recognized his features.

"Ares!" she said, her voice still a little hoarse. "But they said you had been killed."

"They say many things about me," the Bloodmaster said, supporting her on one arm.

"But what are you doing here?" she asked, her gaze sweeping the camp again. "Who are these Opiri?"

"Anu's army," he said, hatred glittering in his pale eyes. "I am its commander."

"I don't understand."

"You were never meant to." He guided her in among the tents and to a field chair. "I sent men to follow you once you left Tanis. I'd heard that someone in the city wished you ill enough to threaten your life."

"You *heard*? But how—" She looked more carefully into his eyes and gave a brief laugh of astonishment. "You are the one who warned me that Anu meant ill for the humans of Tanis. You were in the city all along."

"Only when Anu and the others called for me to attend them," Ares said. "I couldn't let myself be seen talking to you."

"But why did you—" She broke off, remembering that she had more urgent concerns. "If you followed me, you saw the exiles. Did you observe what became of them?"

"I had men follow them, as well," Ares said. "They should be here very soon."

"But why would you bring them here?" She got to her feet, swayed, and sat down again. "What do you intend to do with them?"

"Help them find a safe place," Ares said, "before what almost happened to you happens to them."

"You mean that someone is out to kill them?"

"They have all been deemed troublemakers, have they not?"

A sudden thought crossed her mind, and she exhaled sharply. "One of them—Daniel—was looking for you. He seemed very anxious to find you, and even when he was told that you had left the city—"

"I know," Ares said, his expression very serious. "I learned that he was in Tanis only after his arrest. He should never have mentioned my name."

"He said you had been his master in Erebus, and that he was concerned for your well-being."

"The young fool," Ares said, shaking his head. "If he came to Tanis to look for *me*—"

A commotion from the rear of the camp cut off his words. Dozens of Opiri soldiers turned to look. The human exiles walked into camp and made their way between the tents toward Ares, Daniel in the lead and Opir scouts around them.

Daniel came to a dead halt when he saw Ares. Ares rose to face him.

"You're here," Daniel said, in a voice almost too soft to hear.

Isis witnessed a very peculiar thing then. All the brooding ferocity seemed to go out of Ares, and for a moment his expression softened to one of affection and relief.

"My son," he said.

Chapter 22

Daniel found it difficult to speak. Ares looked the same as he always had, as of course he would; the years hadn't touched him, and he exuded as much power and regal authority as ever.

And he was alive.

"Ares," he said, swallowing. "Father."

They came together, gripping each other's shoulders. Ares's brief smile quickly turned into the kind of frown that had always terrified his serfs; not because they feared he would hurt them, but because he had so seldom turned it on them.

Now Daniel bore the brunt of it. Still holding his shoulders, Ares set him back and looked him over critically.

"It is fortunate that you are still alive," Ares said. "Did Avalon send you to complete my mission?"

"I volunteered," Daniel said, holding his father's gaze. "I suspected soon after I got here that you hadn't left Tanis."

Ares made a sound of disgust and opened his mouth to speak again, but Daniel looked past his shoulder and saw Isis walking toward them, a little unsteady on her feet. He squeezed Ares's arm and ran to meet her, catching her and holding her against him.

"Are you all right?" he asked, turning her face up to his

with his fingertips. "What are you doing here? Have you been sick?" He looked at Ares as the Bloodmaster came up behind him. "Where did you find her? What was—"

"Your father?" Isis said faintly. She straightened and pushed against him. "Your *father*?"

"I am certain his failure to tell you is not because of any lack of trust, Lady Isis," Ares said in a wry tone. "I was under the impression, from my brief observations in the city, that the two of you enjoy an unusually close relationship."

Daniel's face heated, though he had no reason to feel any embarrassment...except for concealing such an important fact from Isis. "I thought it was best that you didn't know," he said to her.

"Know that you aren't human at all?" she demanded, pulling away from him. She included Ares in her challenge. "Or is there some other essential fact I am missing?"

Ares glanced at Daniel with grim amusement. "Tell her, Daniel," he said.

"I am half human," Daniel said. "Most of the rest of what I told you is true. My mother was impregnated before the War began. It was a consensual relationship."

"But my old enemy Palemon frightened her away," Ares said. "Daniel neglects to mention that by failing to find her, I was responsible for what happened to her and our child in the twenty years before I obtained Daniel from Palemon."

There was an awkward, painful silence. "Your son does not seem to hate you, Lord Ares," she said.

"He has forgiven much," Ares said.

"It's in the past," Daniel said.

"But your enemies remain," Isis said. She looked at Ares. "Whatever the purpose of this army, it cannot be a good one. You warned me of Anu's ill intentions, and now we know what those intentions are. If you work for him, you work against your son and all who support the cause of equality in Tanis. Why did you bother to save these people if—"

"I work for Anu," Ares interrupted, "only because I have no other choice." He included both Isis and Daniel in his gaze. "He forced me to recruit Freebloods from within and without Tanis to form this army, and to train them to fight at my command."

"Disciplined Freebloods?" Daniel asked. "That's an oxymoron."

"Not with *my* troops," Ares said, though he spoke with far more bitterness than satisfaction.

"What does Anu intend for this army?"

"I don't know," Ares admitted. "He hasn't seen a reason to tell me."

"And why did you agree to do this?"

"Trinity," Ares said. "Anu has her prisoner somewhere in the towers. He made clear that if I did not obey him, or if I attempted to challenge him, she would die." He glanced over his shoulder. "Let me inform my troops that they are to make our other guests comfortable, and we will discuss this at greater length." He smiled at Isis, a rare glimpse of softer emotion. "You will need blood—"

"She'll have it," Daniel said.

"Good." He pointed out what appeared to be an officer's tent. "You may rest there for the time being."

He gave Daniel one more stern, relieved glance and started for Daniel's fellow exiles, who looked more bewildered than frightened. Daniel and Isis entered the tent Ares had indicated.

"What happened?" he and Isis said at nearly the same moment.

Daniel guided her to the cot and crouched beside it. "We were heading west, to one of the human colonies I passed on the way to Tanis. Early on I had the sense that we were being followed, so we lay low for a while. Around noon today we were ambushed…or so we thought. The Free-blood soldiers who found us claimed they meant us no harm, but that there were others nearby who did. We didn't have much choice but to go with the soldiers." He glanced toward the tent flap. "I had no idea Ares had sent them."

Still clearly shaken by the day's events, Isis relayed her own story. "On the way back to Tanis I was given poisoned blood and left to burn in the sun."

"Anu," Daniel said, thinking very black thoughts. "There's no question now of you returning to Tanis." She looked down at her hands, and he took them between his. "Isis, I should have told you of my relationship to Ares as soon as I knew I could trust you. The moment I saw Hannibal, I realized that he could expose me, because he was in Erebus when Ares acknowledged me as his son. But he didn't, for reasons I can't fathom, and I hoped to maintain the fiction that I was fully human, in part so that Opiri like Anu would underestimate me."

"This explains how you were able to fight Opiri and defeat them," she said, her hands tense and resisting his touch. "Even so, you are like no dhampir I have ever seen."

"I'm a freak," he said, "a mutation. No one knows why I look as I do, though I've heard speculation that it's because an Elder was my father." He touched his mouth, with their unremarkable cuspids. "I don't need blood, but I have the speed, strength, night vision and reflexes of Opiri. The best of both worlds."

"And the means to masquerade as human." She sighed. "You would have given yourself away soon enough, if you had continued to fight. Someone would have realized the truth."

"I know. But I'd hoped to collect more information and find Ares before that happened."

"And so you have." She withdrew her hand. "Your father is a powerful Bloodmaster. He is also one of the ancient gods. But now Anu has power over him, and he could be a great threat to us if Anu chooses to turn Ares and these Freebloods against those who defy him."

"If that's Anu's intention," Daniel said. "But I guarantee that Anu won't use Ares lightly. He's a deadly weapon that could easily turn in Anu's hand."

"But Ares will do anything to protect his mate."

"Yes," Daniel said. He rose and paced across the tent. "When was the last time you saw Trinity?"

"When Ares was preparing to leave Tanis," Isis said. "I have no idea where Anu could be holding her." She began to rise. "I must return to Tanis and find her."

Ares walked into the tent while Daniel tried to make Isis sit again. "You do not condemn me for refusing to sacrifice my wife?" the Bloodmaster asked, letting the tent flap fall.

"No," she said, relaxing under the firm pressure of Daniel's hand on her shoulder. "I..." She glanced sideways at Daniel. "I understand. Better than I could have believed."

Daniel released Isis, half afraid that she would feel the intensity of his emotions. He realized that he was with the two people in the world he most cared about; two people who could easily become opponents in a terrible game.

"You're not going anywhere," he said to Isis, and then addressed his father. "How much control do you have over this army?"

"Complete," Ares said. "I have the loyalty of all my soldiers, and they know of the blackmail." His voice simmered with anger. "They would die for me, if I let them."

"So if we can free Trinity, they will still obey any order you give them?"

Ares nodded, anguish in his eyes. "I cannot free her if I can't find her," he said.

"Isis showed me another way into the city," Daniel said. "Where is Tanis relative to this camp?"

"Ten miles to the southeast," Ares said. "But it's a moot point, because—"

"I'll go back in and find Trinity."

"Daniel—" Isis began.

"No," Ares said. "Trinity will be surrounded by Opiri, and you would have no way of getting near her. I won't lose you, as well. We will find another way."

"*I* can still get into the towers," Isis said. "If Anu failed to kill me once, he will hesitate to—"

"Enough!" Ares growled. "Neither of you is going back into Tanis, even if I must hold you prisoner here."

The tent flap rustled, and a uniformed Freeblood poked his head through the opening. "Sir," he said to Ares. "There is a matter requiring your urgent attention."

With a grunt of annoyance, Ares got up and left the tent. Isis and Daniel sat in tense silence for several minutes, Daniel listening to the voices outside. After a moment, Ares reentered the tent. His expression was grim.

"You cannot remain here indefinitely," he said. "You will rest here for a day, and then we will find you another place to hide." Both Daniel and Isis began to object, and he raised his hand to silence them. "We will not discuss this any further tonight. I have set aside another tent for the two of you, if that is acceptable. If you require separate lodgings—"

"We do," Isis said. She glanced at Daniel, her face expressionless. "It would be best."

"Whatever the lady wants," Daniel said, wondering if she was still angry with him because he had lied to her about his origins and true nature. Or was it because she knew he'd do everything in his power to keep her from going back to Tanis?

"I'll see to it," Ares said. "You may have this tent, Lady Isis."

Ares left the tent. Daniel lingered by the tent flap.

"Are you trying to punish me?" he asked Isis.

"Punish you?" She shook her head sharply. "No."

"Then why do you want separate tents?"

Color surged into her cheeks. "I…feel the need to be alone for a while. It has nothing to do with you."

Daniel knew she was lying. She was afraid of renewing their intimacy, even though the reason for keeping it secret had passed. Was it because she believed she could no longer trust her own judgment, especially about him?

Could he trust his own?

"You need clean blood," he said.

"I will ask Ares for what I require," she said. Her fists clenched on the sheets stretched across the cot. "Please, Daniel. Do not ask more of me now."

Daniel pushed at the tent flap, torn between insisting on answers and leaving Isis to recover in peace. After another long moment of silence, he walked out of the tent.

He moved among the Freeblood soldiers, noting again how disciplined they were…the complete opposite of the ones he had dealt with when he'd lived in Avalon and Delos.

Not even all Freebloods are alike, he reminded himself. Under a strong leader fighting for the good, these Opiri would be a formidable force.

But Anu would not be fighting for the good.

Near midnight, a respectful Freeblood soldier found Daniel, saluted and led him to a small tent that had obviously been recently occupied. Daniel began to protest that he could sleep anywhere, but the Freeblood insisted that this was Ares's wish. An orderly arrived with fresh bedding and hot food.

After he ate, Daniel wondered if Isis had requested blood from the army supply. He thought again of having it out with her, but in the end he gave way to exhaustion and lay back on the cot. When he woke, it was still dark.

Moving to roll off the cot, he found that one of his arms was caught on something and tried to jerk it free. Metal pressed against his wrist. He twisted around to find that he had been cuffed to the cot in a way that made it impossible for him to get up.

He cursed and fought the restraint, first working to break it and then to force his hand through the cuff. The panic of remembered confinement and bondage turned him half-mad, and he continued to struggle until his wrist was bloody and his thumb almost dislocated.

The tent flap opened, and Ares stepped inside.

"Stop," he said, catching Daniel's arm in an iron grip. "Doing yourself harm will change nothing."

Daniel flailed at his father with his other fist, making contact with Ares's jaw. Ares didn't release his grip, though he jerked back out of Daniel's reach.

"Gone back to your old ways, Ares?" Daniel spat.

"This is for your own protection."

"You haven't let Isis leave?"

"No. And I will not let you go, either."

Daniel pulled his bloody wrist from Ares's grip. "I'm not your serf anymore... Father."

"No," Ares said, crouching beside the cot. "But you are precious to me, and I will not throw your life away."

"And how do you plan to hold Isis here? Chain *her* up, as well?"

"She will not be going anywhere," Ares said. "She has had a relapse. One of my soldiers found her nearly unconscious. She has developed the Opir equivalent of a fever."

"What?" Daniel struggled again, but he realized that he was only hurting himself. "What's wrong with her?"

"Apparently the tainted blood she drank is still affecting her. She will have the best care and as much fresh blood as she needs."

"For God's sake, let me go to her!"

"Later, when I know you've come to your senses." Ares rose to leave. "I will send someone to look after your wrist."

Then he was gone, and Daniel lay back on the cot, breathing hard with anger and fear. Ares seemed to believe that Isis would be all right, but no one knew the full affects of whatever poison she had been given.

No one but the Opir who had poisoned her. The spider crouching at the center of this vicious web.

Calming his racing heart, Daniel waited for the medic to clean and bandage his wrist. As soon as the man was gone, Daniel concentrated on doing deliberately what he'd nearly done by accident…dislocating his thumb so that he could slip his hand through the cuff.

The pain was blinding, but he'd become accustomed to dealing with such discomfort long ago. He pulled his hand free and carefully pushed his thumb back into place. It would be useless for a while, but he could work around it.

He continued to evade the patrolling Opiri and made his way to Isis's tent. She was deeply asleep on her cot, undisturbed by his arrival. Her skin was pale, and there were dark circles under her eyes.

Daniel knew better than to wake her, though his fear for her curdled in his gut. He knew Ares would do everything within his power to help her, and Daniel had a task that wouldn't wait.

He knelt beside the cot, brushed his lips across her hot cheek, then left as silently as he'd come.

Somehow, he got clear of the camp and started southeast toward Tanis.

Halfway to the city, Opiri guards from Tanis ambushed him. He was outnumbered six to one; they took him down, bound him and threw a day coat over him to disguise his identity. They kept him surrounded like a living cage as they marched to Tanis, refusing to identify themselves.

Daniel could already guess that they were Anu's men. And when they entered Tanis, moving past what seemed like countless Lawkeepers and armed Opiri, he could smell the sharp, mingled scent of fear and rage in the air.

His captors made it impossible for him to observe more closely, and the human sector of the city was quiet. But he had no doubt that things had gotten worse in the short time he and Isis had been absent from Tanis. As he and his captors made their way toward the tower of the Nine, he could hear shouts of anger and pain, and glimpsed open struggles between Opiri and humans.

Anu's suite was empty of all but the "god" himself and a handful of his supporters, including Hannibal. Daniel cursed himself again for letting Hannibal escape, but he had little time for regret. The guards pushed him to his knees and held him there when he would have struggled to his feet. Anu examined him with the interest of a snake regarding a small rodent, his gaze sharp beneath hooded eyelids.

"You had one chance," Anu said, "but you did not take it. Why were you returning to Tanis?"

Daniel didn't answer. The guard bearing down on his shoulder pulled him up by his jacket and struck him across the face. Daniel's teeth cut the inside of his lip, and he tasted blood.

He knew, then, what was coming.

Anu asked again, with the same result. Daniel picked himself up off the floor.

"Where is Isis?" Anu said, leaning forward on his throne. "She left with you and the exiles and never returned. What is she doing?"

It was a strange question from the one who'd presumably tried to kill her. "I don't know," Daniel said, holding the Opir's gaze. "I didn't see her after we left the vicinity of Tanis."

"You are lying," Hannibal said, stepping forward to stand beside Anu's chair.

"I didn't know you were so concerned for Isis's welfare," Daniel said, his mouth beginning to swell.

He was ready for the next blow, and the next. He told Anu nothing, and he didn't ask if Anu had tried to kill Isis. He kept silent until he would have found it difficult to speak in any case.

"This gains us nothing, my lord," Hannibal said, gesturing for Daniel's guards to let him slump to the ground. "This man was a serf, accustomed to receiving punishment for his defiance. We will require stronger measures."

"Then by all means, use them," Anu said. "I give him to you. But keep him apart from the others. He must remain isolated until he tells us what he knows of the human resistance and any other information that may be used against us."

"No limits, my lord?"

"None, as long as he does not die. We may still use him against Isis if she returns and proves troublesome."

Hannibal nodded, a satisfied smile on his face. He gestured for the guards to drag Daniel out of the suite. He was only half-conscious as they took him to some other part of the tower: a dark and empty former Household, evidently long abandoned by its original owner. Someone had knocked down the walls between the antechamber and the central hall, and built many small rooms that looked like prison cells.

The guards hurled Daniel into one of them, throwing him against the back of the cell. There were chains and manacles attached to the wall. The Opiri forced him to stand and shackled him so that he had no means of sitting or resting his legs. They closed the cell door and left him there with his pain.

He had been alone for an indeterminate length of time when Hannibal arrived, carrying a whip.

"A pity that Palemon isn't here to see this," he said, playing out the whip. "He would have enjoyed seeing you reduced to what you were before Ares saved you."

Daniel didn't give him the satisfaction of a response. He didn't fight when Hannibal's guards unshackled him, turned him around and bound him again. He didn't make a sound when the punishment began, or when Hannibal questioned him with greater and greater impatience.

Gradually, he stopped feeling the pain. He gave himself over to the numbness of semi-consciousness and felt himself with Isis again, lying with her, feeling the healing warmth of her body against his.

But that wasn't right. "Stay away," he mumbled, his cheek against the wall. "Stay…"

The words trailed into silence, and so did his mind.

Chapter 23

Daniel came to when the cell door opened again. He peered through swollen eyelids from his position on the floor, struggling dimly to prepare himself for more pain.

The cell door shut quietly, and the person who had entered, breathing rapidly, pressed herself against it.

"My God," she said.

Daniel managed to lift his head. Even through a nose clogged with blood he could smell her; he knew her, though he couldn't seem to remember from where.

"Daniel?" She knelt beside him, her hands reaching out to touch him. He flinched back, rolling toward the wall.

"It's me," the woman said. "Trinity."

Her name awakened a strange urgency in Daniel's muddled thoughts. He *did* know her. She was important.

"How did you get in here?" he croaked.

"I broke the lock," she whispered close to his ear. "I didn't know you were here until I smelled you. If I hadn't…" Her voice broke. "Why in God's name did you come to Tanis? Did Avalon send you to find us?" She rested her hand on his damp hair. "It doesn't matter. I'll get you out." Her head jerked over her shoulder. "This is the first time I've managed to escape, but they'll notice I'm missing soon. We have to move."

Her tug on his arm brought fresh waves of excruciating pain, but he tried to get up. He was remembering now. He was supposed to find Trinity. Bring her out of Tanis for Ares, so he wouldn't have to—

"Easy," Trinity whispered. She took Daniel's weight against her own body. "I'm sorry, Daniel, but we'll have to move fast. Fast and quiet. Do you understand?"

He managed a nod. She dragged him out of the cell, and he fought to set his feet one after the other, wondering how long it would take for the smell of his blood to attract whatever Opiri were in the vicinity.

"Leave me," he said, standing fast against her pull. "Get…out of Tanis. Ares is in the northwest, with…an army. Find him."

"I'm not leaving my husband's son to die here alone."

Her agile strength was too great for him to resist in his current state. They crossed the hall and approached the outer door to the suite. It was unlocked. Trinity released a loud breath and opened it.

There was nobody in the lobby. Trinity pressed the down button on the elevator, her head darting this way and that.

"Listen," she said close to his ear. "There are things you have to know if I don't make it and you do. Anu's supporters live the old way in secret, with dozens of men and women they've stolen out of the human wards to keep as serfs. They want Tanis back the way it used to be. They're preparing to take over."

"We…know," Daniel said hoarsely as the elevator reached their floor.

"I had help, Daniel," she said. "There's a resistance in the city, and serfs here who've risked their lives. Get out, and find the rebels. Look for a man named Hugh, but don't let yourself be seen. Tell Ares…that I'll do what I can from here."

"No," Daniel said, shaking his head wildly. "Come with me."

Instead of arguing with him, she tried to push him into the elevator. He resisted with uncertain strength, turning his weight against her to reverse their positions. Someone shouted from a corridor off the lobby.

The elevator doors closed on Trinity. Daniel turned and braced his feet, watching the guards emerge from the corridor. He struggled as they dragged him back to his cell, hoping that the guards' focus on him would allow Trinity a better chance at escape.

They shackled him in such a way that he could lie down, and exhaustion claimed him soon after. When he woke, Hannibal was there.

"I am told that you tried to help a prisoner escape," he said, almost mildly. "You might be interested to know that she has been taken, and so have the humans who helped her."

"The serfs," Daniel croaked. "You're…so sure you can win."

Hannibal cocked his head. "Palemon never could break you. I will succeed where he failed." He gestured to the guards behind him. They pulled Daniel to his feet, and Hannibal sank his teeth into Daniel's neck.

After that, there was nothing but darkness.

Isis woke to the sound of the camp bustling with activity, voices shouting commands and gear being moved. It took a moment for her to focus her eyes and realize that she was staring up at the roof of the tent, and that she was lying in the same cot they had given her when she had become sick again. She wore a sack-like sleeping gown, slightly damp with perspiration.

"Daniel?" she said, trying to sit up. Dizziness overwhelmed her, but she persevered until she was firmly braced on her arms and could make her voice heard.

"Daniel?"

No one answered. She tried calling Ares, but there was still no response. A little short of breath, she swung her legs over the side of the cot and staggered to the tent flap.

The camp was in disarray as soldiers moved quickly this way and that…not many, she saw, compared to the number she'd seen earlier. They were like ants left behind to tidy the nest after the others had gone raiding.

She looked out of the tent, blinking against the light. One of the hooded soldiers paused as she saw Isis and hurried to join her.

"What is going on?" she asked, grasping a tent pole for support. "Where is Ares?"

"Gone," the soldier said. "Lady Isis, you should not be out of bed."

"Gone where?" Isis demanded, refusing to budge.

"To Tanis. He was summoned by Anu with most of the troops."

"For what purpose?"

"We were not told, Lady." The woman hesitated. "Lord Ares left a message for you. You are to remain here and rest until he returns. You suffered a long illness because of the poison, and you cannot risk moving about too quickly."

"A long illness?" Isis said. "*How* long?"

Once again the soldier hesitated. "Two weeks," she said with obvious reluctance.

Isis felt a swell of alarm. "Where is Daniel?"

The soldier looked genuinely concerned. "We only know that he tried to return to the city alone. We have heard nothing from him since."

Nothing, Isis thought. Either he had made it into Tanis, or he had been captured attempting to do so.

Curse him.

"I must go," Isis said, slipping back into the tent to gather her clothes and her day coat.

"Ares gave orders—" the soldier began, following her into the tent.

"He is not here to enforce them," Isis said. She looked hard at the woman. "And *you* cannot."

The soldier flinched at the hardness in Isis's tone and the push of her influence. "I beg you, my lady…"

Isis began to dress. "I will know exactly what is going on in my city, and if Daniel is there, I *will* find him."

There was nothing more the woman could do, and she knew it. She and her fellow remaining soldiers watched helplessly as Isis donned her day coat and commandeered one of the three horses left in camp.

She reached Tanis at sunset. The fields were abandoned—no humans and Opiri changing shifts, no signs of life outside the city at all save for the presence of the Opir guards outside the gate. They started when they saw her and looked at each other uncertainly.

"Do you not recognize me?" Isis asked. "Open the gates."

With haste, the guards obeyed her. Isis rode into the courtyard and left her mount with the first Opir she met. There were no humans here, either.

When she entered the city proper, she knew that things had gone very wrong in the time she had been away. She walked through her ward, noting broken windows and discarded signs, burn marks on buildings and the utter absence of humans.

But there were Opiri here, most drifting about as if they had no idea where to go. Isis was preparing to approach one of them when Athena rushed up to her, her gray eyes wide and worried.

"Isis!" she said. "Where have you been?"

Isis took Athena's hand and led her away from the street. "What has happened here, Athena?" she asked.

"Are you all right?" Athena asked, as if she hadn't heard Isis's question. "Nobody knew what had become of you."

"I am fine," Isis said. "Have you seen Daniel?"

"Not since his exile. Why do you—"

"Tell me what's happened here."

"The city is in the grip of madness," Athena said. "In just the past two weeks, everything we worked for has come undone."

"How?" Isis asked, grasping Athena's hands.

"The fighting became much worse after you disappeared," Athena said, her gaze darting across the central avenue. "There were more riots and protests by the humans and more attacks by Opiri. Most claimed they fought in self-defense, but there were many instances of humans found with their blood taken against their wills, even a few deaths."

"Killings?" Isis said, horrified but not wholly surprised.

"And increasing reports of humans disappearing," Athena said, distress in her voice. "Humans have avoided the depository, and the stores of blood have diminished. Opiri have panicked." She clutched Isis's arm. "I was asked to take over your ward, but—"

"Where are the humans now?" Isis asked.

"Most of the humans who resided and worked here retreated into the other wards."

"Because I was not here to help them," Isis said. "Where is Anu?"

"He remains in the tower, sending his agents to investigate the troubles."

"And what has he done to end these troubles?"

"He has brought in armed Freeblood soldiers from outside, a force he has kept in training to handle any attacks on Tanis. They are presently protecting the humans."

"Protecting? These soldiers would fight against other Opiri?"

Athena hesitated, lips parted, and Isis knew she had to take the risk. "Athena," she said, "I believe that Anu tried to kill me."

"What?"

"I was poisoned after I accompanied Daniel out of Tanis. Tainted blood. That is why I have been gone so long."

"By the infernal Styx," Athena swore. "Why? How can you be sure?"

"He now views me as an enemy, because he knows I will stand firm against his plans for Tanis."

"His plans?"

"These troubles did not come about on their own. Someone set them off."

"And you believe Anu is involved?"

"Yes. Athena, Ares never left the city. Anu blackmailed him into training an army by threatening his wife, Trinity, who is incarcerated in Tanis. The army is under Anu's command. I do not believe it is here to protect humans, but to hold them prisoner."

"But what does Anu want?"

"To be a god again, with thousands of humans at his feet. And to get that, he has bribed the most influential Opiri in Tanis with new Households and serfs stolen from the human population."

Clearly astonished, Athena looked toward the tower. "I believe you," she said suddenly. "I would not let myself see how Anu was changing. But if he built an army without telling us, and forced Ares to serve him..."

"There is more," Isis said. "Daniel is Ares's son—I will explain later—and he has returned to the city to try to free Trinity."

"I am sorry, Isis," Athena said, clasping her hands. "I know nothing of this."

"Then either he has managed to get in and stay free,

or he was taken in secret. Anu will surely question him if he can. I must get to the tower and try to find out what is happening."

"You will go to Anu, knowing he might try to kill you again?"

"He will be thrown off his guard by my appearance. And I must know if he has Daniel."

"Then I will go with you."

"If you show yourself as my ally, your life may be in danger."

"If what you say is true, I would not be your only ally," Athena said.

They walked directly and openly to the tower, Isis making certain that the Opiri they passed saw their faces. Their only real protection now was their visibility, and the questions that would be asked if either or both of them disappeared.

They met not a single human along the way, and Isis fretted over Ares and the army. What orders had they been given, and would Ares carry them out?

Trust us, Ares, she thought. *We will find a way to free your mate.*

No one tried to stop them as they ascended to Anu's suite. The guards posted there seemed surprised to see Isis, but they quickly let her and Athena enter.

The room was populated by its usual contingent of favorites, courtiers and liveried guards…many of whom, Isis thought, must be among those who had returned to the old way of serfs and masters. Anu surged out of his seat when he saw Isis.

"Isis!" he said, extending his hands. "You are well! We feared that—"

"I am grateful for your concern," Isis said, striding up

to the throne, "but I am astonished at how bad the city has become. How could it get so far?"

Clearly taken aback, Anu dropped his arms. "Where have you been, Isis? You left to observe the expulsion of your human lover and could not be found by any of my searchers."

"I became very ill," she said. "I did not recover for two weeks."

There was no sign of guilt on Anu's aquiline features, nor did he ask her who had taken care of her. "What illness could keep you away so long?"

"It was almost as if I was poisoned with tainted blood."

Anu's courtiers murmured among themselves. Anu silenced them with a downward sweep of his hand.

"Did you take anything from the exiles, from any human?" he asked.

"No. The last blood I took was from Lawkeepers who were escorting me back to Tanis."

Stunned silence fell over the room. Anu took his seat and rested his chin on his fist.

"Lawkeepers," he said. "No Lawkeeper would harm one of the Nine."

"Yet I can find no other explanation," Isis said, holding Anu's stare. "I was left to die."

"If this is true, it is only more evidence of a conspiracy within Tanis," Anu said.

"A conspiracy?" Isis said.

"You asked how the city could have descended so far. It did not happen by accident."

"You think the Lawkeepers are involved?"

"Not until this moment." He lifted his head from his fist. "Can you name these half-bloods?"

"I would know them if I saw them again."

"I will have Hermes call them to the tower in small

groups, so that none will suspect that they will be questioned."

Isis inclined her head, but her mind was racing. So Anu was suggesting a conspiracy, when he himself was surely at the center of it?

Why shouldn't he speak of it? she thought. Who would seriously suspect Anu unless he or she had Isis's experiences and knowledge…or was one of his allies among the Opiri or the Nine? He could so easily deflect any idle suspicion by acknowledging that something had turned rotten at Tanis's core.

"Where does this conspiracy originate?" she asked him.

"I fear that human rebels are involved," Anu said, "though what they intend remains unclear. We will soon know the truth. And now that you have returned safely, you must join with us in presenting a united front to our people."

"What of the army guarding the humans?"

Anu glanced at Athena. "That is an unfortunate, but temporary, necessity, both for security and protection. I have explained to the others why it was necessary to keep the force's existence secret, so that no outsider spy could learn we had readied defenses against an attack."

"And what is being done with Opiri who injure or kill humans?"

"This situation will not last," Anu said, absolute confidence in his voice. "I have called a meeting of the Nine and the Council for midnight. Everything will be explained there. For now…" He smiled at Athena. "Please attend Isis in her quarters here. We would not wish her to become ill again."

"Of course," Athena said.

"I will send servants to collect your things from your ward apartments, Isis," he said. "Rest while you can."

With that, Anu seemed to dismiss them, though Isis

could feel his stare on her back as she and Athena left the suite. They took the elevator to her long-unused quarters. As Isis was considering what next to try, human servants entered to remove the dustcovers from the furniture and pad quietly about the suite, making it fit for habitation. Isis waited until they were finished and drew Athena to a couch in the sitting room.

"What are your observations?" she asked Athena.

"Anu is hiding something," Athena said. "I have no reason to disbelieve anything you have told me. I will give you whatever help I can."

"You said you wouldn't be my only ally."

"I will approach Bes, and my most trusted companions. Without further proof that Anu has actually caused the troubles in Tanis…"

"He isn't alone. Hannibal is part of it, but he must be afraid of what I might say of him to Anu. He is the one who told us about Anu's scheme, under duress. But he could also do us much damage." She touched Athena's arm. "I must find Daniel, and Trinity if possible. You've heard nothing about prisoners in the towers?"

Athena clasped her hands in her lap. "There is a place in the tower that I have not seen," she said, "an abandoned Household. I have heard rumors that special prisoners are being kept there, the worst of the troublemakers. If they caught Daniel attempting to return to the city, he might be there, as well."

"You have no idea where it is?"

"If anyone else would know, it would be Hermes, since he still guides the Lawkeepers."

"Could he have known that some of his half-bloods tried to kill me?"

"I cannot believe it. They must be working directly for Anu."

"Then speak to Hermes, if you can find him. I do not

care what you tell him, but see if he knows anything about Daniel."

"I will," Athena said, rising. "Be patient, Isis. Remain here. I will return as soon as I have learned anything of use."

Isis's patience had almost run out when Athena returned.

"I found Hermes," she said. "I didn't tell him about the incident with the Lawkeepers who attempted to poison you, or of our fears about Anu, but I know he senses that something is wrong. He told me where to find the prisoners' cells. We can only hope that Daniel is there."

Unless he is dead, Isis thought. But her heart told her otherwise.

Only a half hour before the midnight meeting was to take place, one of Hermes's favorites, dressed as plainly as a servant, came to fetch Isis. He led her by back ways between and behind the Household suites through a series of narrow staircases and corridors built so that human serfs could come and go quietly when they served their Opir masters.

One of the corridors opened onto a dim stairwell, and the stairs led to the rear chambers of an abandoned Household that stank of stale urine, blood and perspiration. Isis's hair stood on end. She tried to breathe evenly, and caught a single thread of scent among all the others.

Daniel. Alive.

Chapter 24

"Go," Isis whispered to Hermes's Opir. "I will find my way back."

Without hesitation, her guide vanished. Isis crept into a wider corridor with cell doors, dozens of them running along each wall. Groans and cries followed her progress as she followed the scent, and she felt as if she had been poisoned all over again.

She found Daniel in one of the cells midway down the hall. The smells of sweat and blood were almost overwhelming, and she choked as she put her hand on the lock and pulled.

The door refused to move. "Daniel?" she called. "Can you hear me?"

There was no answer. She pulled harder, using all of her strength, and the door creaked. Righteous rage coursed through her, and she nearly tore the door off its hinges.

Swallowing again and again, she stepped into the cell and looked down at the shape huddled on the filthy floor. Daniel was curled in on himself; his bare legs were a mass of bruises and raised welts, and his face was a patchwork of black and purple. One eye was swollen shut, but she knew when the other one saw her.

"Isis?" he croaked, bracing his arms against the wall. He struggled to stand, but she fell to her knees and stopped him.

"Daniel," she whispered. "Oh, Daniel."

"You…should not be here," he said, his voice as ravaged as his body. "They will find you."

Isis had no intention of getting into a pointless argument. She pulled him up, doing her best to disregard the ugliness of his condition, and half supported him to the door of the cell.

From some inner reservoir, he found strength to help her and take most of his weight on his own legs. Isis guided him toward the rear of the Household, stepping in anytime he stumbled, and all too slowly they arrived at the stairwell.

"Go…ahead of me," Daniel whispered, the words sawing in his throat. "I'll catch up."

Isis stepped in front of him. "Move slowly. I will be here if you fall."

Daniel must have recognized the futility of disputing her. He began to descend, bracing himself against the side walls of the stairwell. Isis remained close enough to feel his ragged breath on the back of her neck.

But he never lost his balance or stumbled again. At the foot of the stairs, he leaned heavily against the wall, his body trembling and fresh blood running from his more recent wounds.

Though it was dangerous to take the time, Isis knew that she had to help him heal, even if just enough to stop the bleeding.

She helped him to sit and, ignoring his faint protests, bit his neck as gently as she could. She released the healing chemicals into his bloodstream, praying that her efforts would bear fruit.

After several minutes he pushed her away weakly. "I'm all right," he said.

Isis saw that his bleeding had stopped, the worst of his wounds beginning to close as if they had been stitched by an expert hand.

She helped him get up and led him carefully along the corridor, constantly listening for sounds of discovery or pursuit.

They were following a curving passage that ran just inside the wall of the tower when she heard the voices. They were barely audible, but they were not far ahead.

She didn't ask if Daniel could fight. He would try; he would most likely attempt to protect *her*, as if she were the one who had been tortured. Retreating was out of the question; they were as likely to meet guards in the cell block as they were in this corridor, and here, at least, only one enemy could come at them at a time.

They would have to keep moving.

"Stay behind me, Daniel," she said. "If you try to fight, you will put us both at risk."

He shuddered. "Not for me," he said. "Go back, Isis."

The sound of softly moving feet stopped abruptly just around the curve of the corridor. She heard rough breathing and footsteps approaching from just out of sight. Isis prepared herself, knowing that she would use her influence to the fullest extent to save Daniel.

"Who are you?" a voice called out softly.

So there would be words instead of immediate attack. Isis didn't let down her guard. "I know you," she said in the same low tone. "Loukas?"

"Isis." The Opir came into view, his pale skin like a beacon in the darkness. "Daniel?"

"Why are you here?" she challenged.

"Athena sent me to find you, and I quite literally ran into these humans." He gestured behind him, and she recognized another familiar face: Hugh, the human who had so gruffly asked for her help, along with his companions

Kevin and Jessica. She could see several others with them, hear their shuffling feet and fast-beating hearts.

"Serfs," Loukas said. "We're getting them out of the tower." He peered past her uneasily. "Someone could find us anytime."

"How are you getting out?" she asked.

"Follow us."

Loukas turned and disappeared around the bend. Isis had already made her decision. She glanced at Daniel, who nodded, and they fell in behind Hugh, Jessica, Kevin and—ahead of them—a ragtag group of five humans.

Moving at a fast pace, they began to descend successive sets of stairs. She turned frequently to check on Daniel, whose face was drawn with pain and exhaustion. He met her worried glances with eyes blazing defiance, and she knew he would falter only if his body collapsed under him.

Still, she was profoundly grateful when they reached the bottom of the stairs and found a regular corridor again. It was short, and ended at a door that might lead anywhere.

"Lady Isis," Hugh whispered. "We're on the bottom floor of the tower. From here, we go underground."

Without waiting for her reply, Hugh turned away again and helped Loukas pull up part of the floor, the edges so well disguised that Isis might never have noticed the trap-door.

"There is a ladder here," Loukas told her, frowning toward Daniel. "Can he make it?"

"Don't worry about me," Daniel said. He swallowed a cough. "Go ahead."

One by one the humans descended into darkness. Loukas followed. Hugh remained behind.

"I'll go last," Hugh said. "Go on."

Isis dropped into the hole, gripping the rungs of the ladder and pausing until she was sure Daniel was strong enough to follow. Blood dropped onto her cheek. She continued down, watching Daniel carefully place his feet and clutch at the side rails with clawed fingers.

Somehow, they made it to the bottom and to a tunnel just high enough to allow the tallest of them to walk upright. Then began a journey in darkness, Loukas in the lead to guide the humans, Hugh still taking up the rear. They moved through tunnel after tunnel, and Isis sensed that they were approaching the center of the city.

Abruptly Hugh took the lead and guided the party into a much lower tunnel that opened into a small, dimly lit but well-built room furnished with simple chairs and a table. There was a door on the other side, and Isis realized that they had probably been paralleling the official network of tunnels once used by serfs and poor Freebloods during the heyday of the Citadel.

The humans fell into the chairs without any prodding, and Daniel slumped against one of the stone walls. He slid to the ground, his chest heaving, and Isis knelt beside him.

"I'm all right," he rasped, flinching away when she tried to touch him.

"He needs medical attention," Isis said, looking toward Hugh.

"We'll do what we can," Hugh said, "but we're not in any position to contact a human physician now." He crouched before Daniel. "Can you keep going?"

"By the Eldest, let him rest!" Isis cried. "He was beaten to within an inch of his life."

"So were some of the other serfs."

Isis kept her rage inside. "How many Opiri are keeping serfs now?" she asked.

"We don't know," Hugh said. "But one of them escaped, and he was able to confirm that Anu's behind this." He turned his head and spat. "A few Opiri have offered to help us. We have some in the resistance now, and we've managed to get a few more serfs out of the towers."

"Do you know about the quarantine of the human citizens by Anu's secret army?"

"Yes," Hugh said heavily. "And Loukas has told us about the hostage being held here to ensure the commander's cooperation."

"Trinity," Daniel said, bracing himself on his arms. "She escaped. She found me...in the cell. She was in the elevator heading down...when she left."

"Where was she going?" Isis asked.

"I told her to...try to find Hugh."

"She never got to us," Hugh said.

"We must get to Ares."

Daniel pushed himself to his feet, blocking the shriek of pain along his nerves. Isis stared at him with open concern, but all he felt was shame.

For two weeks he had been a prisoner, treated with less dignity and compassion than a rat in these tunnels, and all the old memories had come flooding back. The man he had been since he had escaped Erebus was drowning in those memories, and he wasn't sure he could ever find his way to the surface.

And yet he hadn't stopped fighting. Not as long as Ares and Trinity and the others in danger needed any help he could give.

Not as long as Isis believed in him, even when he couldn't bear her touch.

"Will telling Ares about Trinity not put him in an impossible position, when we still don't know her fate?" Isis asked.

"He must know," Daniel said, his voice almost unrecognizable to his own ears. "His men can help search for her, and no one will question them."

Isis carefully took his bloodied hand, and he managed

not to pull away in self-disgust. "Hugh will also alert the resistance to watch for her," she said.

"And there may…also be a way for Ares to pretend to obey Anu and still…turn the army against him," Daniel said.

"Wouldn't Ares have done that already, if he could?" Hugh asked.

"Only if he's thinking clearly. Under the circumstances…" Daniel shifted his weight and held very still until the waves of pain passed through his body. "Isis… you stay with Hugh and the others."

"You know I will not stand idly by," she said, her delicate chin jutting defiantly. "I will not be separated from you again."

Daniel looked away. He knew why she was so afraid for him. He knew why she would never let him out of her sight, because he knew what it had been like for his father where Trinity was concerned.

Isis loved him.

And he knew he wasn't worthy. He never had been.

"Can you assign someone to get us to Ares's soldiers… in the quarantined wards?" Daniel asked Hugh.

The big man nodded. "It'll be risky, because we'll have to move into the main tunnels to get there."

"If you can tell us the way—"

"No. I'll see to it myself." Hugh turned to Jessica. "Get these other people to the safe house. Kevin, inform our people about Trinity. Tell them I'll be back as soon as I can."

They reached the human wards an hour later, moving cautiously from the narrow tunnels used by the resistance to the paved passages dug out at the time of the founding of Tartaros. They were extremely lucky not to have been seen.

Even so, Daniel kept as physically close to Isis as he

dared...as if he could defend her better than she could herself, he with his battered body and unstable mind.

Ares's army had cordoned off two of the human neighborhoods, Bes's and Hera's, to contain most of the city's human population. But when Hugh, Isis and Daniel cautiously emerged from a passage hidden in an uninhabited apartment, they soon found that only a fraction of the army had been left to "protect" their charges.

Isis convinced Daniel that she should be the one to approach Ares's soldiers, since she would attract less attention than a known resistance member or a bloodied human with torn and dirty clothing. Daniel watched from cover as she boldly walked up to one of the Freebloods and spoke to him with a familiarity that suggested she'd met him when she had been recovering in Ares's care.

She hurried back after only a couple of minutes, her expression strained with worry.

"Ares has been commanded to meet Anu at the tower," she said, holding Daniel's gaze. "His troops are supposed to have been secretly deployed to the other towers inhabited by Opiri."

"Why?" Daniel asked. "Why guard the Opiri when he intends to give the Citadel back to them?"

"I do not know," Isis said.

"Hugh?" Daniel asked.

"It makes no sense," the human said.

"Whatever the reason," Daniel said, "Anu may have sudden doubts about Ares's loyalty. If Trinity escaped, he wouldn't want Ares to know about it. But if he recaptured her..." A crazy thought came into his mind. "We have to convince the remaining soldiers here to come with us to the tower."

"I do not understand your reasoning," Isis said, alarm evident behind the even tone of her voice.

"Deception won't work, and neither will secrecy. Ares

virtually controls the city now. Anu won't be expecting us to march right in with the soldiers left to watch the humans."

"And then?"

"With the humans unguarded, the resistance will have a little breathing room, at the very least. If Trinity is still on the move, we'll buy a little more time for her."

"And if Trinity has been recaptured?"

"We'll deal with that problem when we come to it."

"Why would you put yourself in Anu's hands again?" Isis asked.

"I won't hide anymore, Isis. If I have to, I'll challenge Anu himself."

"You want revenge, even at the cost of your own life."

"I want to give this city a chance at survival."

"You know that you are quite mad."

More than you can understand, Daniel thought. "There's nothing sane about any of this."

For a while she simply stared at him. "How do you expect to get the soldiers to obey you?" She hesitated. "I shall have to use my influence to—"

"No," he said. "*I* need to do this, Isis. I'm Ares's son."

Isis closed her eyes. Daniel was a natural leader. Men *did* listen to him.

And he was half-god. Now he would have to play the part.

"I believe in you," she said.

He smiled, dissolving all her remaining doubts. "Hugh," he said, "stay back. We may need you to arrange a distraction if this doesn't work. Isis—"

"Do not even ask," she said with a crooked smile.

He wanted to kiss her. Filthy and beaten as he was, he wanted to make love to her. But this was hardly the right time.

Moving cautiously from the abandoned building, Daniel and Isis crept toward the soldier Isis had questioned before. He had been joined by several others, who were deep in conversation. They looked with surprise at Daniel, but made no hostile move. To the contrary, their attitudes were respectful, and Daniel began to believe that their loyalty for Ares extended to him.

"You are safe," one of them said. He looked Daniel over with a flash of anger. "Lord Ares feared for you. He has been trying to find you since rumor came to him that you had been captured. He gave orders that if you made contact with any of us, we should protect you."

"I don't need protection," Daniel said. "I need your cooperation." He scanned the area and dropped into a crouch. "Why was Ares summoned by Anu?"

The young Freeblood's expression hinted at rebellion. "Something has changed." He hesitated. "There is a new rumor that Anu intends to kill all the Opiri in Tanis."

"That is impossible!" Isis said.

Daniel touched her, though it was one of the most difficult things he had ever done. "There's more to his plan than we knew," he said. He addressed the four soldiers. "I need you to gather the others watching the human wards and bring them to me. We're going to Anu's court."

The soldier's eyes lit with astonishment. "You want us to disobey orders?"

"Orders Ares was forced to give," Daniel said. "If he's been compelled to slaughter a third of Tanis's population, I have to try to stop him." He stared at each of the soldiers in turn. "You can come with me, or stay behind. The choice is up to you."

Drawing apart, the soldiers consulted in hushed voices. Daniel didn't try to listen. He took stock of himself, of the wounds finally beginning to heal and the strength returning to his body. He looked at Isis, who gazed at him with such deep emotion that he was momentarily caught up in his feelings for her, feelings he could no more control than he could influence the movement of the tides or the turn of the seasons.

"You may die," she said in a harsh whisper. "Daniel, think again."

"Would you take the risk of seeing your own people murdered?"

"Would you make me pit your life against theirs?"

"*Your* life means Tanis's survival." With all his courage, he took her hands in his. "Your dreams represent everything that was good in Tanis. If you come with me—"

"Again, Daniel?" She smiled tenderly. "The argument is already settled."

"If I knew how to stop you—"

"You cannot." She leaned into him, oblivious of the dirt and blood. "Daniel, I love you."

Chapter 25

Isis watched Daniel's face for his reaction, her heart leaping into her throat. She had known it for so long, but to say the words, to admit to what so few Opiri seemed capable of feeling…

Her heart seemed to stop when she saw the look in his eyes. There was a change in him she hadn't recognized until this moment. In spite of his boldness and courage, no matter how much he'd tried to hide it, the imprisonment and torture had had their effects. A gulf had opened up between them: a goddess on one side, a serf on the other.

And he was afraid to cross that gulf. Old wounds had been reopened. Her people had done this to him. He would overcome the pain and shame as he had before, but what would be the price of that recovery? Any hope of love between them?

"I should not have spoken," she said, looking away. "I am sorry."

Daniel reached out for her, stopped, then dropped his hand. "No, Isis," he said. "Your feelings…mean a lot to me. I just don't know who I am anymore."

"Then I will try to help you find what you have lost. We will face Anu together, whatever may come of it."

Daniel opened his mouth to speak, but he closed it

again when the soldiers returned. "We will obey you," the spokesman said to Daniel. "We will gather all the soldiers we can."

"Then scatter," Daniel said, "and meet us at the base of the tower as quickly as you can get there."

The soldiers dispersed, and Daniel, Isis and Hugh began to make their way back to the tunnels. It took them the better part of an hour to reach the tower. Daniel's face was a study in stubborn determination as he struggled to keep pace.

Hugh led them to another covered shaft that ended beneath the overhang of the ramp that led from the lower city to the elevated base of the tower. The sun had risen over the open part of the city, muffling Tanis with its brightness.

About two dozen of Ares's soldiers were waiting, hiding wherever they could find convenient shadows.

"We can't go in using the hidden passages we escaped by," Daniel told them, his breath coming short. "This will be a frontal assault. Have your weapons ready, but don't use them unless I order it." He turned to Hugh. "You've done enough. Get yourself to safety."

Hugh nodded and vanished back down the shaft. The soldiers fell into ranks behind Isis and Daniel.

"We don't know what's going to happen," Daniel said, holding Isis's gaze. "I only know that whatever we risk now, it's better than the alternative."

She caught his face between her hands, very gently, and searched his eyes. "Remember what I told you, Daniel."

"I will never forget it."

Daniel looked away, and they entered the lobby with its three evenly spaced elevators. The area was still deserted, as if Anu could not imagine needing guards at the tower.

That, Isis thought, was not a good sign.

"Half of you come with us in the elevator," Daniel told the soldiers. "The rest follow as soon as you can. If there are obstacles at the top, do whatever you have to do to take them out."

Isis winced at his ruthlessness, but she knew mercy was a luxury now. She had chosen to follow Daniel, and she would not question his decisions.

They met no one until they entered the lobby outside Anu's suite. A dozen Opiri stood guard there, weapons raised as the elevator doors opened.

The ten soldiers who had squeezed into the elevator with Isis and Daniel rushed out, and Isis quickly stepped between them and Anu's guards.

"Stop!" she cried, raising her hands. "I command you to put your weapons down. We would not have your blood on our hands."

Anu's guards faltered and lowered their weapons. Ares's soldiers quickly took advantage of their hesitation and moved in fast, slamming into their opponents and disarming them with little struggle.

"Is Anu inside?" Daniel asked one of the defeated Opiri.

"You," the Opir said with belated recognition. "He will kill you."

The second group of Ares's soldiers arrived, and Daniel ordered several of them to stand watch over the captives. "Shoot them if they move," he said.

Isis joined him and the other soldiers as they burst into the dimly lit room, coming upon a tableau she had never expected to find. It took her a moment to realize what was wrong.

The dark-haired Opir who sat on the throne was not Anu. At first she didn't recognize him. The sharper features, the toothy smile, the bare chest and bullet-shaped crown. He had Anu's coloring, like most of the Nine. He was familiar, and yet…

"Hannibal," Daniel said.

Isis followed his gaze from the heavily armed guards

behind Hannibal to the new set of courtiers and the four members of the Nine who stood below him on the dais. Sprawled across the floor in a wide semicircle knelt at least a hundred humans, foreheads pressed to the floor. Men in the garments of ancient priests stood among them, chanting songs of praise.

And between them and the dais stood a lovely young dhampir woman with auburn hair and hazel eyes, her expression defiant and fearful, chained to the floor by a collar and manacles around her wrists.

Trinity, Isis thought. She could guess the reason for the woman's fear. Ares faced Hannibal with clenched fists and the clear desire to tear the Opir's throat out.

"If you attempt to harm me in any way," Hannibal was saying, "your mate will die."

"Where is Anu?" Daniel demanded, striding up to the dais.

"Indisposed," Hannibal said. "Welcome to my court, Daniel."

"Who *are* you?"

Ares spun around, taking in Daniel's battered appearance with a single hard glance. Isis came to stand beside Daniel.

"He calls himself Ba'al," Ares said. "Lord Ba'al, who once posed as Palemon's right hand in Erebus."

"Posed, indeed," the Opir now called Ba'al said with a slight inclination of his head. "It is simple enough to change the color of one's skin and hair by chemical means. And to change them back."

"Ba'al," Isis said. "God of Phoenicia." *And as ancient*, she thought, *as any of them*. An Elder as powerful as Anu.

"It was his plan to conquer Erebus and rule as a tyrant," Ares said. "I knew nothing of this when I defeated him and cast him out of the Citadel."

Ba'al shot Ares a poisonous glare. "*You* are the defeated

one now," he said. He looked from Isis to Daniel and back again. "When I was exiled from Erebus, I searched for another Citadel to take as my own. It was remarkably easy to gain Anu's confidence. I manipulated him as he manipulated others, because he was not aware of my power. He did not know that I was also a god. And his superior."

"You've killed him, haven't you?" Daniel asked, his head high.

"He learned of his mistake too late," Ba'al said. "He did not expect that a mere Opir could destroy the mighty leader of the Nine." He clucked his tongue. "Perhaps if he had cooperated, like my most loyal servants…" He waved his hand toward Ereshkigal, Hera, Hermes and Bes.

Bes, Isis thought. *Not you.*

And why had Hermes helped her find Daniel in his cell, if he had committed himself to this new and highly ambitious usurper? Had he felt a moment of regret?

"Where are Athena, Hephaestus and Ishtar?" she asked Ba'al.

"I will find them."

"The way you found Isis when she disappeared for two weeks?" Daniel asked. "Or did you believe she was already dead?"

"I did not need to find her," Ba'al said. "She has returned to me." He flashed his teeth at Isis, showing off cuspids filed to even sharper points. "Anu knew you would be first to oppose his plans, Lady Isis, as he knew that you had the power to draw humans and Opiri to you. But he hesitated to take action against you. I was the one to convince him to give you the tainted blood."

"You failed to kill her," Daniel said through clenched teeth.

Ba'al narrowed his eyes. "And what of you, Daniel? Even in exile, I learned everything about the time after your escape from Erebus—how you became a leader of humans and even Opiri, a person of some distinction among your colonies." He toyed with a golden bracelet on one arm. "I helped Anu to understand that you, mere human that you appeared to be, were dangerous even apart from your relationship with Isis."

"Did *you* try to kill Daniel at the Games?" Isis asked, giving Ba'al a clear glimpse of her own white teeth.

"A warning," Ba'al said. "One neither of you heeded." He narrowed his eyes. "Did you think Anu would have shown you mercy?"

"Anu was returning Tanis to the old ways," Daniel said. "But you want something else, don't you?"

"Anu thought like a human," Ba'al said with obvious contempt. "He saw only small things. He imagined a city where his chosen servants and allies would regain their serfs and Households, and he would still hold a third of the humans for himself, to worship him as he so desired."

"He wanted both," Isis said. "Opiri to rule, and humans to conquer with his will."

"Yes," Ba'al said. "He created chaos in Tanis so that he would have the excuse to bring in his secret army to round up the humans and confine them until he could put his plan into effect."

"But most Opiri in Tanis would have opposed him!" Isis said.

"Many, yes. But Anu had a plan to be rid of the rebellious ones once he had the humans in hand. A plan I have gladly taken up."

"To kill the Opiri in the towers," Daniel said.

"Except those who have sworn allegiance to me," Ba'al said. "Those who have agreed to aid my army will help eradicate the rest."

"He lies," Ares said, addressing the courtiers. "He won't allow his supposed allies to keep Households. Like Anu, he intends to return to the ancient past and rule as a true god. But he'll permit only a handful of Opiri to survive, including these four—" he jerked his head toward the other members of the Nine "—as his acolytes."

"He can't control two thousand humans," Daniel said, "no matter how powerful he thinks he is."

"I am *not* Anu," Ba'al said. "His limitations are not mine. Before the coming of the upstarts like Yahweh, I controlled hundreds of thousands. I will again."

"You forget that you're not really a god," Daniel said. "You're still only an Elder Opir. You can't make the rain fall or the moon rise."

Ba'al ignored him and turned to Ares. "You have your orders. Obey them, or I will make this female suffer."

"No, Ares!" Trinity said.

Ares took a step toward the throne. Daniel caught his father's arm, while Ba'al grabbed Trinity's chain in his fist and yanked her toward him. Trinity's face went white.

"Will none of you oppose him?" Isis demanded of her former peers.

"They understand their own interests," Ba'al said. "And so they will survive when you are dead." He pulled Trinity very close and smiled at Ares. "I can destroy her in an instant. Your time has run out."

Isis stepped forward. "Not if I challenge you for rule of Tanis."

The priests' chanting stopped. The guards shifted their weapons. Someone gasped.

"You would fight me?" Ba'al said with open amusement. "Isis the gentle, the good, the loving mother?"

"No," Daniel said, stepping between her and Ba'al. He turned his back on the god and faced her. "You can't," he said softly. "I told you before, Isis. You were never meant to kill."

"You would say or do anything to protect me."

"Anything, Isis. For *you*."

She stared at him, trying to make him feel what she felt: her love for him, her pride in his courage, her determination that he would not have suffered in vain. But her efforts were interrupted by the crack of a whip, and the curling tail of leather tore the remaining rags of Daniel's shirt from his back, laying bare old scars and newer wounds.

With a cry of unbridled anger, Isis leaped between him and Ba'al. The god smiled as he coiled the whip. Daniel caught Isis, blood running down his fingers, and put her behind him again. She felt him gathering his strength, his heart pumping, his breathing labored.

"You will not fight him, Lady Isis," he said. "*I* will."

Ba'al burst into laughter. "You—a serf, a piece of property?"

"You said I was dangerous," Daniel said. "Are you afraid of me?"

Ba'al sprang to his feet, his expression twisted with contempt. "You would die in a heartbeat."

"Then you have nothing to fear."

In sudden rage, Ba'al cracked the whip at Daniel. Daniel caught the fall of the whip in his fist and dragged Ba'al halfway off the dais before the Elder stopped himself and pulled free.

"Kill him," Ba'al instructed the guards.

Immediately Ba'al's Opir guards took aim. Isis cried out. Ares charged toward the dais and only stopped when the guards trained their rifles at Trinity's head.

"If you will not accept a challenge from a half-blood," Daniel said, standing straight and unbowed, "you must accept one from another god."

His face a mask of fury, Ba'al gave an ugly laugh. "Ares cannot touch me," he sneered. "Guards—"

"You know what I am," Daniel said. "Ares is my father."

"I remember the great revelation in Erebus," Ba'al said, "and the shame it brought down upon Ares's head."

"Shame?" Ares asked. "You were as poor at observation then as you are now." He smiled. "He is half-Opir, and he has the right to challenge you."

Isis expected Ba'al to laugh again, to declare that a half-blood—son of a god or not—was no fit opponent...to remind them that no dhampir or Darketan had ever formally challenged a full Opir in living memory.

Because, Isis thought, no half-blood in the Citadels had ever been given the chance. But Ba'al was far from stupid. He *could* refuse, but it would paint him a coward in the eyes of the few allies he might actually need...the four of the Nine below him on the dais. He noticed when Hera and Ereshkigal shifted and exchanged glances, waiting for his answer.

He had to believe that he had every advantage, Isis thought. Challenges were fought hand to hand, body to body and teeth to teeth. Daniel was lacking one essential weapon.

Daniel looked at Isis and smiled with warmth and encouragement—he exchanged glances with his father and then walked between the genuflecting humans to stand at the foot of the dais.

"I challenge you, Ba'al," he said formally, "by the ancient traditions of the Opiri. If you refuse or I defeat you, you will surrender your property and be expelled from this Citadel."

"What?" Ba'al asked, nearly spitting the word. "You would not *kill* me?"

"Only if I must."

At this moment, Isis thought, Ba'al appeared less enraged than genuinely confounded. But as Daniel stared at him, he began to smile.

"By all means," he said, removing the jewelry from his arms and around his neck. "Since I am challenged, I choose the time. It will be now."

Ba'al descended from the throne and disappeared through a door in the wall behind it. His guards followed close on his heels.

"Boy," Ares said to Daniel, his voice unsteady, "you're a fool."

Trinity stared from her mate to Daniel with tears in her eyes. "I'm sorry," she whispered.

"It's done," Daniel said.

Ares met Isis's gaze. He *knew* how she felt. He knew because he couldn't bear to lose the woman on the dais.

But he wouldn't try to stop Daniel, and neither would Isis. They wouldn't dishonor him by taking his choices away from him. They wouldn't steal what remained of his pride.

The humans kneeling on the floor looked up with bewildered faces as Daniel returned to Isis. He reached for her hand, noticed the streaks of blood on his skin, and dropped his arm.

She grabbed his hand as it fell to his side. "You will not escape me so easily, Daniel," she said. "Ba'al still does not realize that he cannot control you with his influence."

"I know." He gazed into her eyes, blinked and looked again.

"You're crying," he breathed. He brushed his thumb across her cheek and caught an errant tear. "That's impossible."

"It isn't so for the Elders," she said, glancing away. "It makes us different from other Opiri, like our skin and hair."

"God." He took her face between his hands and kissed her cheeks, one and then the other. "Don't weep for me, Isis."

"Because you are not worth it?" She pressed his hand against her chest, just over her heart. "You say I am not a fighter, but if Ba'al harms you—"

"You'll run the instant he pulls me down," he said. "You'll find allies. You'll survive to take Tanis back."

"Perhaps I do not wish to survive without you."

"But you will." He kissed her very lightly on the lips, as if he feared he would soil her. "Knowing that will give me strength."

"You will not lose," she said fiercely. "I have faith in you."

They fell silent as a human servant approached with a clean tunic and pants. Surprised by the gesture, Isis helped Daniel find a place where he could change. The closest they could get to privacy was in a darker corner of the room.

Daniel began to remove his torn and bloodied clothing. The ragged shirt stuck to his skin when he tried to pull it off, and there was hardly an inch of his body that hadn't been injured. The marks of Hannibal's whip had barely stopped bleeding.

"It doesn't matter," he said, noticing her stare.

Isis clenched her fists until her nails bit into her palms. The anger was there. Oh, yes. And it was powerful, this searing rage, this desire for revenge.

In Egypt, Sekhmet the lioness had been a deity of war and vengeance. If Isis gave way to this anger, she would become exactly like the goddess whose mask she had worn at the Festival.

But Sekhmet was also a goddess of healing. "You know that I can help with your wounds," she said to Daniel, keeping her voice level and calm.

Working his left shoulder, Daniel couldn't quite hide a wince of pain. Isis didn't wait for his permission. She locked her arms around his waist and bit him through the scar tissue and the more recent bites, releasing the healing chemicals into his veins. He jerked free after a few moments, holding her away from him.

Then he lifted her head and kissed her—hungrily, desperately, with a sense of finality that chilled Isis to the bone.

Chapter 26

The rising hum of voices drove them apart. Isis tried to hold Daniel, gripping his hand as if she could keep him from the inevitable. But he only kissed her forehead and eyelids with great tenderness, worked his hand free of hers and walked out into the room.

Ba'al had returned to the foot of the dais. He wore only a kilt and padded gracefully on bare feet. Isis knew that he was a true predator, more than Anu had ever been, and he clearly intended to fight like one.

But Daniel was also prepared. He moved with surprising agility in spite of his wounds, his head slightly down, his face expressionless. Isis walked beside him to the dais, holding her anger in check. If the worst happened, she would need the element of surprise, the chance to reveal the full force of her nature when it would be most effective.

The room seemed to have one heartbeat now, both the humans' and Opiri's pulses falling into a single, terrible rhythm. Ares lightly rested his hand on Daniel's shoulder, careful not to put pressure on his wounds, and clasped the back of Daniel's head in a gesture of deep affection. Then he stepped away, and so did Isis.

Ares's soldiers formed a loose circle in the center of the room, creating a living arena. Ba'al and Daniel faced each other in the center. Half-crouched, Ba'al's fingers curled into claws. He bared his teeth to expose his cuspids.

Daniel had none to display, but he flashed Ba'al a mocking grin. It was enough to provoke the god into attack.

Isis's gaze remained fixed on Daniel: each feint, each retreat, each time he scarcely avoided the bite that could take his life. She watched him seem to weaken, and then suddenly find enough strength to force Ba'al back; his kicks and punches were almost too fast for the eye to detect, even though Ba'al retained the advantage of natural weapons Daniel didn't possess.

But if Ba'al tried to use his influence to slow Daniel or daze him, the effort failed. Each time his teeth snapped close to Daniel's neck, Daniel dodged and counterattacked. Red stained his shirt where his deepest wounds broke open with his exertion, but he paid no attention to blood or pain.

It soon became clear that Ba'al would not attain victory as easily as he had expected. With every minute, his frustration became more apparent, his attacks less measured. Daniel maintained a detached sense of calm, as if he had no stake in whether he lived or died.

Perhaps he doesn't, Isis thought in panic, remembering Daniel's kiss. Perhaps part of him would be relieved to lose all the pain, the humiliation, the shame of being treated no better than a caged animal.

But he was no coward to surrender to his own fears. When Ba'al raked his shoulder with his fangs, Daniel fell with the attack, rolled and catapulted Ba'al over his shoulders.

Ba'al scrambled to his feet with a roar of rage and charged Daniel, muscles rippling under glossy skin. He barreled headfirst into Daniel's stomach, carrying Daniel several yards before forcing him to the ground.

It was all Isis could do not to leap into the fray. But to do so would forfeit the fight to Ba'al. She held her breath and bit her lip and mourned in her heart when Daniel failed to rise, lying still as Ba'al pummeled him with fists and raking fingers. Then he swooped down like a hunting hawk and sank his teeth into Daniel's neck, not to take blood but to rip out Daniel's throat.

In a moment Daniel would be dead.

But then something remarkable happened. Daniel's arms shot up, his hands catching Ba'al around the throat and squeezing hard. Ba'al reared back, eyes wide in surprise, but Daniel continued to bear down on the god's throat with greater and greater force. Ba'al began to wheeze, his hands battering at Daniel wildly, his fingers digging into Daniel's wounds, his feet scrabbling on the tiles.

An instant later their positions were reversed, and Daniel was knocking Ba'al's head against the floor, muscles straining. Isis knew he was no longer himself, but truly the son of the god of war, expert in the art of death.

Ba'al's struggles began to weaken. He gasped and flailed; two of his guards began to descend from the dais, but a trio of Ares's soldiers surged forward to hold them back. Daniel positioned himself to snap Ba'al's neck.

Isis almost cried out. Ba'al could not remain alive; the threat he posed was too great. But she didn't want his blood on Daniel's hands.

Too late, she moved to intervene. Ba'al's body jerked once and went still. Daniel straightened, his hands still around Ba'al's neck, and drew in a deep, shuddering breath.

As Daniel got up, one of the priests knelt beside Ba'al's body and touched his neck. He let out a wailing cry, and the other priests took it up.

No one spoke, but Isis was aware of movement throughout the throne room, courtiers and humans stirring as if they had just wakened from a dream. Ares practically leaped up on the dais. Daniel took an uneven step toward Isis and then suddenly stopped, his breath ragged.

He stared at her for a moment and then looked down at Ba'al's body. Four priests were already lifting it in their arms, chanting in an ancient tongue as they ascended the dais again.

"Is he dead?" Daniel asked hoarsely, stepping back.

"You don't remember?"

"No."

Isis tried to take his hand, but he flinched and tried to pull his newly torn shirt up over his shoulders.

"You did what you had to do," she said, feeling that he was slipping away from her.

He met her gaze briefly and then looked over the astonished audience. Ares's soldiers had disarmed Ba'al's guards. Ereshkigal had fled; Bes and Hera stared almost fearfully at Daniel and Isis. Isis could understand their wariness of Daniel; he seemed to have grown in victory, sweeping his gaze around the room as if he owned it.

The humans were in disarray, some on their feet, others still kneeling, shaking their heads and murmuring in shock. Ares and Trinity were embracing with all the passion and relief of long-separated lovers.

"Ba'al's influence is broken," Isis said. She raised her voice. "Are there any others who would challenge the victor?"

Bes was the one who answered. He approached Isis and Daniel with wary meekness, as if he expected to be torn apart himself.

"You have defeated Ba'al," he said. "We did not believe it was possible."

"That is clear," Isis said.

"I am sorry," Bes said, bowing his head. "I was afraid when he killed Anu and Ishtar."

"Ishtar is dead?"

"Among other courtiers who would not bow to him." He lifted his head. "Now all must bow to you, Daniel."

"There will be no need for bowing if you do what I tell you," Daniel said.

"What do you wish us to do?"

"Hermes," Daniel said.

The red-haired Opir was not nearly as resigned as Bes. His movements were sharp, almost defiant as he came to Daniel. Isis could barely stand to look at him.

"The Lawkeepers are your responsibility," Daniel said coldly. "You've used them against the interests of this city, especially its human citizens."

"Hanni—Ba'al threatened me," Hermes said, "just as Anu threatened Ares. He promised to kill all the half-bloods if I did not do as he commanded."

"They won't be taken into custody if you do what I say," Daniel said. "Find them wherever they are and restrain them. No human in the city will trust them now. Keep them out of the way."

"Yes," Hermes said. He darted off. Daniel beckoned to the soldiers who had come with him to Ba'al's suite and disarmed the guards. Ares's troops gathered around Daniel expectantly.

"We must move quickly to get things under control, or there will be further chaos," Daniel said. "The humans in this room can leave. Hold the guards, the Opiri and Hera until I or Ares give you further orders. Some of you go look for the priests who took Ba'al, and recover his body." He glanced at Ares and Trinity as they descended the dais, Trinity free of her chains but still wearing her collar. "Ares," he said, "send orders to secure the towers and tell your soldiers to free any serfs and arrest the Opiri who've been keeping them. Tomorrow morning, I want every citizen of Tanis we can find gathered at the main plaza."

"Many will be in hiding," Ares said, deferring to Daniel without resentment. "There will be resistance from the humans, who will have no reason to trust my Freebloods."

"Then we get as many as we can persuade to come without using force. Our prisoners, of course, will have no choice."

"The Nine still have the power of their influence," Isis said.

"Then some may escape. I don't plan to hunt them down. Their time of power is over."

"What will you do with the prisoners?" Isis asked, touching his arm.

He looked at her through shuttered eyes. He was a leader now, focused on the many things that must be done to bring Tanis under the rule of law again. He would bring peace, though he could have set himself up as absolute ruler of Tanis without facing objection from anyone in the room.

"That will be for the people to decide," Daniel said distantly. "Tanis as they knew it has fallen. The human citizens and the Opiri who helped and supported them have a decision to make."

Isis's chest tightened. Along with the gratitude she felt that Daniel had won without suffering a major injury, she was almost frightened by his ruthlessness. If he left the fates of the prisoners to the humans, they might face worse than exile.

And do they not deserve it? she asked herself. Would she not choose the same fate for them?

But what of the Opiri who had not kept serfs but had declined to stand against Anu or Ba'al? They could not entirely be blamed; they would have become victims themselves if Ares had been driven to give the order to kill them.

Could any of them ever be trusted again?

There must be a way. There *must* be.

"I will need your help, Isis," Daniel said, seemingly unaware of her distress. "You can walk among the people and try to persuade them to accept that the violence is over. The Opiri behind the troubles are dead."

"Perhaps they will not listen to me."

"Find Hugh. He'll help you spread the word."

So Daniel was sending her away. To do important work, yes, but he had moved so far from her that she felt as if they existed on different planes.

He had changed after he had been taken and tortured. Now he had changed again.

It didn't matter. She had to reach him before he moved beyond her grasp.

"You said that Tanis, as the people know it, has fallen," she said, demanding his attention. "You said they have a decision to make. But you have *saved* Tanis, Daniel. Because of your faith and courage, it has not been destroyed."

"Not my faith," he said, still very far away. "And it hasn't been saved. Its end has only been delayed."

"And what if the people decide differently?"

"Tanis would never have succeeded," Daniel said. "Ares and I have the answer to the question we came here to find. All we can do now is protect the innocent and give them the means to seek their own way in the world."

"Their own way?" Isis asked. "Returning to the dangers they faced when they were the prey of any rogue Freeblood or Citadel patrol in search of serfs?"

Daniel shook his head. "I'm sorry, Isis. The dream you nurtured is gone."

Stunned by his dismissal, Isis retreated until she found herself outside in the elevator lobby, surrounded on all sides by bewildered humans and Opiri attempting to flee. Even as she watched, Ares's soldiers seized the courtiers and dragged them back into the suite. She pushed her way past them toward the door to the stairs.

Ares caught up with her just as she reached the stairwell.

"Isis," he said, grasping her arm. "You can't leave him now."

She jerked her arm free. "He does not need me," she said. "He needs your army to complete his conquest."

"Conquest?" Ares said with a harsh laugh. "And you pretend to know him?"

"He has already determined that Tanis is dead," she said.

"Isn't it?"

"What do you care for this city or the people here now that you have your mate again?"

"I'll assist Daniel in any way I can." His stare was unforgiving. "Do you realize what he suffered here while you and I were unable to help him? How he was forced to relive the life he endured in Erebus, before I found him? How much pain and humiliation must a man endure before he strikes back?"

"I have not given up," she said, "even if *he* has."

"Does he love you?"

She turned her head away. "If he ever did, it is gone now."

Ares's lip curled, but she didn't wait to hear his response. She flung herself into the stairwell and descended, breathless, to the ground floor. Freeblood soldiers ran this way and that along the causeway, and she could see figures milling about the bases of the two nearest towers and along the central avenue.

Isis descended the ramp, sank down against the wall—out of sight of most passersby—and looked at her hands. They were stained with Daniel's blood. The blood he had given to stop Ba'al, the blood of punishment he had endured for her sake.

How much pain and humiliation must a man endure before he strikes back? How could Daniel see anything but the bad, when he had met so few Opiri who supported the dream upon which she and the Nine had founded Tanis?

The Nine, she thought. Daniel had seen them betray their own ideals. Athena had worked to help him and Isis, but, in the end, Bes and Hermes had turned their backs on all they claimed to have believed in. The others had either been too afraid to challenge Ba'al, or they had wanted the human serfs he would have allotted to them.

And some of them had surely known of Anu's intentions, as well. They had simply exchanged one tyrant for another.

After a while, composed again, Isis let her thoughts return to Daniel. To what Ares had said.

Does he love you? he had asked. Clearly Ares had believed it possible—more than merely possible—but Daniel had never told her.

Did it matter? Were her feelings for him dependent upon his for her, or upon what path he chose to take to help the people of Tanis? Could she be such a coward, when he had set aside his own pain to restore peace to the city?

Slowly she rose, climbed the ramp, and pressed the button for the elevator. When it reached the bottom, two more soldiers and three Opiri prisoners spilled out: two of Ba'al's courtiers and Hera. It was clear from their appearance that they had fought their captors; Isis knew that Hera, like the other "gods," would have tried to use her influence against them. Either her will hadn't been strong enough, or she had simply been outnumbered. It remained to be seen what had become of the other conspirators.

At least Daniel would not keep the prisoners in the cells where Anu and Ba'al had imprisoned *him*. He had not lost all his compassion.

She entered the elevator and rode it to the top.. Daniel's suite now, if he chose to claim it. Which he would never do.

Half expecting to find the rooms still seething with soldiers and blank-faced humans, she was surprised to find it nearly empty. None of the Opiri remained, and the humans had either left of their own accord or been escorted to a safe place.

One man stood in the center of the reception room, his blood-caked hands at his sides, his expression empty. It was as if he had used up all his energy giving orders to those who needed direction, and had nothing left for himself.

Isis crept into the room, approaching him as if he were a stranger. "Daniel?" she said.

He turned his head toward her without meeting her eyes. "Isis?" he said in a tone of dazed exhaustion.

She continued toward him, waiting for him to come alive again. He was still in a state of shock when she took his hand and led him toward the rear of the suite. All Households had been built on much the same plan, and she knew where to find the bath.

The small, dark room was eerily silent, echoing with her and Daniel's footsteps. The bathing pool was rectangular, with a slightly sloping bottom, and filled with warm, clear water.

"Let me help you," she said. While he stood at the edge of the pool, unresisting, she carefully removed his torn shirt and trousers, close to weeping again at the sight of his scarred body. He seemed utterly unaware of her touch, even when she led him to the stairs descending into the water and helped him enter the pool.

He slid down into the water automatically, as if his body understood what he needed better than his mind did. Isis found the cleaning oil and cloths, shed her clothes and slipped into the pool beside him.

For a while she did nothing but lie by his side. He closed his eyes and breathed deeply. Little trails of blood meandered away from his body.

"I am going to touch you now," Isis said. She gathered a handful of oil and gently spread it across his chest. He inhaled sharply, and she thought he might bolt from the pool. But he settled again, staring straight ahead, enduring the sweep of her palm as she worked the oil into his skin and brushed carefully over recently healed wounds. His heartbeat slowed, and she began to work on other parts of his body: legs and arms, neck—so terribly abused—and shoulders. He resisted a little when she turned him over, but he relented and let her bathe his back with all its layers of scars, washing the dried blood from the most recent lashing.

When she had finished, she urged him to turn over again. With even more care, she began to wash his face, dabbing at the scrapes and cuts, working the cleanser into his stiffened hair. She rinsed him off with a basin at the pool's edge and thought of leaving him there to recover, believing that he would come back to himself when he had a chance to rest.

But as she moved to go, his hand clasped her wrist. She looked at his face and closed eyes, holding very still.

"You haven't finished," he said, his voice a rasp.

Chapter 27

Isis felt a flood of moisture between her thighs that had nothing to do with the warm water's caress. Still watching Daniel's expression, she slid her hand down into the water and took his half-erect shaft into her hand. Immediately it came to full attention. She massaged the oil into his skin, heard his breath catch, felt gentle waves slap against her as he shifted. She took her time, and he seemed suspended between relaxation and tension, pleasure and pain.

She knew then that he would take everything she could give. She moved to straddle him, welcoming him inside as easily as a lock accepting a key. Erotic sensation burst through her. She eased up and down, her hands spread across his chest where the skin was least marked. He made a sound low in his throat and caught her waist in his hands, thrusting up to impale her again and again. Then he cupped her breasts in his hands, drew her down and kissed her mouth, probing urgently with his tongue. She opened to him, always aware of her teeth, and he bent his knees to hold her astride him while he speared his fingers in her hair.

The kiss ended at last, and she grazed her lips over his brows and cheekbones and chin, thinking only of healing, of restoring some small pleasure to his world. He continued to stroke her hair, wordless, giving in return. He took another long, deep breath, and she was certain, as his hand dropped from her head, that he would sleep.

She was wrong. He opened his eyes, his gaze searching her face. She offered her breasts to him, and he suckled her, kissing and licking her nipples until she was gasping with delight. He lifted her in his arms with easy strength and turned her over, placing her on her hands and knees at the foot of the stairs.

Isis shuddered. Daniel braced his hands on her hips and thrust into her, gently rocking her forward, driving so deep that she thought it impossible that they should ever separate. She moaned as he caressed the most sensitive area between her legs in time to his thrusts, and she knew she would soon lose control over her body's desire for completion.

But he showed no mercy. He withdrew and turned her over again to pick her up in his arms, carrying her up the steps and setting her on her feet. He found a pile of feather-soft towels, tossed them on the tiled floor and laid her down on top of them.

Then they were face-to-face, Daniel braced on his arms over her, his hips cradled between her thighs, his blue eyes no longer distant but deeply tender. She wrapped her legs around his waist at the moment he entered her, preparing herself for the full force of his passion.

But this time his movements were not urgent, not marked by the almost desperate hunger that had imbued their other encounters. Now he was as gentle as his gaze, caressing her inside and out, kissing her nipples and her face and her lips. It was an act of love, of gratitude, of desire…and above all, of acceptance of everything she was or had ever been.

"I love you," she whispered as he brought her to climax. But as he finished and rested against her, his face pressed into the hollow of her shoulder, he did not answer. He would not speak the words. Perhaps, Isis thought with profound grief, he could not. Perhaps those feelings were locked up inside him with the pain of his past, entangled so that he could no longer tell one emotion from another.

"Take my blood," he said, positioning himself so that she could reach his neck. She knew this was another act of the love he couldn't accept, and she bit him with great care, piercing the healed flesh, shuddering with fresh ecstasy as his blood rolled over her tongue. Daniel began to shudder, but not with horror or disgust; he stiffened again, and as she drank he thrust into her, carrying her up and up, bringing her to another full completion. She ran her hands over the shifting muscles of his back as she sealed the wound.

And suddenly it was over. Daniel rolled over and rose to fetch another towel. He helped Isis to her feet and wrapped it around her, engulfing her in warmth and safety.

"I have to go back out," he said, regret breaking his voice. "I still need you, Isis."

Need her, yes, she thought. To pacify the city without violence. To gather the people to hear his pronouncement of Tanis's fate, as if only he had the right to determine it.

She shrugged out of the towel and put on her clothes again. Daniel watched her, his eyes following every motion. When she was finished, she took his hand.

"There will be clean garments in the suite," she said. "Will you wear them, even if they belonged to Anu?"

"As long as they don't look like a god's," he said.

Her loins still aching, Isis led him from the room.

Word had spread quickly throughout the city.

Daniel stood on the steps of the Hall of Justice, the administrative buildings and multistory apartments rising on either side. Ares, Trinity, Athena, Bes, Hermes and a dozen soldiers stood just behind him. To one side, Ares's soldiers guarded Hera, Ereshkigal, Hephaestus and as many of Ba'al's and Anu's supporters as they had been able to find and overcome; their serfs had been freed and taken into the care of human physicians. The Council, too, were under guard, until such time as their part in the recent events could be established. Certainly, Daniel thought, the human members would be absolved, and possibly the Opiri, as well.

Hundreds of citizens had gathered to hear him—men and women, Opir and human and half-blood were bathed in morning sunlight. But the crowd was divided. Humans had assembled on one half of the plaza, hooded Opiri on the other. Puzzled, half-hostile glances were exchanged. Information about the captive humans and Anu's ultimate plans for Tanis were still filtering through the ranks, provoking confusion, anger and fear. Ba'al's part in it was still little more than a rumor, but every human and Opir knew that a half-blood outsider had defeated the leader of the Nine and taken his place.

Scanning the plaza, Daniel searched for Isis. She wasn't there. He remembered every moment of the previous morning, the way Isis had cared for him when he had nearly lost himself, the joinings both urgent and gentle. She had spoken words to him she had spoken before, and again he had been unable to answer.

He laughed at himself. Here he was, with hundreds of people ready to hang on his every word, and the one thing he wanted was lost to him. Her love wasn't enough.

Daniel understood. She had given him that last time together. But she had clearly made a decision. She couldn't support his plans for the citizens of Tanis, and so she had left him.

He was alone. As he *must* be.

Daniel raised his hand. The crowd went silent.

"My name is Daniel," he said. "I am the son of a human woman and the Opir Bloodmaster Ares, who commands the Freeblood army that freed the human serfs and took the law-breaking Opiri into custody."

A murmur rose from the crowd, comments and questions rising like a stiff wind. The soldiers behind Daniel shifted their weapons. Daniel raised his hand again.

"I speak to you now as one who has been a serf and has also led colonies where Opiri and humans live in peace. I come to tell you what has happened to Tanis, and what lies ahead for all of you."

"What gives *you* the right to speak?" a voice called from the Opir side of the gathering.

"He defeated the usurper Ba'al in formal challenge, after Ba'al killed the leader of the Nine," Ares said, stepping forward. "And he has my army behind him."

Those humans and Opiri who had known little of recent events reacted with sounds of surprise and confusion. Someone from the human side raised his voice above the chatter.

"The army protected us," he said. "Let him speak!"

His exhortation was echoed by a hundred other humans, and gradually the crowd grew quiet again.

And then Daniel told them. He told them how the chaos in the city had been deliberately but subtly provoked; how humans had been stolen from their wards to become serfs to Anu's favored Opiri lords; how Anu had planned to return the city to the old ways and how his favorite, Hannibal, once known as the god Ba'al, had killed him in order to rule once more as a true deity, unchallenged and omnipotent in his own world. He spoke of Isis and Athena and the human resistance, and how they had helped to defeat the enemies of Tanis. And, without shame or pride, he explained how Ba'al had died, laying the fact before them plainly and letting them absorb it as they realized that everything had changed.

"The Nine founded Tanis on an ideal," Daniel said. "Some intended to carry it through. The Lady Isis has always been devoted to all the people in this city."

There were a few cries of "yes!" and a hum of approval from the audience.

"If it were not for her courage, either Anu or Ba'al would surely have succeeded. She—"

He stopped as Isis approached from the rear of the crowd, walking directly down the center of the plaza between humans and Opiri. She was every inch the goddess, and the watchers seemed to hold their breaths.

She's come to challenge me, Daniel thought. Not in battle but with words. She would try to persuade the people of Tanis to begin again in this place where so much evil had occurred. She would do it because she believed with all her heart and every one of her long years that the city could still succeed.

He would have no choice but to argue against her.

"In spite of all she has done," he said, "in spite of the good work of her allies and the humans and Opiri who stood against Anu and Ba'al, Tanis can never become what it was meant to be. Someday, it may be possible for humans and Opiri to live together in a city like this. But that time hasn't come. There are too many obstacles that face both peoples, decades of tradition and habit to overcome, pain and anger to be set aside."

"You say we have failed," Isis said, her voice carrying clearly across the plaza as she gazed up at him, "but for six years we lived in peace."

"Yes," Daniel said. He met her gaze, concealing all emotion in his eyes and voice. "But it didn't last, because a city is too big to nurture the dream of peace. People become anonymous to other citizens; Opiri and humans have room to live apart. There's no need for them to learn to understand one another."

"But the will was there," Isis said. She spoke to the entire gathering, but her gaze was for him, and she spoke of more than the city's fate. "The desire to live as equals—"

"Was not enough," Daniel finished for her. "Not when the desire itself was unequal."

"Do you blame the Opiri?" she challenged.

"I blame nothing but the system," he said. His gaze swept over the crowd again. "There is another way. There are places in the west where humans and Opiri and half-bloods truly do live in peace. Settlements where each colonist knows every other, regardless of race. Where misunderstandings are worked out before they cause disputes."

"Are humans forced to give blood?" a man shouted.

"They choose to do it, because there is no cause for resentment."

A single sigh seemed to ripple over the divided audience. Relief, uncertainty, anxiety all intermixed along with hope and disbelief.

"I can take you to the west," he said, raising his voice. "I can show you the colonies where you would be welcome, every human and Opir who still desires true equality."

"All of us?" another human asked.

"When a colony grows too big, we form daughter colonies," he said. "All are run the same. Some of you would become members of those daughter colonies, free to establish your own community."

"And if what happened here happens again?"

"There is always sanctuary for those driven from their homes by violence and unfair laws," he said. "But you must have the courage to try."

He looked at Isis, asking her to hear him, to understand. The wide gulf between former serf and goddess might be unbridgeable, but if she was willing to lead her own people to a new life…

She turned her back on him. "Hear me," she said. "You have been given a grave choice between journeying into the unknown with this man's promises to guide you, or rebuilding Tanis with your courage and goodwill."

"Goodwill?" Daniel asked, struggling to harden his heart. "Can any amount of goodwill overcome the taint Anu, Ba'al and their followers have left on this city?"

The silence was painful, cutting Daniel to the heart. If Isis were repudiated by her own people, she would be cut loose from everything she had known during the time she had traveled with the Nine and all the centuries before. Severed from her dream, what would she become? Apart from her peers and her followers, without love…

"I offer a new life to the humans of Tanis," he said, "and for any Opiri who wish to join us. But Lady Isis is a wise leader. Those who want to remain with her here are welcome to do so."

Every voice in the plaza faded. It was some time before the next human spoke up.

"What will you do with the lawbreakers?" she asked.

"That is to be your decision," Daniel said.

"Exile!" the woman shouted.

"Death!" someone called, followed by many other voices demanding the same punishment.

"Your anger is justified," Daniel said, interrupting them. "But to kill them means that you'll be no better than they are. Their fates will haunt you when you try to start a new life, here or in the west."

All over the plaza, humans and Opiri talked among themselves and exchanged wary glances across the aisle that separated them. Isis was still standing in the center, her gaze on Daniel.

"You defeated Ba'al," an Opir shouted. "You make the law."

"It was never my intention—" Daniel began.

"You decide!"

"You choose!"

"Tell us!"

Humbled and disturbed by the power all these people had put into his hands, Daniel descended the steps and stopped at the level of the crowd. Isis was no more than a few yards away, but the yards might as well have been miles.

Some of the humans moved forward to gather around him. They waited, their eyes anxious and stubborn.

"Tell us," Hugh said, working his way forward through the bodies surrounding Daniel. "There's no Council now to make the decision. You've earned the right."

Meeting Isis's eyes over the heads of the humans, Daniel nodded slowly. "Very well," he said. "The lawbreakers and supporters of Anu and Ba'al will be exiled. Soldiers will escort them to the east onto the prairie with day coats and the means of hunting for themselves. What they make of their lives after that will depend on their own resources… without the help of humans or other Opiri. If they make it to another Citadel, they'll have to fight their way back to a position of rank. And they may not find that so easy to do outside the walls of this city."

Hugh looked around at the other humans. "It is a fair punishment," he said.

The humans murmured and nodded and drifted back to their fellows in the crowd, sharing the news. When Hugh announced Daniel's decision to the Opiri, none objected.

Then there was no one between Daniel and Isis, no sound except the thudding of his pulse and the harshness of his breathing. Isis walked toward him slowly and mounted

Dark Journey

the stairs behind him, each step dragging as if her robes were hemmed with weights.

When he saw her eyes, he knew that she had surrendered her own convictions in favor of his. In the end, she'd chosen to trust him.

"People of Tanis," she said, turning to the crowd. "I gladly testify that you may safely trust Daniel with your life. He is a great man. He has lived as a serf, a free human and a half-blood. He knows what it is to serve, and to rule. He has led Opiri in colonies such as those he has offered to you and put his own life at risk many times to save those he has sworn to protect." She paused, her voice catching. "I have no doubt that he and his allies can deliver what they have promised—a place where the dream we dreamed can be fulfilled. If you go, do so without fear or doubt."

Daniel listened with his head down and his hands clasped behind his back, confounded by her testimony. He wanted to sing her praises, as she had sung his; stand by her side and declare that Tanis was not a lost cause, after all.

But he believed with all his heart that Tanis's foundation had rotted under the feet of its people, and it would never be sound again, no matter how much Isis wished it so.

He turned to thank her for the words she had spoken on his behalf, but she had already climbed the rest of the stairs and was striding alongside the hall, headed toward the center of her ward. Athena, who had been standing quietly at the top of the steps, followed her.

A flood of people from the audience demanded Daniel's attention, and he had no choice but to let Isis go. He spoke to Ares and reassured dozens of humans, and more Opiri approached him with questions and concerns. He became again what he had been in Delos, far in the Northwest: calm, confident and unmoved by distracting emotion. It was almost noon when he answered the last question and assured the crowd that the more practical aspects of the journey would be discussed at length over the coming days.

As the Opiri adjusted the hoods of their day coats and the humans drifted back to their homes, only a few remained. Hugh was among them.

"They'll follow you to Hell and back," Hugh said, admiration in his voice. "Anyone would."

"You give me too much credit," Daniel said stiffly.

"And you give yourself too little." He nodded to his people, and they headed toward Bes's ward, openly and without fear.

"Well done," Ares said, resting his hand on Daniel's shoulder. "The army will help make the preparations. We'll need all the livestock, and wagons to carry the supplies—"

Ares continued to speak, but Daniel barely heard him. "Please excuse me," he said. "I have something to do."

Climbing the stairs to join his wife, Ares let him go. Daniel jogged toward Isis's apartment building, no longer thinking of grand, dangerous journeys but of a single woman who meant more to him than life itself. A woman he worshipped—not as a serf or inferior, but because she was the one he loved.

He found her in her apartment, stepping out of her gown in the darkness. She turned as soon as he entered, making a futile grab for her clothing as if she were ashamed to let him see her.

"Isis," he said, closing the door behind him.

"Why have you come?" she asked, her voice small and soft.

"To thank you," he said, his courage momentarily deserting him. "For supporting me, when you could so easily have done otherwise."

She smiled. "But you were right, Daniel. I clung to a dream because I did not wish to admit failure. I did not wish to believe that everything the Nine had done was a lie."

"Your part was never a lie," he said, moving closer to her. "Without you to temper their ambition, Anu or Ba'al would have acted long ago."

"Would they?" She stared at the rich carpet under her feet. "How could I have been so blind?"

"I was the one who was blind," Daniel said, taking another step.

"You saw the futility of my hopes," she said, looking away. "And you were right."

"No, Isis." He moved so close to her that he could see the pulse throbbing at the base of her throat, feel her warmth, smell her natural perfume. "What you wanted was right. Was, and still is. If you'll give the seed a chance to grow in a new field..."

"You have the seed, Daniel," she said. "It is yours."

"But it's nothing without someone to nurture it. That is your skill, not mine."

"Now you are the one who is blind." She met his gaze. "You are everything I said you were. I admire you more than I can say."

Admiration. His blood turned to ice. "That's not what I want, Isis," he said.

"What more can I do?" she cried. "You need nothing, no one. They tried to destroy you twice, and both times you emerged stronger than before."

"And you think I did it alone?" He touched the tears on her cheek. "I could never have survived the first time without Ares. Or *this* time without you."

"I cannot give you—"

"You already have. Unless your feelings have changed." He searched her eyes. "Have they, Isis?"

She backed away. "No. If you ever trusted me, you know they could not."

"Neither have mine. Isis…" For a moment, in the presence of this stunning, warm and loving woman, he almost lost his courage. She would always be a goddess to him and to everyone who had the good fortune to know her. And he had been indelibly marked by the past, no matter how highly she thought of his courage.

"I want you to come with us," he said at last. "You carry the heart of this city inside you. Without that heart, it will be an empty journey."

"There will be enough who believe," she said. "You will help them. I am not necessary."

"I didn't say the journey would be empty for *them*." He moved in close again, cupping her chin in his hand. "I loved you from the moment I saw you. But trust came hard to me, Isis. The memories kept their grip because I couldn't accept my own feelings. But you gave me a new life with your love. I want that life with you, for as long as we live. I never want to take another step without you."

Her eyes glistened. "Say it, Daniel."

"I love you."

Their lips met, and the new journey began.

* * * * *

MILLS & BOON®

nocturne™

AN EXHILARATING UNDERWORLD OF DARK DESIRES

MILLS & BOON®

Mills & Boon have been at the heart of romance since 1908... and while the fashions may have changed, one thing remains the same: from pulse-pounding passion to the gentlest caress, we're always known how to bring romance alive.

Now, we're delighted to present you with these irresistible illustrations, inspired by the vintage glamour of our covers. So indulge your wildest dreams and unleash your imagination as we present the most iconic Mills & Boon moments of the last century.

Visit **www.millsandboon.co.uk/ArtofRomance** to order yours!